Collateral Hearts

By Margaret Tipton

Margaret Tipton

Before smart phones and e-readers, were newspapers and books.

In loving memory of my parents, who filled our home with both.

Chapter 1

"Collin, get in the car! And help your brother buckle up!" Libby had said that a thousand times. She was sure she would say it a thousand more, but at the moment, she would just appreciate some compliance.

She slammed the rear door of her SUV and walked toward the cart return. She was hot, tired, and sick of feeling like the only parent in her household. How in the world did she ever convince herself that she could really "have it all?"

Libby opened her door and hopped in just in time to watch her youngest son aim his grape soda at his brother and pop the top. A great purple fountain spewed across the back of her car amid a host of shouts and giggles. Her anger and frustration erupted from her as swiftly and as violently as the soda.

"What is WRONG with you? You know better!" She jerked the half-empty can from Ben's hand and put it in the cup holder. "You'll clean this up if it takes you all night."

"But Dad's taking us to the ballgame."

"I don't care. He can sit and wait for all I care. You should have thought about that before you squirted your brother."

"Mom," Collin whined, "why do I have to wait all night when Ben did it? That's not fair! You're mean!"

"Yeah, yeah. Mean old Mom. I'm sure you did something to provoke your brother, so you can either help him or wait with your dad. I don't care!"

The car settled into uncomfortable silence on the heels of her outburst. If her own unhappiness with her life wasn't enough, she was compounding it by lashing out at the boys. She felt horrible. She would make it up to them later. Right now, she just needed to get them home and ready for their daddy to take them to the high school football game. It was the biggest draw in town on Friday nights, and Matt was a former star.

He had been taking his "boys" to the game since they were potty trained. It was tradition.

First, she had to unload the groceries and put them all away. She had planned to mow the yard this afternoon, but Collin had football practice and Ben had soccer practice. To make it even more impossible, she had been the room mother for Ben's class party today. The house was wrecked, and she doubted if she could get some sort of dinner on the table before Matt strolled in from work. He was sure to have some flip remark over the state of affairs in their home. She didn't care. If he didn't like it, he could help.

Life had been so much easier when the boys were younger and not quite so involved in everything. She only worked PRN as a nurse in Labor and Delivery, but the constant need to play chauffer and champion volunteer was wearing her down. Matt kept the boys while she worked one or two nights a week, but he had so many responsibilities at his family's construction company that he was barely able to do more than occasionally mow the yard or treat the pool.

Summer was still in full swing; the yard was a jungle and the pool was turning an ominous shade of green. Summers were long and hot in rural West Tennessee where she had made her home with Matt McDonald, and she knew that the swimming pool would be nasty and the yard would need to be baled if she didn't get them under control in a hurry.

She pulled into the driveway of their home. Matt had designed it himself. He had spent his evenings fiddling with the plans for years. When they decided it was time to build, he had agonized over every detail. Most days, it was more house than they needed and certainly more than she could ever keep up with.

She parked in the garage and yelled at the boys to grab a bag. Truly, they were good boys. They made good grades and always received good conduct marks at school. Libby and Matt had done everything they could to give their boys the perfect childhood. It was killing her. She baked, chauffeured, wrapped, planned, chaired, and volunteered until she was ready to drop; then she went to work.

Today was like any other day, except for one thing. Last night had been the last straw for her. Their fighting had increased over the past year to the point of hopelessness. Libby had thought that it was a phase they were going through; that somehow they would come out at the end of this long, black tunnel and find a ray of light. She was wrong. There was no ray of light. There was only resentment and indignation. Their relationship had deteriorated so slowly that neither of them realized how bad it had become. They had managed to hide their problems from themselves and the rest of the world.

Libby was withdrawn and frustrated. Her marriage seemed a sham in the face of their problems over the last year. It didn't start that way. They had known each other for a few years and had dated for several months when she became pregnant with Collin. They had married two weeks after graduation; Collin was born five months later. She supposed they loved each other, but theirs had never been a relationship filled with passion or romance. They never talked much about love. The first few years of marriage had been crammed with Matt's pursuit of his Master's Degree and his growing involvement in his family's construction business. She worked one or two days a week to keep her nursing license current and provide some extra cash. They had forged a comfortable friendship and a quiet coexistence that seemed to outsiders to be the perfect marriage.

For over 10 years, it had been enough, but even their friendship had withered away in the past few years, as the boys demanded more of Libby's time away from the house. Matt was exhausted from work and expected more from her as he became unable to keep up with the yard and pool. He made constant biting remarks about her apparent misuse of her time and refused to help with any of the household chores. The busier they became, the more her frustration mounted. She was tired of him. She was tired of it all.

Last night they had argued about money. He had long ago dumped their finances on her. He had an excellent salary, and she contributed a significant amount with her part time job, but he spent as much as they made. She tried to warn him that they were becoming overextended, but he continued to spend. Last night she had finished balancing the checkbook and had warned him not to spend any more money until their next payday. He hadn't taken it well. He had even accused her of spending all of the money or stashing it somewhere so he couldn't get to it.

The argument had lasted for hours and had eventually included accusations and insinuations she hoped the children hadn't heard. She was embarrassed and frustrated. Most of all, she was exhausted. Carrying the burden of their finances for so long had worn her down enough, but the constant strife had completely drained her. Last night had been the knockout punch. She was finished. She had made the decision to end their marriage.

She went upstairs to the boys' rooms and started digging for their Milton County Mustangs shirts. She was sure Matt had his on today. He always wore it on game days.

Matt let himself in through the garage door and made his way from the kitchen into the den. He scratched Collin's head as his oldest son ran past him and slung open the door to the garage. He couldn't quite make out what the boys were yelling at each other as the door slammed behind Collin. He dropped his briefcase and a set of blueprints on the sofa and went to look for Libby. He could hear her rummaging around upstairs.

She was digging in a drawer of Collin's dresser. At this angle, with her shorts hiked well up, he could see her great legs. Despite having given birth to his two boys, she managed to look as good from behind at 32 as she had when he had met her at 19. Nice, slightly muscled calves eased into shapely well-defined thighs that disappeared under her shorts to form a perfectly rounded bottom. Her hair was some mixture of brown and gold. He knew she had it done that way, but it always looked good. She pushed the soft, short curls over her ear in a habitual gesture he had always found extremely sexy. Sexy, hmmm. They were both so tired their love life had slipped away without much thought. It had never been earth shattering, but it had been regular and familiar. He was so busy he didn't have energy left for much more anyway. It had obviously been too long since they had made love. He couldn't resist the urge to grab her butt.

She jerked up and looked at him. "Hey. We just got home. It'll take a few minutes to get them ready to go." She swatted his lingering hand away from her rear and gave him a disgusted look.

He put his hand in his pocket and puzzled over the look on her face. Was she mad at him for grabbing her? Struggling to recover from his embarrassment, he blurted the first thing that came to mind, "Is there something wrong with the mower?"

Shaken, she stared at him. "What?"

"Is the mower broken or what? You could make crop circles in the yard. I thought you were going to mow today."

She looked at him in disbelief. The sight of him dressed in soft khakis and his blue chambray Mustangs shirt temporarily distracted her. He was as perfect as ever. With sandy brown hair and crystal blue eyes, he usually looked like the All-American boy. Shaking off the thought, she snapped back at him, "No, it's not broken. I've been a little busy chasing your children around this week."

He crinkled his brow and looked around the room. "Not much time to keep house either, I guess? Have you backwashed the pool? You need to get that done or it will cost a fortune to get it cleaned." He walked over to the window overlooking the backyard.

"Good grief, Libby! The pool is disgusting. What's wrong with you? You've never let things go like this. Are you somehow taking care of my kids in the midst of this disaster?"

He threw his hands up and turned to face her. "What the hell is happening here?" What was he saying? He should be relaxing with a cold beer while he waited for the boys to get ready, not starting a fight with her. Again.

"I don't know what your problem is." She was NOT going to cry. "You have no right to talk to me that way. You know darn well I take care of OUR children. I'm a good mother. I can't believe you said that to me!"

"Look around you, Libby. What else am I supposed to think?" He shook his head and walked next door to Ben's room. He had to get out of there before this turned into something ugly. He had had a helluva day and he just wanted to get to the ballgame and relax with the guys.

"You know I'm busy with things at their school and with ball practice." She was shouting at his back as he disappeared around the corner. "I don't think they'll be scarred for life because their yard wasn't mowed this week. And you COULD help me out. I think you know how to use the mower!"

She was certain he'd lost his mind. This was the sort of argument that had become routine for them. She felt consistently inadequate as a wife, as a mother, as a woman. She knew that it wasn't true, but it was hard to keep convincing herself when she heard it so often. Sometimes she just wanted to throw up her hands and get the heck out of Ainsley. She could find a nursing job anywhere. Memphis and Nashville paid much better. She could work a Baylor plan and let Matt have the boys on the weekends. It wasn't out of reach. No one would say she hadn't tried to make it work. She knew plenty of couples who had divorced for lesser reasons. She was always afraid she would be stuck in a bad marriage in Ainsley, Tennessee forever.

"Bloom where you're planted" had been her mantra since the day she married Matt and moved to Ainsley. The town was large, and situated on a nice lake, so they had some shopping, a big movie theater, and a performing arts center. She was grateful for the hospital and the employment opportunity it gave her. She would have made more money in the city, but she enjoyed her work and the few friends she had made there. She missed having a mall, an airport, a symphony, and her family.

The sacrifices she had made to create a home and family for Matt seemed long forgotten as he stormed down the stairs carrying Ben's shirt. "I just can't get over the condition of this house. And why is Ben out there cleaning your car?"

"Ben is cleaning my car because he sprayed his brother with grape soda."

"Wonderful. They're just out of control anymore. I don't know what's going on around here." He grabbed Collin's shirt from her hands and walked toward the living room.

"Matt, I don't think this is the time or place for you to start something like this with me. The boys are coming in the garage door. Besides, I'm doing the best I can. It would help if you would pitch in a little!" Her anger was beginning to get the best of her and she could feel the tears swimming in her eyes. "The boys are perfectly fine. The house is messy, but it's not filthy. I'm the only one around here who seems to be able to do anything. Must be nice to have someone to pick up after you, cook, take care of the kids, and do your laundry. Oh, I forgot...you've had ME for all these years. I guess you can just get a little nookie on the side and you'll have everything you always wanted." Libby didn't know what she was saying and she was quickly losing control of this situation.

He threw Collin's shirt at him. "Get dressed. Go upstairs and wash your face and hands." He jerked Ben's dirty t-shirt over his head and threw it on the floor. He pulled the navy Milton Mustangs shirt over the boy's head and straightened it. He patted Ben's bottom and pushed him toward the stairs. "You, too. Get cleaned up."

Libby stood, arms akimbo, and seethed at his apparent dismissal of their conversation. How could he say those things to her and just go on without a second thought?

In her anger, she grabbed his arm and turned him to face her. "Well, I'm sick of it. I'm tired of the way you talk to me. I'm tired of feeling like nothing I do is ever good enough for you or your family. I'm tired of this town. And I'm tired of YOU. I want out. I want this to be over." The tears were flowing hard and hot now. She couldn't remember ever being so mad at him or losing her temper like that. What *was* wrong with her?

"What you do and how you live has an impact on the boys. I won't let them live in squalor because you're too busy flitting about town being the social queen to act like a mother. You've obviously lost control of yourself and my boys!" This was not how he had intended to start his weekend. He had to get out of here in a hurry. He had no idea what he was saying or why he was even arguing with her. Things were so much better when they just ignored each other.

"Don't talk to me that way!" Neither of them was making any sense. Libby looked up in time to see the boys coming down the stairs. "Just go," she said quietly.

"I'm going." Matt herded the boys out the door and into his truck. He backed out of the driveway and squealed the tires as he pulled into the street.

"Asshole," Libby muttered as she slammed the door and stomped back to her room. She had to get ready for work.

♥ ♥ ♥ ♥

Libby collapsed in the tub and reached over to turn on the jets. She had almost an hour before she needed to be at work. It was time to make some plans.

What was wrong with their marriage? She was so aggravated all of the time. Sometimes she looked on their life and thought it was perfect. They had everything most couples their age dreamed of. A beautiful home, wonderful children, a close family. What more could anyone ask for?

Libby wanted more. She wanted to work. Not the type of work she did most often now. Not driving the kids around, keeping the house and yard, volunteering at the church, school, and hospital. Not all of those things that satisfied her but left her just short of complete. She wanted more. She wanted a career. A chance to end each day with the feeling that she had made a difference. Not just a feeling that she had picked up and dropped off everyone on time today.

They had bills. Lots of them. She was responsible for their finances, but she hadn't spent the money. Matt had. She never mentioned to him that he was breaking them. She didn't want to argue about it. He was used to having money, so he spent. He took trips, he went to sporting events, and he bought toys for himself and toys for his kids. He spent what he made. She was expected to pay the bills and keep his fairy tale alive.

She hadn't been raised to do this. Her mother didn't do this. Her mother was a career woman. Even her mother-in-law was a professional who had raised her children in the offices of McDonald Construction. Who had formed this plan where she had to stay home and become the epitome of the 70's housewife? Why had she gone to college only to end up as a domestic engineer? Anyone could be a chauffer and chaperone. Was there more to her than this? She just wanted the chance to find out for herself.

Matt wouldn't understand. He was so resistant whenever she mentioned working more. He didn't have any crazy, antiquated ideas; he just wanted her at home with him when he was there. He worked hard, starting his day early and often coming home after 6 o'clock in the evening. He wanted to come home like Ward Cleaver and have his little family gathered around him for a nice dinner and a quiet evening of television. Maybe his view of family life was a little outdated.

It was a beautiful picture. The problem was that they hadn't had a quiet night of dinner and TV in years. With all of the activities the boys were in, they were lucky to get a nice meal around the kitchen table once a week. Once they landed at home from their whirlwind afternoon and evening, homework took up the rest of their time. Baths and preparations for the next day completed the night. By the time the boys were in bed, Libby was exhausted and Matt was asleep in his recliner, usually with some sort of paperwork on his lap. They would drag themselves to bed and collapse. Sometimes they made love.

She had tried to talk to him about her feelings, but they somehow ended up in a fight each time she mentioned it. Their fights had begun to form a chasm between them that seemed unbridgeable. Once one of them said something hurtful, the other would start in and they would launch into an ugly barrage of accusations and name-calling. Each argument surpassed the last in intensity and pain. Lately she dreaded any encounter with him. They hadn't made love in weeks. They hadn't had a long enough truce.

What could she do to put their marriage back where it belonged? Was there anything she could do? She was not prepared to stay on their present course. She couldn't. She recognized the signs of depression beginning to ravage her mind and body. She didn't care about her appearance. She either ate too much or forgot to eat at all. Often, she was so consumed with anger, anxiety, or sadness that she wasn't sure she would get through her day.

Nobody knew. She kept her smile in place and performed as expected. She had avoided her parents for the last few months. Her mother would know. She could always tell when something was wrong.

What was the answer? Divorce? Marriage counseling? She doubted Matt would ever talk about their problems to an outsider. He probably didn't realize they had problems. He just thought she was being an unreasonable bitch. Maybe she was. She didn't care; she just wanted to feel better. Right now, divorce seemed the most likely option. She didn't know how she could manage that, either, but she had to try something different. This life wasn't working. She had so many problems, she couldn't think about them all at once without making herself sick.

She got out of the tub, dressed and drove to work with a heavy heart. Her frustration level seemed to grow, rather than abate, as she reflected on her life and her options. By the time she pulled into the parking lot of the hospital, she had worked herself into a fine state. She dragged herself into the hospital and took the elevator to the Maternal-Child unit. The Labor and Delivery floor looked busy. She dumped her things on the floor and plopped down in a chair.

"Who yanked your chain?" Amanda Morris was one of Libby's best friends and a coworker. She knew Libby better than anyone and had never seen her quite as moody and disgruntled as she appeared to be today.

"You look like you could take someone's head off. You're going to scare the patients."

"It's nothing, really. Matt and I had a little disagreement this afternoon. I'm sure it'll blow over." Amanda knew about their problems. Libby sometimes discussed their fights, but never elaborated. She felt disloyal mentioning it now.

"What do you mean, 'a little disagreement'? You and Matt seem to be 'disagreeing' a lot lately. What's going on?" She pointed her finger at Libby like an angry parent. "And don't lie to me. I'll know."

"He's just mad at me because I can't keep the house and the yard and the pool and the kids. He said I was a bad mother because the yard isn't mowed, the house is dirty, and the laundry is piled up on the couch." Libby took a deep breath and sighed. "He says I'm too busy flitting around town playing social queen or something. As if. But I do volunteer at the school and church a lot. I'm rarely home. Sometimes I wonder myself. It does sound bad when I say it out loud. Maybe he has a right to question me." Talking out her problems made them seem silly, even to herself.

"Get real, Libby." Jessica Bennett walked up to the desk and dropped down in a chair to work on her charts. "This is the 21st Century. Nobody is allowed to judge you on the cleanliness of your house. As long as it isn't unsanitary, he'll get over it. You don't have a housekeeper like he's used to. I doubt if he even knows how to run a vacuum cleaner. I know he's never cleaned a toilet! I've told you a hundred times, you need to leave him."

Jessica had known Matt all of her life. She constantly teased Libby for stealing her high school boyfriend. When Matt had brought Libby, his "sorority babe," home for the first time, Jessica was surprised that Libby didn't run screaming back to the city. She had tried desperately to hate her for getting the one guy

Jessica had always wanted. After all of these years, though, she actually liked the city girl. Jessica had married a great guy she met at college and they had a son Collin's age. Seth was often in Collin's class, so they had been forced to get to know each other. They worked together in L&D for most of the ten years Libby had lived in Ainsley. They sat on school committees and worked on the county fair. Libby was a good nurse, a good mother, and a good friend. It was easy to like her.

"I know, I know. Tonight was as bad as last night, except this time, he yelled at me in front of the boys. I'm not sure how much they heard. I don't know what to do. I still won't be able to get that stupid yard cut until Monday. By then, I'll have to get out the tractor and bush hog." Libby looked at Jessica and Amanda and threw up her hands. "I don't understand why he refuses to help me do anything anymore. He works until after dark unless he has some sports thing to do with the kids. He can always come home for that! I guess I'm lucky he spends any time at all with them. When he is at home, he's looking at drawings or poring over project documents. He's busy. I understand that, but I could use some help, too."

"That's crazy. You mean he doesn't even mow the yard anymore? Just exactly what does he do? I suppose he's at least good enough in bed to keep him around for the sex." Jessica rolled her eyes and snarled at her friend.

"What sex?" Libby shrugged her shoulders and looked sheepishly back. "We barely touch each other anymore. And you're right, it IS crazy." She put her arms on the desk and laid her head down in defeat.

"Oh, that's just ridiculous! I had no idea things had gotten so bad between you two." Jessica was on a tare. "A little less sex after so many years is normal, but NONE! I guess he's at least good for the money." She put her hand on Libby's shoulder in support.

"Women have put up with more for a lot less cash. The McDonald money has to be worth something."

"If we didn't have a new house, two new cars, a country club membership, three credit cards, two cell phones, karate lessons, piano lessons, a four wheeler, a boat, a slip at the lake, and a ridiculous utility bill, all of that money would be grand. As it is, it barely keeps us afloat." Libby raised her head to check the reaction from Jessica.

"You've got to be kidding me!"

Amanda shook her head and gave a cynical chuckle. "I can't believe it either. No money, no sex, no domestic support. I believe you have to have at least one of those for a successful marriage."

"I don't know." Libby was starting to get a little embarrassed by this conversation. "It's not as bad as it sounds. We've been married for a long time. Things change over time. We need more things, the boys need things. They all cost money. We aren't broke, but we just don't have what everyone thinks we do."

Amanda jumped back into the conversation. "When was the last time you bought something for yourself?"

"Well, last week I bought some new uniforms."

"No, Libby, that's not what Amanda means. When did you buy something besides scrubs and sneakers?"

"I guess it's been a long time. It doesn't matter, as long as the boys have everything they need. I can't complain. I don't want to be critical of him. It's not so bad. I wish I had never brought this up. I don't want to talk about it. It's depressing me even more."

"It should! You need to do something. I'm serious. You need to go tell his parents what's going on. If you can't get some help from them, you need to leave his lazy butt. You deserve better. I can't believe he's turned out to be such a useless jerk. I'm just glad I didn't end up with him." Libby could tell that Jessica was not going to let this go.

A call light went off in a patient room and saved Libby from having to answer any more questions. She should never have mentioned any of this to her friends. She hated to say bad things about Matt in front of other people. He was a good man; he just didn't understand what her life was like now. Things were hard at work. He was tired and frustrated like she was. She was wrong to think divorce was the answer to their problems. She was being ridiculous. She would get the house in order and help him with the bills and everything would be just fine.

♥ ♥ ♥ ♥

"Hey! How's it going?" Chuck McDonald picked up Ben and gave him a big hug. "Collin! Come sit by Uncle Chuck."

Matt shook hands with the group of friends he always sat near at the Mustang games. The talk around him was all about the new season. What did the new sophomore class look like? How many returning seniors were there? It was always the same. It had been the same when he had sat in these same seats with his father when he and Chuck were boys. He made his way up the bleachers to where his brother and father were settling the boys into their seats.

"Hey, Dad. Chuck." He nodded a greeting at his brother and sat down next to his father. "Big crowd for the season opener. Always good to see support for the team."

"Yeah, I think it's going to be a good year." Charlie McDonald had played for the Mustangs nearly forty years before. He was still built as well as his sons. He had dark, salt and pepper hair and green eyes. Chuck looked like a younger version of his father.

Chuck and Matt had grown up here. Both had played football in high school. They had engaged in this same conversation for as long as they could remember. It was fall. It was football time in Tennessee.

Charlie looked at Matt, "Tomorrow is a night game. Mom wants to leave around ten in the morning so we don't have to rush. Do you all want to ride together or do we take separate vehicles?"

Matt hesitated. His family had maintained season tickets to University of Tennessee football for three generations. He knew they were expected to go. Hell, he wanted to go, but he wasn't sure what was going on with Libby. He didn't know what to tell his family. He had to tell them something about tomorrow. "I guess we'll ride with y'all. Libby's working tonight, so she'll need to sleep for a little bit. I hope she can get some sleep on the road. She might not want to go. She's been sort of tired lately." There. Maybe that would placate them if she threw a fit about going. They really hadn't discussed it at all. They hadn't discussed anything.

"What do you mean, 'She might not want to go?' Is she sick? I can't believe anything short of the plague would keep her away from the first game of the season!" Charlie McDonald looked at his son and shook his head.

Chuck looked around Ben and his father to where Matt sat with his head down. "What's going on?"

"I don't know. I don't want to talk about it." He looked at the boys, then at his family. "Boys, why don't you go play some ball with the rest of the gang. It looks like all your buddies are here, now."

"Cool, Dad. We'll be back in a little while." Ben and Collin jumped up and sprinted down the bleachers toward the grassy area where the "future stars" played their own games during the varsity game. Sometimes, their games were more exciting than watching the "big boys."

19

"Okay, they're gone," Chuck leaned in and shot his younger brother a concerned look. He knew something was amiss. "What gives?"

"I don't know. We're just having a rough patch, I guess. Everything's a mess. We fight all of the time. She can't even stand for me to touch her anymore. I don't think we're going to make it through this. You can't fix something if you don't know what's broken. Sometimes I think we just did this all wrong. I'm not even sure if I want to fix it. Maybe it would be easier just to kill it before it gets even uglier than it is."

"What do you mean, son?" Charlie looked around at the people nearby and lowered his voice. "You can't mean that you want to split up! Good grief, what in the world are you thinking? She's your wife!"

"Yeah, I know that part. Only, I don't think she wants to be anymore. And I don't think I can muster up enough energy to care. I'm just tired of fighting. I'm tired of coming home to a dirty house and a fight every night. I have enough problems at work without coming home to more. I don't think it's fair to the boys, either. I'm sure they can sense that something's wrong. It's only a matter of time before they start to ask questions, or worse, start to have problems because our home is in such turmoil. I just don't know what to do." Matt dragged his hand through his hair and hung his head down, resting his elbows on his knees and putting his head in his hands.

"Oh, God. I had no idea things were so bad. Is there anything Mom and I can do to help?" Charlie shook his head and leaned back so Chuck could talk to his brother without anyone hearing.

"Me too. I'll be glad to do what I can. I hate to see anything happen to your marriage. I don't think the boys deserve that kind of a mess. And Libby's just as much a part of this family as you are." Chuck straightened back up in his seat. "Hell, I'd rather keep her than you. At least she's got great legs!"

"Thanks. I really appreciate the support." Matt reached across his father to smack Chuck on the shoulder. "I don't know what anyone can do. I'm beginning to think it's too late. We just let it slip away without even recognizing the signs. If there were signs. I'm just at a loss here. I plan to apologize for being an ass, but I don't know if it will help. I think it'll just be too little, too late."

"All you can do is try. Half the solution is up to her. It took two of you to make your marriage. It'll take two of you to break it." Charlie put his arm around his son's shoulders and gave him a fatherly squeeze. "I know you'll do everything you can. If you need your family, you know we're always here for you. Just make sure you don't hurt that girl. She's pretty special to us, too."

"Thanks, Dad. I appreciate it. And I know how you and Mom feel about Libby. I always have. Maybe that's why we've made it as far as we have." He hesitated, then looked at both of them before he continued. "She's been talking to the girls at work about how bad our marriage is. I had one of the foremen for our tile contractor ask me if we were getting a divorce. I was floored! Can you imagine? It took me forever to track down the source of that rumor. It's coming from the hospital. It seems the girls at work are encouraging her to leave me. It infuriates me that she's discussing it with other people. I never thought she would do something like that."

Chuck leaned in to his brother, "That doesn't sound like Libby, but you could be right. I've heard around town that y'all were having some problems. I didn't want to say anything to you. I figured you'd tell me when you wanted me to know."

Matt closed his eyes and raked his fingers through his hair again, groaning. "This is great, just great."

They dropped the subject and turned back to the football game. Matt tried to keep his mind on the game, but it drifted back to that afternoon and the events of the past few months. He tried to think of when his marriage had started to turn sour. He couldn't pinpoint a single date or time; it seemed to have been a slow, miserable slide into hell. Had Libby noticed? How did people like his parents manage to stay married forever? Not many of their friends had done it. Perhaps it was simply easier to let it go than to suffer the trials necessary to hold it together. Was there anything left to save? A building needed a solid foundation or it would slowly crack and crumble until it collapsed. Had they built their marriage on a solid foundation? He wasn't sure. And that couldn't be good.

Chapter 2

Libby dragged herself to her SUV and slid into the driver's seat. The shift had been grueling, but she was more tired from lack of sleep. She hadn't managed a nap yesterday, so she had been up for more than 24 hours. Her nice warm bed beckoned. She could just imagine curling up in her dark, quiet bedroom and sleeping until afternoon.

She pulled into the garage around 7:30 and parked, wondering if Matt was up yet. She didn't want an altercation with him today. It was all she could do to get her body to bed; she certainly wasn't up for a fight. Maybe he would be in his office working and she could avoid him altogether.

He was still in bed. From the look of him, he was still very much asleep. The boys weren't even stirring this morning. The game had probably been long last night and they had gotten to bed late. He was on his stomach with his arms under his pillow. All she could see were his bare shoulders and the top of his head. She dropped her scrubs, threw on a t-shirt and slid into bed, trying not to wake him.

He stirred and rolled toward her. He pulled her to him instinctively as he slowly broke through the fog of heavy sleep. She felt good. Really good. He ran his hand up her thigh and under her t-shirt to caress her side, sliding a hand over her belly and toward the top of her panties. Her skin was cool against the warmth of sleep. He pulled her closer to him and snuggled her into him. He opened his eyes and stared at the back of her head as he became fully awake and realized that she was completely still. Like a rock. Like a big, icy glacier. Not only was she not responding to his obvious advances, she was trying to ignore him.

He groaned. He would tell her whatever she wanted to hear. He just wanted things to be settled between them. "I'm sorry about yesterday. I don't know what came over me. I'm just tired from work. I know we have a lot to do around here. I'll try to get home earlier so I can get some of the yard work done." He nuzzled her neck. She still didn't move.

How could she have married such an idiot? He couldn't possibly expect her to want to fool around after the things he had said yesterday. And that apology! What a joke. He honestly expected her to just forgive and forget...and give him a little to get his day started off right. What an ass. She'd like to give him a piece of her mind. But she was exhausted and, at the moment, couldn't come up with a good enough retort to make him understand how upset she really was. So, she decided to take the coward's way out.

"Okay, I'm sorry, too. I'm really tired now, and I need some sleep. If you'll just make sure I'm up by about two so I can get something together for dinner, I'd appreciate it." She tried to scoot out of his grasp, but she was already hugging the edge of the bed, and only succeeded in rubbing her bottom against him. He responded by pulling her even closer. As mad as she was at him, it still felt good. Comfortable. Familiar. She needed to feel close to him. It had been so long since they had been this close.

"Um, aren't you going to the Vols game with us today? Mom wants to leave around ten."

"You've got to be kidding me!" Tears welled up in her eyes. "I'm so tired I feel like I could barf. I can't imagine that I'm going to get one hour of sleep, then drive more than four hours to Knoxville for the game. I wish you would have reminded me that it was this weekend. I could have changed my shift." She rolled over to face him. He held on.

"I'm sorry. We haven't exactly been communicating well lately. It just slipped my mind. I guess I expected you to know that today was the season opener, and to assume that we would be going. If you don't want to go, it's okay. I'll take the boys and get out of your way so you can get some rest. I know you're tired." He pulled her left leg toward him and slid it over his, then ran his hand up her body. He smiled when she closed her eyes and bowed her body toward his.

Her mutinous body was responding to his hands even as her mind told her this was going to be a long, miserable day. She brushed a kiss on his lips and ran her fingers into his hair. "Mmmm. I wish you'd quit that. You're not fighting fair." He caressed her bottom, rubbing her against him. "I'm tired, but I know how your mother feels about having everyone there for opening day. I'll go, but I've got to at least get a nap."

He rolled her onto her back with minimal effort. "I'll make sure you get a super nap. God, you feel good."

She caressed his back. "You, too." Knowing her body, feeling her response to him, he eased them through a smooth, sexy ride. Short and sweet, comfy and cozy. Complacent. She was supposed to be mad at him, but it felt so good to be a part of him if only for a few minutes. Was this enough? Could a little physical contact solve their problems? It was her last thought as exhaustion robbed her of consciousness.

"Sweet dreams, baby." He kissed her cheek as he rolled out of bed. She was asleep before he reached the bathroom. He turned and looked at her sprawled out on her back. She was so beautiful. And still so mad at him. What was he supposed to do about that?

♥ ♥ ♥ ♥

Matt woke her up an hour later, just after nine. He had fed and dressed the boys and packed up their things for the trip to Knoxville. At least he was trying to help. She jumped in the shower, fixed her hair, and put on her makeup. He brought her a cup of coffee while she was ironing her Tennessee orange polo shirt and her khaki shorts. He was dressed in an identical polo and khaki shorts, with an orange ball cap sporting the familiar white "T". He was adorable.

She dressed quickly, packed a clean set of clothes and cosmetics for Sunday and dragged herself to the living room to wait for his parents to pick them up. Matt was standing in the kitchen with the boys when she walked in. The sight of her boys, dressed up just like their daddy, and obviously giddy with the excitement of the new season, made her choke with sorrow over the thought of splitting up their family. How could they do such a thing? But was it fair to them to live in the constant uproar their fighting was causing? They didn't fight in front of the children now, but it wouldn't be long before they became so accustomed to it that they would. It frightened her to think of it.

"Hey, baby." Matt moved toward her and took the coffee cup from her hand. "I'll get that. Do you need some more? I packed a pillow so you can sleep on the way. Emily and Brad are taking their own car, so you'll have plenty of room in the back of the Expedition. It'll just be Chuck, Mom and Dad, and us riding up now. Emily and her gang left yesterday. She wanted to go do some shopping." He was rattling and he knew it, but he wanted her not to be mad at him.

His attentiveness and chattering were getting on her nerves. She knew he was trying to soothe her so they wouldn't fight. That was as annoying as just fighting with him. She bit back an ugly remark and walked to the boys. She hugged and kissed them both. "Are you ready to go? We're going to have so much fun today!"

"Grandma said we could have pizza for lunch. She also said she would buy us new jerseys today!" Collin's excitement was contagious.

"And Grandpa said I could hold the Big Orange hand during the game!" Ben had started to hop from one foot to the other. "Can I have a frozen lemonade at the game?"

Libby laughed and ruffled his hair. "We'll talk about that later. Do you have everything you need for today?" When they both shook their heads, she stood up and walked to the garage door to look out the window. Her in-laws were pulling into the drive. "They're here!"

They piled in, with Libby and Matt taking the back. They sat with a seat between them so she could stretch out. Matt had even packed an afghan with her pillow so she could nap in comfort. She took advantage of the temporary solitude and attempted to sleep. It was hard to block out the family chatter, but fatigue took over and shut her brain down long enough to allow her a few hours of rest. When she woke up, they were stopping at Crossville for a restroom break.

Matt gently touched her leg to wake her. "Do you want anything? I'm going to get the boys a drink."

"Thanks, but I'll get something for myself. I need to get up anyway." Libby crawled out of the back and stretched next to the car. She made her way into the restroom and waited in line next to Mary Beth McDonald. Her mother-in-law was as much a mother to her as her own was. Proximity had encouraged a close relationship. Standing with her now was a little uncomfortable. With the end of her marriage looming on the horizon, she was certain their friendship would be ruined. How would she ever manage without Mary Beth to share her life with?

She looked admirably at her husband's mother. It was easy to see where he got his sandy brown hair and beautiful eyes. At 58, Mary Beth was fresh and attractive and appeared much younger than she was. Her soft, Southern charm made her easily likable. She was wearing a pair of khaki slacks and white t-shirt with an orange cotton sweater covered in white, sequined T's. Her purse was orange and white canvas to match her sneakers. Her hair, once the color of Matt's, was now tastefully highlighted to cover the encroaching gray. She wore a short bob that she occasionally updated to fit the current styles. She was wonderful. Libby had always envied her ability to run her family and their growing construction company with equal success.

"What's going on between you and Matt?" She held up her palm when Libby started to protest. "Don't start that with me. I know both of you and I can tell something's wrong. You can cut the tension in the back of the car with a knife. That, and my grandsons are noticeably stressed about something."

"They can't be. We haven't said anything to them. I've tried hard not to fight in front of them. I don't want anyone to know."

"To know what? That you're having some sort of marital crisis? It happens. You just need to talk about it and get through it. Do you think we've made it through almost 40 years of marriage without problems? Get a grip!" She crossed her arms at her chest and looked to Libby for a response.

"It's not just a crisis. I think we should never have married. It was all wrong. We've made it this far because we've been too busy to have problems. Now, we're too busy to have anything but problems. And who has the time or energy left to deal with them?"

They were drying their hands on hard, brown paper towels when Libby turned to her mother-in-law and sighed. "I don't think we're going to make it. It's been over for a while. We're just too stubborn to kill it." She put her head down as if in shame. "I don't know how this is all going to go, but you know I'll miss you. You've been so good to me all these years. I hope when all the ugliness this causes gets better, we won't hate each other. I would definitely not like that."

"Oh, honey." Mary Beth grabbed Libby and hugged her. "It can't be that bad. But if it is, I promise we'll be okay. You'll always be my grandsons' mother. That's a pretty important job in my book. It ensures you a special place in this family. Especially if Chuck continues to refuse to marry and give me some more grandchildren! Since Emily has only girls, you have my only boys. But just so you know, you'd be special to me even if you hadn't married my baby boy and given me such handsome grandsons. I'll always love you like you're my own daughter."

"Thank you." The tearful duo left the restroom and piled back into the vehicle with the rest of the family. Libby had seen too many of her friends' divorces to believe that everything would be okay, but she could at least hope it wouldn't be horrible.

"Do you need to nap some more?" Matt asked her as he crawled into the back seat. "The boys are going to put in a movie. Will it bother you?"

"It's okay. I'll just nap a little if I need to. I'm so tired I could probably sleep through anything." She poked and pounded her pillow into the window to try to get comfortable. Pulling the afghan over her, she snuggled in to nap.

A short time later, she woke up in the parking lot of Itza Pizza. The boys were clambering out of the Expedition like they had arrived at Disney World. Grandma and Grandpa had been taking them to Itza Pizza before Tennessee games since they could remember. To them, it was the best place on earth. Emily and Brad were waiting at a huge table. Their girls, Meghan and Allysan were nearly the same ages as Collin and Ben. They, too, were wild with excitement. They ran up and jumped into Grandma and Grandpa's arms.

The boisterous family meal was cut short when Collin began to ask when they would be going to the stadium. "We'll miss EVERYTHING if we don't hurry. We've already missed the Vol Walk. If we don't get there soon we'll miss the band and the pregame warm ups. I don't want to miss that."

"Okay, okay." Charlie was always ready to get to the stadium as soon as possible. "Let me take care of this check and we'll be going."

Matt reached out and grabbed the check. "I'll get that, Dad. It's the least we can do since you drove." Libby gasped and looked at him with wide, unbelieving eyes. She stopped herself from making a scene, but she was furious. They barely had enough in their checking account to buy groceries next week. How did he think he could afford to feed his entire family pizza and beer?

When they reached the parking lot, she grabbed his arm. "What was that all about? Don't you ever listen to me? We can't afford a bill that big. We can scarcely afford groceries. As a matter of fact, you just spent our grocery money. Now we'll just have to do without. We have to stop trying to keep up with the rest of your family. It's going to send us to the poor house. Is that what you're trying to do?"

"Get off my case." He pushed her hand off his arm and strode away from her. "I'll cover the bill; you just stop worrying about it. I can take care of my family. Now hush before you embarrass me in front of everyone."

She rushed to catch him before he got into the vehicle. "Don't talk to me that way. Do you have some secret bank account I don't know about? If so, I have a stack of bills you need to pay. I'll have them on your desk first thing Monday morning. I'm tired of worrying about them. Your spending is way out of control. I'm thinking of picking up a fulltime slot at work just so we can make ends meet."

"You're not going to work fulltime. That's ridiculous. You can't get your chores done as it is. If you go to work fulltime, we'll have to shovel out the house. Hell, it's a junk pile now. What's it going to look like when you have more excuses not to clean it?"

His voice was low and hateful. It started a surge of anger that ripped through her like a lightning bolt.

"You arrogant, male chauvinist pig." She matched his tone, but injected it with a degree of spite that tore him in two. "How DARE you. I've worked my ass off to make a home and a life for you and the boys. All I get from you is criticism and complaints. I'm sick of it. I'll go back to work fulltime, and I'll take care of my children and myself. I did not spend four years in college to work one day a week. I need more. I need ME! I damn sure don't need you and your crap anymore. I think it's time we ended this farce we call a marriage and went on with our lives."

"Well, I'm glad you finally got around to discussing that with ME. I think you've talked to everyone in town about our problems, except for me! I couldn't agree more that this marriage is doomed, but I would like to have known before everyone else did. You've lost your mind. Get your job. Get your divorce. Just whatever you do, get the hell out of my life!" He pushed her into the car and climbed in after her.

They rode in silence to the stadium. The entire vehicle was soundless. Libby was sure they had all heard at least part of what had transpired between them. It was humiliating for her, but if the boys had heard too much, it would be devastating for them. Maybe they just sensed the tension and responded to it. Surely if they had heard the talk of divorce, they would have said something by now.

Charlie parked the Expedition and they joined the rivers of fans all flowing into one huge sea of bright orange. Everything in and around Neyland Stadium was orange. Shirts, shorts, shoes, slacks, faces, hair, and purses were orange. Generations of Volunteer fans assembled here in their favorite orange attire to show their support for the team. Welcome to Big Orange Country.

Libby was temporarily distracted from her marital problems as the family made their traditional walk down James Agee to the stadium. Every game, she was fascinated by the dedication of Big Orange fans. She had been coming here, becoming a part of the Big Orange experience, since she was a child. Her grandparents had been alumni and always season ticket holders. Her mother had received a scholarship to Vanderbilt and had met her father there. Her parents had been a little disappointed, but not surprised, when Libby had chosen Tennessee over Vandy. Big Orange Pride was a hard habit to break.

She watched her boys. Ben held tightly to Grandpa's hand as he tried in vain to see and hear everything. Collin, with his hand in Matt's, jerked his head from left to right attempting to take it all in. It was a magical place. Some of their best memories were here. Neyland Stadium was family, friends, and fun. It was tradition, and she was not going to ruin it by fighting with Matt all afternoon.

She walked up to Collin, slipped her hand in his, and gave Matt a brief, watery smile. "Truce?" She mouthed to him.

Smiling at her sadly, he gave her a nod. "Okay."

Mary Beth put her arm in Chuck's and whispered in his ear, "What are we going to do about that mess?" She cocked her head in Matt and Libby's direction.

"Stay out of it, Mom." Chuck took her hand and squeezed it. "They have enough problems without us all jumping in. Just leave them alone. If it can be fixed, they'll find a way to fix it. My brother is hardheaded, but he's not stupid. She's the best thing he's ever had. Surely he'll find a way to put them on the right track again."

"But don't you think they'll do better with a little outside encouragement? I just hate to leave something so important to two people who aren't thinking clearly."

"Don't meddle. I'm telling you, it'll make things worse."

"Oh, you're right. I'll stay out of it. For now. But if they start making a bigger mess of things, I'm jumping in."

Charlie slipped Ben's hand into his mother's and fell back to walk beside his wife and eldest son. "Have you two gotten this figured out yet? I'm a little fuzzy on some of the details."

"Dad, I've just finished telling Mom to stay out of it. I think that advice goes for you, too."

"I'm not butting in; I just want to know what's going on. Why did she get so upset when he caught the check? Are they having money problems? How's that possible? He makes plenty of money. He didn't say anything about that last night."

"I can't figure that either. Chuck, what do you think is going on?" She slipped her other hand in Charlie's and looked ahead at her youngest son and his family as they walked toward the stadium.

"I'm not sure. I do know that he bought that four-wheeler, and the kids are involved in a lot of sports now. One of Collin's new baseball bats cost about $200. I guess maybe it's just starting to add up on them. He never has been one to worry much about money. I think Libby handles most of their bills. He probably just has no clue what it takes to keep them afloat." He shrugged his shoulders and grinned at his mother. "Now you know why I'm still single. It's much simpler that way!"

Charlie smacked him on the back of the head. "Don't tease your mother like that. I'll have to listen to her for a week." He scratched his head and leaned in to make sure they could both hear him clearly. Speaking in a low voice, he declared, "We can do one thing, we can make sure they don't spend any more money. I know it's not the heart of their problem, but I'll bet it's a catalyst for these arguments they're having.

Just keep an eye on them and watch Matt's spending. And try to be discreet about it. Meanwhile, we can try to get to the bottom of it."

"Now, what part of that involves staying out of it?" Mary Beth giggled and kissed her husband's hand. "I think you're worse than I am. Only, I know what their problem is."

"Oh, really? So what's their problem?"

"I'm not telling. I think they can get through this, but it's going to take a little time. It's probably going to get worse before it gets better. You remember how hard our first years were? I believe they've skipped some of that. They need to work through some things. We just need to be supportive."

Libby took their tickets from Charlie and handed them to Matt and the boys. She nudged the boys through the turnstile. "Let's go!"

They managed to put aside their differences for the duration of the football game. Libby caught him staring at her a couple of times, but couldn't quite place the look. Maybe he was as upset and confused as she was. She knew he thought she was mad at him. She was a little mad, but mostly she was just tired. Their marriage was over. It seemed like it had been for a long time. She just didn't know how to end it. It was a bit like euthanising a favorite pet. You know it needs to be done, but you just keep looking for that glimmer of hope.

He could tell she wasn't paying much attention to the game. She was probably plotting her great escape. Or maybe she was listing all his faults. He was sure she had a list somewhere. He hadn't realized it was that bad. He knew it wasn't perfect, but they had always gotten along. Did they really not have any money for groceries? He felt more embarrassed for not knowing that than he did because they might be broke. How had they managed to lose so much? The money was nothing. He could always make more of that. A good marriage, however, was hard to replace. He just wished he could stop saying terrible things each time she provoked him. It wasn't helping.

After the game, they had dinner at a restaurant near campus, then drove to the hotel where his parents had maintained reservations for years. They unloaded their bags and herded the kids up to their rooms. It was late and everyone was tired and grumpy. Ben was barely awake enough to walk to the room. He started whimpering as soon as he got there. That was just the break Libby was looking for.

"I'll lay down with him so he'll get some rest. He's just exhausted. Collin can sleep with you."

Matt gave her a knowing look. "I guess this is where we are now? Separate beds. When do we get separate homes?"

"I suppose as soon as you can pack your stuff and get out, but I don't think this is the place to discuss that." She quickly undressed a sleepy Ben and covered him up, kissing him on the cheek.

"Where do you think we can discuss it, Libby? There never seems to be a time or place that's right for you." He looked to the bathroom to make sure Collin hadn't come out. He walked over to her and put his hands on her shoulders. He softened his tone. "Are you sure this is what you want? I had no idea we had reached this point. I guess that's my fault, but I didn't know. I can't believe you're so ready to do this."

"I can't either, but I am. I can't take anymore. Just the thought that you've been so engrossed in your work that you had no idea we were financially stretched is enough to make me scream. We're broke, Matt. Busted. Negative cash flow. Whatever you want to call it. We've got no money."

"So now that my money's gone you're ready to hit the road, huh? I never took you for the coin-operated type. I guess I should have known." Why couldn't he control the negative flow from his mouth?

He knew it was not going to solve anything.

"Oh, shut up. You know this has nothing to do with the money. It's you. You have no idea what our life is like. I spend my entire day, everyday, taking care of you and the boys. At the end of it all, there's nothing left for me. There's nothing left OF me. I'm tired. I want more out of my life than to drop into bed exhausted every night and wonder what you're going to complain that I didn't accomplish for you"

"It's not like that and you know it. I'm tired, too. We have so much work we can't keep up with all of it. You work one day a week. How can you possibly be so overworked? I guess you're right; I just don't get it."

Collin stepped out of the bathroom and went to the sink to brush his teeth. Matt shook his head at Libby and walked into the bathroom, slamming the door behind him. Collin hesitated before climbing into the empty bed.

"How come Ben gets to sleep with you, Mom?"

"I thought you'd like sleeping with Daddy. You got to sleep with me when Daddy was out of town last. It's Ben's turn."

"Okay." He giggled. "I better hurry up and get to sleep before Daddy does. He snores."

Libby bent to kiss him goodnight as Matt opened the bathroom door. He came out dressed in nothing but his boxers. She averted her eyes to the suitcase she had packed. She dug out a pair of cotton pajamas and walked past where he was brushing his teeth at the sink.

He looked up at her in the mirror as he stood up and leaned back to stretch. She quickly shut the door and leaned back against it. He was trying to get past her resolve and get her into bed. Their love life had all but dried up over the last few years, but all of a sudden, he was trying to seduce her. Well, it was not going to work. She could be strong if she needed to. Their marital problems went beyond the bedroom and she wasn't going to give in to the nagging physical urge he was stirring in her. It wouldn't solve anything to jump into bed with him and go a round or two. No matter how good he looked. Or how bad she wanted to.

She walked out of the bathroom and dropped her dirty clothes onto the open suitcase. He was sitting slightly up in the bed with the sheets down to his waist. The dim light from the television cast shadows across him, accenting his well-defined chest. He had one hand behind his head. She mustered every ounce of energy she could to walk past him and get into bed with Ben. She fluffed and puffed the pillow and rolled onto her side away from him.

She was either made of stone or she didn't want him anymore. How could she parade around in those little shorts and that tiny shirt and expect him to just lay here? That was just cold. Matt slumped down in the bed and pulled the covers up to his chest. Maybe she was serious about this separation. She could be very stubborn when she set her mind to something. He just wished he had had the good sense to see this coming so he could have tried to do something about it. Now, she didn't seem very willing to work out whatever problems they had. Not that he knew what her gripe was. He was still confused about the whole business.

Chapter 3

They stopped in Nashville on the way home and went for their traditional shopping spree with Grandma. She bought new school clothes for the boys and spoiled them by letting them pick out their shoes. As they got older, the price tags on their sneakers became more ridiculous. Libby was glad Grandma was willing to pay so much for shoes for them; she sure wasn't going to.

After an exhausting afternoon at Opry Mills, the family sat down for a good meal at the Rainforest Café. The kids loved the atmosphere and always stayed on their best behavior so they would have this special treat. The adults were just happy for a reprieve from Grandma's shopping.

Libby and Matt hadn't spoken since the night before. She was desperately trying to maintain her composure, realizing that this was the last "family" event she would ever attend as a member of this family. It was bittersweet.

Matt was just bitter. She was ignoring him and he couldn't stand it. He was unsure how he was supposed to act. Did she expect him to pretend that everything was fine? The boys were having a good day with the family, but he could tell they sensed the strain in their parents. They were old enough to know something was wrong.

He felt nearly empty. Lost, confused, alone, and empty. He looked over to the where Libby was sitting. She had chosen a seat at the table with the children. Meghan was regaling them with an animated tale of her summer camp. Libby seemed engrossed in the story, laughing with the kids. She looked up at him. She gave him a pensive smile and looked down at her plate. His heart sank. She wasn't just trying to get his attention or punish him. She was serious. Their marriage was over.

The ride home was quiet. The boys were worn out and fell asleep watching a DVD. Mary Beth dozed in the back seat with them while Chuck sat up front with his father and carried on a light conversation about one of their projects. Libby stared out the window trying to avoid any contact with Matt.

She could tell he was stewing. He wanted to talk. That would not be a good idea in a car full of people. Their next talk would be ugly. She had evaded it for as long as possible. She still didn't feel up to it now. As much energy as she could feel coming from him, she doubted he would be reasonable. She wasn't prepared for an intense confrontation. Why did people argue over whether or not to divorce? When one person wanted a divorce, was a fight the way to keep the marriage together?

As soon as they got home, Libby hustled her sleepy sons upstairs to take showers and get ready for school. Matt joined the chaos and helped tuck them in. Collin was unusually clingy, and asked his dad to stay with him until he went to sleep. Matt curled up next to him and pulled his son into his arms.

"Is everything okay, buddy?"

"Yeah, I'm just tired. Are you coming to football practice with me tomorrow? Our first game is Thursday afternoon. I'm starting at quarterback."

"I don't know about practice, but I'll be there for the game. Aren't I always there?"

"I guess." He pulled back so he could look at his father's face. " Are you and Mom getting a divorce?"

Trying to remain calm, Matt gently pushed the hair out of Collin's eyes before he spoke. "What makes you think that?"

"Well, I kinda heard you back at the hotel. I didn't want to listen, but you were sort of loud." Big tears started pooling in his eyes as he looked for reassurance from the one person he trusted most. "Daddy, I'm scared."

"I'm sorry, son. I don't know what to tell you. Mom and I have some things to work out. Sometimes grownups have problems. They don't have anything to do with you. We both love you very much. We're just having a hard time."

He closed his eyes and drew his son in to hold him. Collin smelled like soap and shampoo. He was clean and innocent. And wracked with sobs. "No matter what happens, Daddy will always be here."

He stayed and held his son until he cried himself to sleep. Just the mention of divorce had shattered the child. What would happen if they went through with it? The longer he held the sobbing boy, the angrier he became. How dare she break up their family? What could be so bad that she could tear them apart so easily? When he finally started downstairs, he was livid.

He found her folding laundry on the couch.

"Now, what the hell is your problem?"

"I thought you had figured that out by now." She knew this would not go well.

"Refresh my memory. I seem to have missed something. Or maybe you just told so many other people what our problem was, that you just thought you told me. I don't seem to recall having much of a conversation about any issues so bad they warrant a divorce." He was getting himself worked up. What he really wanted was for her to tell him it was all a misunderstanding. Then they could go to bed and forget about this mess.

"I've told you. Several times. You just choose not to listen to me." She took a calming breath and tried to gather her thoughts. Maybe if she could stay focused on the issues, they could end this thing without saying too many things they would later regret.

"Listen to what, Libby? That your life is hell? That we're broke? That I'm a terrible husband? What? I don't get it." He threw up his hands and walked to where she was sitting on the sofa. He towered over her. He knew the dominant position gave him an advantage.

"Could you just sit down and listen for a minute? It's not going to do you any good to try to bully me. I'm tired of it."

"I'll stand. You talk."

"That's exactly what I'm talking about. You think you can just order me around. I'm your wife. I'm not your employee, or your housekeeper, or whatever else you think I am." She stood up and walked to the other side of the room. "I'm a woman. I am the mother of your children. But I need to be something besides head room mother, chaperone, carpool coordinator, and community volunteer."

She turned back to look at him. "Can you understand that?"

"I understand that you say we're broke and you're ready to leave."

"I'm not leaving, you are." So much for staying focused on the issues.

"WHAT?"

"I want you to move out. It'll be hard enough on the boys as it is. The last thing they need is to be jerked out of their home."

"I'm not leaving my children. This is the 21st Century. I can get custody." He raked his fingers through his hair in frustration and walked toward her. She backed away.

She was talking in a fast, clipped voice as she continued to back away from him. "I'll be working three nights a week. You can have them then. Until this is settled, you can stay here on those nights. It'll be easier for them." He kept moving toward her. The look on his face was frightening. Her heart was pounding. The wall halted her backward motion.

He stopped inches from her. He put his hands on the wall, pinning her. "I hope you know what the hell

41

you're doing." He leaned in; the anger and hurt in his eyes paralyzed her. His voice was low and dangerous. She could feel his hot breath on her face. "Our son is devastated by the thought of us divorcing. I'm still not sure why we've never talked about this before, but I'll tell you this, now. You had better be damn sure of what you're doing, because I'll not let you, or anyone else, hurt my boys."

She gasped for breath. "I'm not hurting anyone. You are. You're selfish and inconsiderate. If you paid any attention to anyone but yourself, you'd realize that we'll all be better off. They're used to being without you on a daily basis. They'll survive. I'll survive." She put her hand on his chest and pushed him away. "Get off me."

He backed away from her. "I'm not on you. You'd know if I were."

"Get out." She pointed to the back door.

"I'm going out, but I'll be back; and I'm sleeping in my own bed tonight. If you can't live with that, I suggest that YOU find another place to stay. This is MY house." He stomped out and slammed the back door behind him.

She shouted after him, "We'll see about that."

Libby slumped into a kitchen chair and put her head in her hands. They still had not discussed the reason she wanted to end their marriage. That was another of their problems. They could never communicate. The list seemed to be growing. This wasn't how she had envisioned their separation. He was never home. They had spent so little time together as a couple in years. Why was he so resistant? Was he so dense that he didn't realize what had happened to them?

She planned to keep the bedroom for herself, but if he insisted on sleeping there, she would make other arrangements. Sleeping with him was not an option. She gathered up some blankets and a pillow and made a bed for herself on the couch. She could have taken the spare room downstairs, but that seemed more like a permanent capitulation to his demands than a pallet on the sofa.

She packed a suitcase for herself and one for the boys. She called her mother and let her know she was coming the following day and would be spending the night. She knew it wasn't fair to leave her mother in suspense, but she didn't want to get into a long conversation tonight. She gathered all of their financial information and made copies of what she would need to take to her mother. The bulk of it she put together to leave for Matt in the morning. She washed her face, took a hot bath, and brushed her hair, trying to relax and clear her mind.

She curled up on her makeshift bed and burrowed under the covers. Sleep didn't seem to be in her immediate future, so she found a good old movie on the television. She suspected that he would go to his brother's, but who knew. She thought maybe a good cry would help, but she couldn't seem to muster the tears. He was so stubborn and hateful. It was hard to cry when you knew you were doing the right thing.

♥ ♥ ♥ ♥

Matt pulled into the parking lot at Ainsley Country Club and found a spot. He turned off his truck and laid his head on the steering wheel. What was happening? She sounded so sure that this was what she wanted. How could he not know she was so unhappy? They had been fighting lately, but he had thought it was just a phase couples went through. He sure hadn't been ready to end it all. They needed to talk, but it didn't seem like they could do that without coming apart.

He saw his brother's truck as he walked across the parking lot. Good. Chuck would be able to help him sort this out. Not that Chuck had such a great record with women, but he was easy to talk to. A friendly ear would be helpful.

The clubhouse had been built in the 70's and remained much as it looked on its opening day. The floors in the entry and ballroom were a utilitarian white terrazzo with black and gray flecks. It had weathered 30 years of wear only through the diligent care of the same caretaker. Jonah had been employed on the day the clubhouse was finished. He had been old when they hired him. Now he was ancient. Each day he swept and mopped and vacuumed the floors with an unappreciated obsession. Nobody noticed the floors at all until Mrs. Barbara Linden tripped on a tear in the carpet and fell down the stairs. Her Bloody Mary consumption was not mentioned. That was in 1985. They had replaced the original carpet with a Vegas-style commercial carpet. It was well worn and fading, but it was not yet torn. It trailed down the stairs and into the lounge.

Matt followed the sound of country music and football coming from downstairs. He walked through the door and looked around for his brother. A pool table sat in an alcove on one side, and was currently occupied by a couple of guys he had gone to school with. The bar spanned one wall. The bartender was leaning on the bar discussing the football game a half dozen of them were watching on the big screen across the room. A few couples occupied the small, round tables scattered around the room. It was a typical Sunday evening crowd.

He walked over to where his brother was sitting with a mixed group of friends. He recognized most of them. One couple was Matt's age. One of the women, Darlene Veazey, was a little younger, and in the middle of a scandalous divorce. He wasn't sure what her last name was today, but he was certain it would be different next time he saw her. Appropriately, she had been called "Easy Veazey" in high school. They said she had "peanut butter legs" – brown, smooth, and easy to spread. He knew it was true. So did the rest of the Mustang football team.

Chuck stood to greet his brother. He gave him a quick, manly hug and started rearranging furniture to make more room for their group. Chuck pulled up a chair beside his and motioned Matt to have a seat. Little brother didn't look so good. The events of the weekend had the entire family worried. Now, Matt was at the club on Sunday night. He never went out.

"What's going on little man?"

"Nothing. I just thought I'd get out and visit tonight. I was hoping to run into you." Now he wasn't so sure he really wanted to talk about it. He just needed a few beers and an hour or two to clear his mind.

"You know where to find me. Do you know everyone here?"

"Pretty much." He gave them all a friendly nod.

"We were just talking about the game yesterday. Hey, you need a beer." He waved his hand over to the bartender. "Can we get a couple of Bud Lights over here? Thanks."

Darlene leaned around Chuck and put her hand on Matt's. She was resting her ample, prominently displayed bosom on Chuck's arm. "What brings you out tonight, baby?" Her drawl was slow, husky, and deliberate. It made him sick to hear her.

"Just bored and wanted to get out for awhile. How've you been, Darlene?" He pulled his hand away from hers to take his beer from the bartender.

"Oh, I'm just fine, honey." She picked up her martini glass, holding the stem carefully between her long, fake nails with the French manicure. Nobody in Ainsley drank martinis. She thought she was being sophisticated. She just looked like a tramp. "Where's what's-her-name? Is there trouble at the sorority house tonight?"

"Her name is Libby, and there's no trouble. I'm just out. Okay." He picked up his beer and stood up. "I'm going to shoot some pool." And get away from you.

"Ooooo, aren't we sensitive tonight. Must be a little trouble in paradise." She flashed a haughty smile at the rest of the group. "I'm sure he'll tell me all about it later."

"Leave my brother alone, Darlene. He doesn't need anything from you. He's married."

"So am I, but that doesn't mean anything, Chuckles. You know how that goes. No purchase necessary."

"I mean it. Stay away." He took his beer and headed toward the pool table.

"Yeah, I mean it, too." She boasted back to the rest of the group. "Matt hasn't been out in ten years and all of a sudden, he's up here on Sunday night with the rest of us mere mortals. There's trouble, and I'm going to make the best of it."

One of the other girls at the table watched Chuck walk away. "He looks good, but so does Matt. Definitely some good genes in that family. I don't blame you for wanting a piece of that. I'd like to take a bite of his tight ass myself." She earned a few laughs from the group.

"If Matt's wife's home alone, I'd like to go keep her company. She looks good." Jimmy Morton was twice divorced and always looking for some action.

"Well, I hate to tell you, but she wouldn't have the likes of you, baby. She thinks she's too good for us. To her, Ainsley is just another Hooterville." Darlene curled her lip in disdain. "I never did like that snooty old bitch. Matt should never have married her and brought her here. She just doesn't belong."

Matt and Chuck joined the group at the pool table and spent the next few hours drinking and shooting pool. Matt was comfortably drunk when

46

Darlene walked up to the table. She plastered her body against his and leaned up to his cheek.

"Hey, baby. You ready to tell Darlene all about it?" Her voice was low and syrupy sweet. Like ipecac syrup, it was enough to make him puke.

"I'm not telling you anything." He turned toward the table and tried to ease her away from him.

"Oh, you don't really have to talk, honey. Talking is always optional. We can go back to my house and make some new memories. The old ones were sooo good." She grabbed his butt and reached up to nuzzle his neck and whisper a nasty suggestion in his ear.

He jerked away like she had burned him. "My God, Darlene. Tell it to someone who cares. And get off me. I'm not interested. Can't you comprehend that?"

He looked at his brother. "I've gotta go. I need to get out of here." He was flushed and beginning to slur his words.

"I'll run you home. You don't need to be driving. We'll get someone to follow in my truck."

"Yeah, whatever. I just need to go."

Chuck arranged for a friend to follow them to Matt's in his truck. When they got in the truck, he turned to his brother. "So, what gives? I know you didn't want to talk in there, but I'm worried about you. You don't look so good, and I could tell this weekend that something is up."

"I really think she's leaving me. Or rather, she thinks she's going to kick me out of my house. She says I can stay there when she's working. Isn't that nice? I build the house with my own hands and she says I can stay there when she's working. Priceless."

"I swear I didn't know y'all were having problems. You sure hid it well."

"We hid it so well, I didn't even know our marriage was failing. You found out before I did, I think. I mean, I sort of knew things weren't perfect, but

I thought we could maybe work it out. Hell, I don't know."

"I'm sorry, man. You know I'm here for you. If you want to crash at my place, you're always welcome. You and the boys can come stay with me. You built my house, too." He tried to add a light chuckle to the statement.

"I'm just tired of it. It's going to kill the kids, but it's hard to fight something you can't identify. Collin's already screwed up by the mess. I'm sure this is going to be pure hell on everyone. I don't know how we're going to get through it. I just wish I had some clue what to do." They pulled into the driveway and into the garage. "Thanks for taking care of me tonight. I needed it"

"Anytime."

Matt staggered in the back door and went to the refrigerator to get himself a drink. He pulled a soft drink can out of the fridge, popped the top, and proceeded into the den. She was covered up to her neck with a pile of blankets. The television was airing a black and white movie. She had obviously fallen asleep watching a classic. He could have guessed that's what she would do. She always buried her problems in a good book or an old movie.

She looked so sweet and vulnerable. Her hair was mussed into a nest around her face. Her skin was the same ethereal, glowing perfection it had always been. For all of their problems, she was still the most beautiful girl in the world to him. He wanted it to be okay. He just didn't know how.

She was aware the minute he pulled into the driveway. She could tell by the way he was staggering that he was drunk. Determined not to have another confrontation with him, she lay as still as possible and pretended to sleep. He came into the den and stood over her. She could smell the beer and smoke from wherever he had been. She guessed he was staring at her. She wished he would just leave. He didn't.

She finally stirred and opened her eyes, pretending to be surprised that he was standing there. "Where have you been?" It came out sounding much more harsh than she intended. She didn't want to provoke him.

"What do you care? I wasn't here bothering you." His words were slightly slurred, but he wasn't as drunk as she had assumed.

"I'm sorry. I was just making conversation. I don't really care." And she didn't. She sat up on the couch, taking the blanket with her, holding it under her chin. She looked up at him.

"Yeah, well, I was at the club playing pool with Chuck. That's all." He turned his head and looked toward their bedroom. She saw the lipstick on his neck and cheek.

"That's funny. I didn't know they had whores at the country club. Must be something new they've added."

"What are you talking about?" His brows squashed together as he cocked his head to the side and snarled at her.

She stood, stepping up to face him. She could smell perfume on him. It made her sick to think what that must mean. They hadn't even officially separated and he was already out catting around. She hadn't prepared herself for that. She should have known he wouldn't stay single for long. Chuck would make sure he had plenty of offers. The women in this town had made it clear from the beginning of his marriage to her that he needn't go far for favors. She had trusted him, and had rarely given it a second thought, until now.

"You smell like a brothel, and you have lipstick on your face. I guess you were shooting a little more than pool tonight." She looked at him with all the contempt she felt. "I would have thought you could at least wait until we aren't sharing a house. Think of the scandal this will cause and what your children will have to endure."

"I haven't done anything wrong - not that Darlene didn't try. It's really none of your damn business, anyway. You've made this decision, so you can live with it. If and when I decide to pursue other interests, it'll be none of your concern. As for what my children have to endure, YOU are the one who has done this to them. I still don't know what's going on."

"What's going on is that I'm tired of living with an asshole. You make me sick. I've never been so insulted in my life as I am this minute. I can't believe you couldn't even wait for the papers to be drawn up before you went out screwing around."

"I told you nothing happened. She's a slut. Chuck won't even touch that. But if I had, it wouldn't matter. I can do whatever I want."

"Well, I'm going to see my parents tomorrow. I'll get the paperwork started on my end. You need to get an attorney and give me his name so we can get this done. I can see we'll need to be quick about it, before you embarrass more than yourself."

"Get over it. You can tell your parents to contact Ham Blankenship. You know the family keeps him on retainer. I'm sure he'll handle this little problem for me. And you can expect a fight. I've already told you about the boys. They're mine. I'm not a weekend dad."

"You've been a weekend dad for years, Matt. I don't understand why you think you can handle being a parent all of a sudden. You have no idea what it takes to keep up with them on any given day." She had dropped the blanket and was pacing around in a pair of cotton shorts and a tank top.

He noticed. He almost forgot what they were talking about. "Oh, please. I think I can handle a few practices. And I can surely drive through the Burger Barn on the way home from practice. Isn't that how it goes?"

"If you had ever offered to do anything before, we might have managed to avoid this situation altogether. Part of the problem here is that this family requires two parents. Not a parent and an additional child." She stopped pacing and turned to look at him. He was staring at her breasts. In her anger, she had forgotten what she was wearing. "Stop looking at me like that. Didn't you get enough of Darlene tonight?"

"How many times do I have to tell you, I didn't do anything tonight? And as long as we're still married, I'll look at you however I want." His long strides closed the gap between them. "As a matter of fact, I'll DO whatever I want."

He grabbed her head with his hand and pulled it up to him, sealing her mouth with his. Despite her protest, he pulled her to him and deepened the kiss. She tasted so good. He was angry with her, but he wanted her more than he ever had. He couldn't remember ever wanting her as much as he did right now. Her protest had died in his mouth as soon as he had molded her torso to his.

What was she thinking? He smelled like another woman, but she was flaming with desire for him. He had never been so forceful with her. Never. Their lovemaking had always been exciting, but sedate. Proper. This was far from either. This was passion. Where did it come from? The other woman? The smell of the strange perfume brought her back to her senses.

"Stop." She pushed him away and fled to the other side of the room.

"If you want. It didn't seem like you wanted me to quit a minute ago." His smugness irritated her more than the way her body so easily betrayed her.

She threw up her hands. "Don't flatter yourself. It's a habit. Like biting your fingernails or smoking. It's hard to stop even when you know it's not good for you."

"So now our marriage is a bad habit? Is that what you're saying?"

"Don't you see it? It's plain as day. Shotgun wedding. Eleven years of marital bliss. It doesn't happen very often. We were stupid to think it would happen for us."

"At the risk of repeating myself, I have to ask. What are you talking about? You're not making any sense to me. I don't understand what you're saying."

"Matt, you do know. Marriages are made of more than a couple of kids and a home. It takes commitment, trust, friendship..." She looked down at her feet and hesitated before finishing. "...and love." She was certain he had never really loved her. Not in the way she thought they both deserved. He had married her because he had to and had stayed in the marriage for convenience. Their biggest problem was that they had a marriage built on all the wrong things. It was destined to fail.

"I, uh, I thought we had most of those things." Did she not feel anything for him anymore? Had she ever?

"Yeah, maybe most of them. It takes all of them to succeed. We've failed. It's time to move on before we destroy more than the marriage. We were friends before I got pregnant. Can't we just be friends again? I don't want the boys to grow up in the middle of hostile parents. They haven't done anything to deserve that."

"Hell, Libby, we haven't done anything to deserve that." He sat down on the edge of his recliner and leaned over, resting his head in his hands.

"I agree. That's what I'm talking about." Maybe now they could discuss this like adults. He seemed to be listening to her. She really wanted to explain her feelings to him. "Our relationship has been less than perfect for awhile now. You know that. Can you honestly say you can't feel it?"

He didn't know how to answer her question. Sure, it felt different. Didn't all marriages feel different after such a long time? Is that what she meant? "I agree that we don't seem to be as close as we once were. I think all couples go through some transition after so many years. It's natural. Don't you think so? Is that what you're talking about?"

She was, but it wasn't as simple as he was making it sound. It was more. It was about a marriage with no love, but she couldn't get him to see that. "Sort of. It's more, though. It's about the boys. It's about me. I want more for me. I want to use my degree for something more than one night a week at the hospital. I could have done what I do now with an Associates in Nursing. I got the BSN so I could eventually go into management. Now, I could even get my Masters and go into advanced practice. I need to use my education. I can't do that without your help at home."

"Why haven't we discussed this before? You've never told me that's how you feel." He was trying to understand, but she was dropping so much on him at once. He couldn't process it all.

"I've tried, but that's another one of our problems. We don't communicate. We never truly talk. I'm not from here. I don't have many friends here. It gets old feeling like an outcast. One of my best friends is your high school sweetheart. How strange is that?"

"I've never thought about it. Jessica's a nice girl. It was just high school. I mean, it was a high school relationship. Nothing more. I didn't realize you felt like an outcast. You can't mean that. No McDonald has ever been an outcast in this town."

"That's just the problem. I'm not a McDonald. Except for a rare few, the women in this town act like I stole you away from them. You're some kind of trophy to them. It's disgusting. I'm sure it doesn't help that I got knocked up and you "had" to marry me. I'm a pariah. Do you know what that feels like?" She was trying to maintain her composure. She had never spoken these words aloud to anyone. She had kept them buried deep in her heart for eleven years. She was close to tears, but determined not to break in front of him.

"I'm sorry, baby. I never realized. I guess that's no excuse." He moved off the chair and stepped toward her to put a hand on her shoulder. He wanted to comfort her, but not scare her into pushing him away again. "I should have figured it out somehow. I've known these people all my life. I can't imagine that they would treat my wife with anything less than the respect any McDonald would receive."

He still didn't get the whole picture. She was determined to get some of it through his stubborn head. "I get respect, Matt. Nobody would openly rebuff me in public. What I don't get are invitations to silly little girl parties, sororities, and ladies clubs, whatever. All my volunteer work is at the school, our church, or the hospital. They're all too desperate to turn me down, or I'm sure they would. It hurts. I'm sure it's stupid to have let it bother me, but I came from a place where I was accepted. I was invited to join every club at school and in the community. I'm tired of feeling completely alone in this town."

The tears came. She was embarrassed and ashamed. This whole situation was completely humiliating. He didn't know. She buried her head in his chest when he pulled her to him. "I'm sorry, baby. I'm so sorry. We'll find a way to make it better. I promise. Mom can fix it. She's in all those clubs. She'll make them invite you."

"I don't want anyone to make them invite me. That's not even the point. The point is, I don't belong here. This marriage is a disaster and I need to move on. I want to go home." She hadn't meant to tell him that. It wasn't even in her immediate plans. She actually planned to stay here for a year until the boys were settled from the divorce. Then she would go home to Nashville. She didn't want him to know, but she had lost herself in his warmth. She had forgotten that he was not on her side in this. He was not going to like her announcement.

He immediately pushed her back, holding her by the shoulders at arms length. He was livid. "You what? You can't 'go home.' Unless, of course, you intend to leave my boys with me. I doubt that's what you mean, is it? Do you really think I'll just let you waltz off to Nashville with my kids and never say a word? You've lost your mind. Your paranoid delusions have obviously reached a fevered pitch. You not only think everyone hates you, you think I'm going to give you my children. I think you need help." He was saying things he shouldn't, but he was so shocked and angry he couldn't stop himself.

"I'm not paranoid or delusional. I'm their mother, and I'm keeping them with me. I'm sure we can work out a reasonable visitation schedule. I want them to have a relationship with both of us. It'll just be more complicated when we move. We'll find a way. I'm not planning to leave anytime soon." She was desperate to keep him calm.

He was on the edge. He was shaking. Every muscle in his body was tight as a bowstring. He didn't know what to say to her next. He had thought they were getting somewhere until she dropped the bomb on him. Could she really take them away? His heart had stopped and his breath was stuck somewhere in his chest. He had to get away before he said or did something stupid. He dropped his hands from her shoulders, turned, and walked toward their bedroom.

The last sound she heard from him that night was the sound of their bedroom door closing.

Chapter 4

Early Monday morning, Libby gathered the suitcases she had packed the night before, picked up a briefcase holding their financial information, and loaded the boys into the car. She dropped them off at school and headed for the offices of McDonald Construction.

The building was new. They had built it three years ago when the old one became too small to accommodate their growing business. Libby had helped with the decorating. It was clean, contemporary, and contained every piece of modern technology available. Charlie McDonald believed that technology would keep his small company in competition with bigger contractors. He was normally right.

Libby stepped through the doors at 7:45. She knew from years of experience that Matt and Chuck were at the gym. Charlie would be in the back part of the building in the shop area drinking coffee and chatting with his superintendents while they watched heavy equipment and supplies being loaded onto trucks for the day. Mary Beth would be in her office attempting to accomplish something before the phones started ringing. Officially, Mary Beth McDonald, CPA was the Chief Financial Officer of McDonald Construction. Unofficially, everyone knew she was heart of the operation. Nothing happened in the office that she didn't know about.

Libby had two reasons for being at McDonald Construction. First, she walked down the hall and into Matt's office. It was cluttered with blueprints, specifications, and piles of phone notes. His screen saver was drawing football plays and squeaked like chalk on a chalkboard. It was obnoxious. He loved it. She dropped the stack of information on his desk and headed down the hall to Mary Beth's office.

Libby stuck her head in and tapped on the door. "Good morning. May I come in?"

Mary Beth looked up and smiled at her daughter-in-law. "Sure. Come on in. Did you stop and get yourself some coffee?" She motioned for Libby to sit down.

The office was cool and comfortable. The walls were papered in a marbled print of muted pastels. A burgundy chair rail surrounded the room. The desk was a huge "U" shape made of dark cherry. Plush burgundy carpet covered the floors. It was the one impractical thing Mary Beth had insisted on. She had informed them that if the workers tracked mud on it, they'd just have it cleaned. Vases of fresh flowers sat on tables and bookshelves completing the feminine feel of the room. It was classic and tasteful. Just like Mary Beth.

"What brings you here this morning?" She was wearing her CPA/CFO clothes today. You never knew. Sometimes she donned an expensive, tailored suit; other days she wore khaki pants and a McDonald Construction shirt. Whatever she wore, she oozed class and style.

"Um, well, I need to ask a favor." She was feeling a little self-conscious. She hated to drag her mother-in-law into this mess, but she had no choice at this point.

"Anything." Mary Beth gave her a concerned, motherly smile.

"I'm going home for the day. I need to talk to my parents about the uh, the divorce papers." She looked around the room, trying to avoid eye contact, but finally rested her eyes on Mary Beth's.

"I hate to hear that. Are you sure that's what you want?" Mary Beth walked around her desk and sat in the chair next to Libby's. She took her hand.

"I feel like I'm doing the right thing. We've tried to talk, but we just keep making a bigger mess of things. You can't have a marriage without love. I don't know how we ever did it. We've made it this far, but it's over. One of us just had to lead the dirge." She squeezed the hand gently holding hers and rose from her chair.

She paced a moment, then looked back to the patiently waiting Mary Beth. "I need for you to pick up the boys this afternoon. They have the usual practices. I've left Matt a note, but he won't be able to help you. Tomorrow there's an awards ceremony for the first six weeks of school. Both boys are getting the "All A's" award. It's at 10 in the gym. I usually try to go. I've called and told them I won't be there to monitor the cafeteria or read to the third grade after lunch. I'll be back tomorrow evening. I also have a job interview." She shuffled in her briefcase and produced a list of the activities the boys had for the next few days.

"I think I can take care of the boys. You know I don't mind. I just hope you aren't getting ahead of yourself. Why are you looking for a job in Nashville? Are you moving?"

"I don't plan to move yet, although it is a possibility in the future. What I'm looking for is a Baylor position where I can work every Friday and Saturday night and get paid for three days. If I pick up Sunday as well, I could get the extra pay, plus insurance. I won't be covered under Matt's policy. It would work out well for visitation. Matt could have the boys on the weekends when he's off, and I could have them during the week when I'm off. I would also make enough money to support us without needing any money from him." She wanted them to understand that she wasn't doing this for the money. She just wanted it to be over. No more fighting, no more rejection.

"Okay, honey. Just don't jump into anything if you aren't sure. This is a big step. It's going to be hard on the boys. It'll be hard on you and Matt, too. I guess it'll be hard on all of us." She stood and halted Libby's pacing by pulling her into a hug. "I love you. I hope you two can get this straightened out."

It felt so good to be comforted. Nobody else had bothered. Nobody else really cared. She hugged back fiercely. "Thanks. I'm not sure that can happen, but I appreciate it. I think we've both said and done some things that have sealed our fate. I just want more. I can't live this way anymore. And it's not just me. He deserves more. He should be in a marriage with love."

"Don't you love him anymore? I had no idea."

"Oh, I do. I always have. This is ripping my heart out."

"So, you think he doesn't love you? Is that what you're saying? Has he told you that?" This was very strange. How could two people live together for more than ten years and not be sure if they loved each other?

"He hasn't said it exactly. I just feel it. I'm a big disappointment to him. I don't know what he wanted in a wife, but I know I'm not it. He is constantly telling me all of the ways I've failed as a wife and mother. I don't fit in here. I don't have many friends. I can't take it. I have to get out before I start to believe that I'm not worth anything as a wife or a friend."

"I don't understand. I can't see him that way at all. Maybe it's just stress or nerves or something. I certainly don't agree with him. Have you tried to talk to him about it?"

"Of course. We just end up in a nasty fight. Let's see. Last night he determined that I am paranoid and delusional. I think that sums it up." She reached down and picked up her briefcase. She didn't want to talk about it. It was time to move on to something else before they got into a discussion that made them both upset.

"I'll put the boys' bags in your car. I packed them in case Matt doesn't get finished in time to help you. It might be easier for you just to take them to your house for the night." She turned when she got to the door of the office. "I know you want to help, but this is a much bigger mess than you can imagine. He's your son, and he'll need you to support him. I don't expect anything from you except to help him take care of the boys. I'm a big girl. I can take care of myself. No matter what he says."

Mary Beth watched her move the bags from one vehicle to another and drive away. Something had to be done. She just wasn't sure what it was.

Matt and Chuck came in laughing around 8:15. They headed straight for the kitchen to get a cup of coffee, a banana, and a bowl of cereal. Emily would be in as soon as she finished running the carpool. They had been doing the same thing since they were children. Except for the weekends, she couldn't remember if any of them had ever eaten breakfast at home. When they were little, she had worried about it, but then she realized how lucky she was to have them with her rather than at daycare. They had both parents with them most of the day. They had turned out well in spite of being raised in an office. She was proud of them. But she was going to kill Matthew Bryce McDonald. He was an idiot.

♥ ♥ ♥ ♥

Libby eased out onto the interstate and merged into the light, weekday morning traffic. She had spent the last 45 minutes on the two-lane highway that took her from Ainsley to I-40. She would have another hour on the interstate until she turned off onto the state highway to get to her parents' house outside Nashville.

Driving provided her with a chance to gather her thoughts. They had been moving toward this divorce for a long time. She was sure she was doing the right thing, but she wasn't sure she was ready. She knew what had to be done. It would be difficult. It would likely turn ugly. Her heart would be ripped from her chest a thousand times before it was finished. But it had to be done. How could they possibly go on now?

She recited her litany of issues as if to convince herself that this was right. She wanted more. He didn't love her. He was irresponsible. He constantly criticized her. He ignored her needs. They didn't communicate. Could anyone survive with such a list of problems? She wasn't sure about that, either. Mary Beth had said that she and Charlie had been through some hard times in their marriage. She was certain her parents were going to give her some sad story about their marriage. It was a perplexing situation. Fortunately, their confrontations over the weekend had pushed them both to the point of no return. It would be over before they knew it.

She turned off the interstate and headed toward her parents' office. They had moved to this small, country town south of Nashville when they both finished law school. It was considered a suburb of Nashville, but it fought furiously to maintain its independent, small town atmosphere. The large Victorian that housed their offices had been their home when she was a small child. Her father, born in poverty, had spent most of his life pursuing unlimited wealth. With the help of her maternal grandfather, a successful financial analyst, he had learned to invest and save. By the time Libby was in middle school, they had built the 'big house' in the country. Her parents had formed their own law firm and had retrofitted the old home into a beautiful, elegant office for their practice.

Her mother's Volvo wagon was in the front space when Libby pulled in. Daddy's spot was empty. Good. She needed time alone with Mother before Daddy became involved. He wouldn't be as objective as her mother. Mother was always objective. Even when it favored someone other than her own family. Once, her mother had battled one of her grandfather's biggest clients in order to settle a land dispute. She felt her client was right and his was wrong. It didn't matter to her that she was going to cost Ellis Dandridge a fortune in lost commissions if his client took his business elsewhere. Her only scruple was that she would not compete against her husband in court. He was glad. She was relentless in her pursuit of justice. Her clients usually won.

Libby was reminded why juries loved her mother when she walked into the office. She could smell the Chanel No. 5 before she could see Lauren Reynolds. She looked as good as she smelled. Mother was wearing a pair of gray, tropical weight wool trousers with a light pink cotton sweater. The sleeveless mock-turtleneck sweater was the perfect display for her pearl necklace. She was appropriately accessorized with pearl earrings, pearl bracelet, and small gold Rolex. Her light brown hair was dusted with natural white highlights and was cut in a modern, tousled look that flipped up in the back in perky points. She looked trim, polished, professional, and 15 years younger than her 60 birthdays suggested.

She rushed to grab her daughter in her arms. "Oh, baby. Please sit down and tell me what's wrong. I've been so worried since you called last night. I cleared my calendar for the morning. Daddy's taken my court cases so we could be alone for a bit. I can't imagine what's going on. I'm just sick."

She held her child at arms length and surveyed her from top to toe. She appeared to be okay, but she looked a bit frumpy in navy shorts and a sweater with little footballs on it. Her hair needed to be cut, her eyes were rimmed with dark circles, and her shoes were worn. What was happening? Libby had always been fastidious about her appearance.

She let her go and motioned toward an antique sofa in her office. "Have a seat, sweetie. I'll just get us some coffee and you can tell me all about it." She walked to the kitchen across the hall and returned with a silver coffee service. She set it on the coffee table in front of the sofa and sat beside her daughter.

Her office was filled with antiques. Her desk was an antique dining table set atop a large oriental rug. A credenza behind her desk held files and office supplies. A buffet and china cabinet held other records and books. A beautiful mantelpiece laden with photos of Libby and her children topped the functional fireplace. It was a look only someone with Lauren's independent spirit would even try. Her office felt more like a home library than the office of an aggressive, callous attorney.

Her mother was such a contradiction. Most of her professional associates feared facing her in a courtroom. They saw only the brilliant, calculating attorney. Libby saw so much more behind her polished façade. She wondered what they would think if they had seen her mother curled up on a pink bedspread drinking cocoa with a heartbroken sixteen year old. They would have been amazed at the tears she shed when she was allowed to witness the birth of her youngest grandson. She was a loving, attentive mother and grandmother. Libby was grateful for that, but now, she needed a damn good divorce lawyer.

"Mother, I need an attorney."

"Oh, honey, what's happened?" She reached for her daughter's hand. Libby pushed it aside and reached for a cup of coffee.

"Just let me get this out. It's hard enough to tell an attorney something like this, but when your attorney is your mother, it's petrifying."

"Okay, I'm your attorney, and I'm all ears."

"I want to divorce Matt." She put her hand on her mother's leg when she started to speak. "You said you'd listen. Now, I'll try to explain. Things haven't been going well. We fight all of the time. Mostly about trivial things, but lately it's gotten much worse." She continued to outline the situation. Her mother listened in stunned silence.

"Have you talked to him about all of this? What does he say?"

"He went out drinking last night and came home smelling like a whorehouse. I guess that says it all." Libby put her arms out, palms up, as if she had presented her case.

"I still don't see what part of all of that should end in divorce, but if it's what you want, I'll take care of it."

"Oh, there's one more thing. We're broke. We've spent what we've made. I don't know how I'll pay you or how I'm going to manage on my own. I've picked up a fulltime slot at home, but I'm applying for a Baylor position in Nashville. I have an interview tomorrow. I'll have to work out your fee later. If that's okay with you." She hung her head in shame when she finished.

Lauren put a finger under Libby's chin and lifted her face to look into her eyes. "You never have to pay me a thing, but if you did, you'd have plenty of money. You will inherit a fortune from us. Daddy and I have moved quite a few of our assets into a family trust in your name for tax purposes. All you have to do is ask and you can have whatever you want. We're not getting any younger. I'd rather see you enjoy it now than after we're gone."

"I don't want your money, now or later." She was immediately defensive. "I will make plenty of money when I start working a regular schedule, I just need a few weeks to get myself together."

"That's fine, honey. Let's just discuss the specifics of the divorce." She rose and walked to her desk. "Come sit over here. I'll get you some paperwork you'll need to fill out regarding custody and visitation. You do know that this is going to be ugly. I can't imagine Matt stepping aside and letting you have custody of those boys."

"I'll share, Mother. I don't have a problem with that. I'll be working every Friday, Saturday, and

Sunday, so he can have them then. I can have them Monday morning through Friday afternoon. What else is there?" She sat down with a plop in an upholstered chair in front of the desk. She felt more like a penitent child than a grown, independent woman filing for divorce.

"Really, there is much more. Tennessee now has a program that encourages both parents to remain active in their children's lives. You'll each have to attend a parenting class, and you'll have to fill out a formal parenting plan. You'll need to designate who will have the boys on which holidays, and who will be responsible for education, medical care, religion, and extracurricular activities. You'll also need to designate who will be considered the primary custodian for government purposes. That's usually a bit sticky, but I'll explain it later."

"Okay, I get it. It's complicated."

"It's more than complicated. We're talking about lives, but we also have to discuss the more crude aspects of divorce. Like money. You'll also have to agree on taxes. You can do that several ways. Since there are two children, you can each claim one every year. Most people just alternate years."

"Oh, gosh. I think I'm going to faint." She covered her face with her hands.

"What about support? That's always a touchy subject. Have you thought about that?"

"Well, actually, I have. I told him I didn't want any." She gave her mother an apologetic look.

"That was bright. Even if the courts would allow it, I wouldn't. We have a formula we use. How much money will you be making and how much does he make?"

Libby outlined the figures for her mother then sheepishly looked at her. "See why I "volunteered"? With the nursing shortage, I'm in demand. With specialty pay, incentives, shift differentials, and bonuses, I can do rather well for myself. If he really knew how much I could make, he would want support from *me*. I don't want him to know that I'll be making as much or more. I guess his father will probably increase his salary now that he knows we're broke, but it will still be close enough that I would rather keep my income quiet if we can."

"And you say he has no idea what your hourly rate is now? I can't believe that." She put her pen down and folded her hands on her desk. "We have several things to think about, then. You'll need to work on the parenting plan and get it back to me. Meanwhile, I'll make some discreet inquiries into the likelihood of getting this filed without any further financial disclosures. If we have to list assets, you're going to have problems as well. Remember, I just told you that we have put quite a bit of ours in your name. Technically, we may have left some of them open for him to get them. If we had known you were having problems, we would never have done any such thing." She gazed off thoughtfully. "Daddy and Grandpa Ellis handled most of that, though. It may be okay. I'm certain they made some contingencies. We'll have to talk to them about that later."

"About Daddy. I know he's going to be mad. I don't want to hear it. Can you help me? Can you run interference so he won't go nuts over this whole thing?" She was twirling her hair in her fingers like she had done as a child. The habit had been squelched 20 years ago. She didn't even realize she was doing it. Her mother did.

"I'll talk to Daddy. I don't think he'll be as judgmental as you think. He may want to kill your husband, but he won't be mad at you."

"Oh, that's what I'm afraid of. I don't want him to blame Matt. It's both of our faults. I'm sure I haven't done everything I could have to make this work. I just don't want this to turn out to be a 'Matt-bashing' session. He's still the father of my children. I have to learn to get along with him. I've indicted his personality enough. I don't need anyone else to jump on the bandwagon." She had twirled her hair into a knot and was unconsciously trying to get it out.

"I see. Well, I'll talk to him. Is there anything else?"

"Oh, yeah. I have printouts of our checking and savings, copies of our bills, mortgages, credit cards, etc. I guess we have to figure out what to do with the bills. I haven't thought much about that. I did tell him I want to stay in the house with the boys." Her twirling was becoming distracting. Lauren couldn't help but stare in dismay. "I told him he can stay there with them on the nights I'm working, but that won't last long. I have to sleep. Especially if I'm still working in Ainsley. Once I go to Nashville, I'll just sleep at your house or in a call room at the hospital. I'll play that by ear."

She handed the notebooks to her mother. "I'll go through this and see what I can come up with. It'll need to be fair. I'll work with his attorney on it. By the way, do you have that information for me? You need to let me handle this with his lawyer from now on. You don't need to discuss anything else with Matt."

"His attorney is Hamilton Blankenship, III. His office information is in the front of the notebook. You might remember him from the wedding. He and Matt were frat brothers. He was my big brother in their fraternity. The McDonalds keep him on retainer. I'm sure Matt will see him sometime today. He's good, but I have confidence in my counsel." She smiled across the desk at her mother.

"Good. Well, your counsel would like to go to lunch and then spend the afternoon on a decadent shopping spree. How about it?" She stood and grabbed her jacket off the back of her chair. "We'll just leave your car here. Daddy can bring your car home and he can ride in with me in the morning. You are spending the night aren't you?"

"Of course! I wouldn't miss one of Velda's meals if my life depended on it. Besides, I do need to talk to Daddy. And there's the job interview tomorrow. It's at 11 downtown. I'll go home after that."

"Let's go. There's a new little café up the street. They have fabulous quiche." Her cell rang and she checked the number on her caller ID. "I'll have to get this. You go on to the car." She handed Libby the keys and turned back into her office, closing the door behind her.

She spent a few minutes on the phone and walked out, shoving it into her purse. She checked her messages with her secretary and headed out the door. She felt like a traitor for taking that phone call, but there were extenuating circumstances. She hoped she was doing the right thing.

They relaxed over lunch, avoiding any mention of the divorce. Lauren enjoyed the tales of her grandsons and promised they would come over for football games and soccer matches in the next couple of weeks. She dragged Libby to the mall and bought her several new outfits. On a whim, they dropped into a day spa where they both received a massage and a facial. Lauren convinced Libby to get her hair cut and highlighted, then paid for their adventure with a smile.

At 6:30, they pulled into the driveway of the Reynolds estate. The expansive home was built on a hundred acres of real estate barely 30 minutes from downtown Nashville. They cruised up the long driveway and stopped outside the front door. Libby bounded out of the car and ran up the front steps to greet the housekeeper who was running out the door with equal fervor.

"Velda! I'm so happy to see you. You look wonderful!" She threw her arms around the elderly lady and squeezed her vigorously. Velda squeezed back.

"Child! You're a sight to see. What have you done with my boys? I can't believe you've come up here without them." She took the girl's hand and dragged her into the house. "I've made your favorite dinner. Your mother told me you'd be joining them tonight."

"Oh, thank you, Velda. It's good to be home. I miss y'all so much sometimes. How have you been? Daddy isn't still harassing you about retiring is he?"

"He tries, but I've refused again. I'm not that much older than your parents, you know. He's a sneaky devil, though. He's hired me an "assistant" to do the heavy cleaning. I'm not much more than a supervisor anymore. I guess I should be thankful. They've been very good to me."

Her parents hired Velda when they moved from the house in town. She had been middle-aged then. Her family had lived in this area since long before urban sprawl had swallowed it up. Her husband had died the year before, leaving her a childless widow with little money and no education. She jumped at the chance to live and work in the big, beautiful house the Reynolds had built. She quickly bonded with their precious twelve-year-old daughter and had been content to stay and run their household ever since. They treated her more like a member of the family than a servant. She was even seated after the mothers when Libby and Matt were married.

Libby suspected that her father had invested Velda's pension so well that she could probably retire and build her own home, but they all knew she never would. She would stay with them until they needed to care for her, or one of them needed her care. She was healthy as a horse and could still cook better than any international chef.

She hustled them into the sitting room and instructed the new maid to take Libby's things to her room. She rushed into the kitchen and returned with a vegetable tray. She opened a bottle of wine and brought them each a glass. "You two enjoy yourselves. Mr. Clay is in his study on a business call. He'll be in directly. He's been pacing for the last hour waiting for y'all to get here. Dinner will be in about 20 minutes." She marched off to the kitchen to complete her preparations.

Moments later, Clayton Reynolds strolled into the room. Cool and confident, he looked more like a country gentleman than an attorney. He wore L.L. Bean khaki slacks and a long sleeve plaid shirt. He had auburn hair, lightened now by a considerable amount of gray, bright green eyes, and a ruddy complexion complete with the freckles one would expect for a redhead. He was tall and rangy, and carried himself like the wealthy man he had become, not like the poor, hopeless bastard he had been born.

Hard work and sheer determination had earned him a scholarship to Vanderbilt, despite being the son of a motel housekeeper and a drunk who had left the minute his mother had conceived. She had done everything she could to give her son what little she could to help him have a future. She sequestered him in their cheap little efficiency room at the motel after school each day and forced him to study. He spent most of the summers reading, and was rarely allowed out of the room to play with other children. She was afraid of the influence they might have on him.

For him, she had been everything. He never faulted her for his upbringing. After seeing the paths chosen by so many of the others from his neighborhood, he was thankful she had been so diligent. He could have wound up in jail or dead. Instead, he had graduated at the top of his class and received the finest education money could buy. He worked his way through college to pay for his living expenses. When he got his first job after law school, he used part of his salary to move her from the motel to a nice apartment in a better part of town. He spent his first raise paying her expenses to vocational school so she could be an LPN. When she retired he purchased a condo for her in a retirement community.

To Libby, Daddy was the world. Every Southern girl held her Daddy in the highest esteem. He was warm hugs and soft spankings. He smelled like woodsy cologne, a Cohiba, and Gentleman Jack. What Mother wouldn't allow, Daddy would indulge. Her daddy had a quick wit, a fierce temper, and an endless credit card. She had never forgotten or taken advantage of any of them.

She jumped up from her seat and threw herself into his arms. "Oh, Daddy, I've missed you so much." She buried her head in his neck and inhaled the familiar scent. She was so glad to be home. She could almost forget what had brought her here in the first place. Almost.

"I've missed you too, princess. What brings you home on such short notice? Not that we aren't glad to see you, but you've come without my boys." He broke the embrace and led her by the hand to his big leather chair. She sat on the floor at his feet. "Now, tell Daddy what's wrong so I can fix it."

"She's not 12, Clay. She does need to talk to you, but you need to listen to her and hold your temper. She doesn't need the additional stress of a temper tantrum from you." She reached over and put a hand on his arm. "Am I making myself clear?" She raised her eyebrows and gave him a threatening look.

"I think you have. I'll be quiet and hold any comments until you finish." He looked down at his daughter and stroked her hair. She wasn't 12 anymore, but she was still his baby and she looked tired and unhappy. He was not pleased.

"I'm divorcing Matt." She rose from the floor and sat on the edge of the ottoman in front of his chair. She looked into his eyes and saw the difficulty he was having holding his tongue. "It's not anyone's fault. We just can't do it anymore. We're fighting, money's a problem, I'm not happy in Ainsley, and we just can't seem to communicate. I know it probably sounds silly to you, but I want more from life than to be stuck in that town with a loveless marriage and no future. The boys deserve better. Even Matt deserves better than to be saddled with me. I don't fit into his world. I never have and I never will. It's an impossible situation, best resolved by a quick and painless divorce."

"Well, you make it sound so final. And so simple. I hope you understand, sweetheart, that I've never, in nearly 40 years of law, seen a "quick and painless divorce", particularly where children are involved. I'm assuming you've asked your mother to handle it?" He gave them both knowing, disapproving looks. Lauren shot him a look that suggested he hold back any other unnecessary comments until they talked.

Libby felt sick. She knew her father longed to say more, but her mother was determined to rein him in. She was somewhat grateful, but she could feel how much it hurt him for them to be going around him. She didn't want him to be hurt. "Well, there are a few things she'll probably need help with. We've had some financial setbacks, which I'm sure his father will settle before this is finished. However, as I've explained to Mother, he has no idea how much money I'll be making when I go fulltime. He is also unaware of the assets you and Mother have transferred to my name."

"Damn!" He got up and started moving around the room. "I wish I had known about all of this." He flailed his arms as he paced. "A little warning could have saved us some trouble. He could claim some of what we've set aside for you and the boys. I think I've locked up most of it in the family trust, but some could be exposed. I will have to look at that. I'll call Grandpa Ellis and see what he has to say."

He paused in his pacing and looked at her. "And how much money will you be making, young lady? Is it more than he makes?" He grinned and reached down to pull her to her feet.

"Yeah, it's a little more," she answered quietly. "I've just never been able to work fulltime and show what I can do. I'm actually quite in demand and I'm ready to put my education to good use." She hooked her arm through his and aimed him toward the door. "Let's go see if Velda has our dinner ready. I'm starved"

Chapter 5

Matt wandered into his office around 8:45. He had a fresh cup of coffee and was ready to face the mountain of work on his desk. He had four projects he was managing simultaneously. They were in four different phases of construction and each came with its own set of problems. He sat down at his desk and set his coffee on a coaster.

He saw the note from Libby sitting atop three notebooks. It was handwritten on a piece of notebook paper.

Matt,

I have gone to see Mother so she can get the paperwork started. As I promised, I have left you all of our bills so you can take care of them. The green notebook is our banking information and printouts from our online banking program. There's a CD of the info in the pocket if you want to load it on your computer at work.

The blue notebook contains all of our credit card statements with receipts attached where applicable. The red notebook contains our mortgage and the notes on our vehicles, the 4-wheeler, and the boat, along with the lease agreement for the slip at the lake.

If you have any questions, I'll have my cell on me.

Your mother has a copy of the boys' schedules for today and tomorrow. Try to help her if you can. They have to be in two places at once. Collin mentioned that you were going to his football practice today. Please don't disappoint him.

*I'll be home tomorrow afternoon.
I'll pick them up from school or I'll call
your mother if I'm going to be late. We'll
need to talk to them as soon as possible.
Plan to do it tomorrow night. The sooner
the better.*

Libby

A pink sticky note from his mother was attached: *You'll need to take care of the boys this afternoon. I have a meeting. Mom.*

He opened the green notebook and looked at the printout of their checking account. It was easy to see that there wasn't much left after all the bills were paid. He leafed through the pages and noted the declining balance over the course of the last year. The blue notebook was frightening. All but a few charges were his. The guns, new helmets, baseball equipment, Titans tickets, Braves tickets, hotel rooms in Atlanta, the list was endless. It made him look like more of an ass than he knew was possible. Why hadn't she told him they were struggling so? She had kept it all to herself. He could easily have stopped spending, or taken more salary. He was embarrassed and frustrated. She should have told him. Sometime in the last year, she could have shown him all of this. Why did she have to wait until it was time to show their attorneys?

He tallied up the amounts they owed on credit cards and personal loans and went across the hall to his father's office. Charlie was fixing himself a cup of coffee. "Can I talk to you, Dad?"

"Sure, come on in, son. I have a minute or two before I need to leave. I have a meeting with the owners on the Lakeside Inn project.

They can't seem to understand what a deadline means."

"I'll just make this short and sweet. I'm embarrassed to tell you this, but I've been extremely irresponsible with my money. My only defense is that I didn't know." He sighed heavily. "If I had a nickel for every time I've said that in the last three days, I could probably pay off my debts without borrowing from you. It's ridiculous, but that's the truth."

"Is that what's happening with you and Libby? Is it money?"

"No, it's not really the money. That I didn't know about the money is probably the most telling. We just haven't communicated. There's more, like the fact that she's unhappy here, but mostly, we just don't have it. Whatever it is that makes a marriage, we don't have it."

"It takes love to make a marriage. Do you two not love each other?"

"I love her, but I don't think she loves me. She keeps talking about how you can't have a marriage without love. At the risk of sounding like an even bigger idiot than I already feel, I didn't know. I thought what was happening was just normal stuff. I guess I was wrong."

"I can't believe that. I think you two need to talk."

"We've tried. My mouth overrides any sense I might have. I think hers does, too. We start out trying to have a serious discussion, then we get off on some trivial thing and we start saying awful things to each other. I think last night put us over the edge. She's gone to her mother's to start on the paperwork."

"I had no idea it had reached that point." He could sense his son's encroaching depression and his heart ached to help him. He took a long drink of his coffee and shook his head sadly.

"Me, either. Do you think I should call Ham? I need to get myself prepared for this. I don't know what I'm supposed to do. She wants me out of the house. She also says she wants to go home. I don't know what the hell we're doing, and I'm not sure she does, either." There was another list of, 'I don't knows.' The situation was becoming more uncomfortable by the moment.

"Oh, God. This is terrible. How in the world are you going to tell the boys? They'll never understand." He closed his eyes and leaned his head back on his chair.

"Collin's already asking questions. He was hysterical last night. She wants to tell them tomorrow when she gets home. I guess we'll have to before it gets around town and some kid announces it in gym class. I can't put them through that. I wish I could shield them from this whole mess." He leaned an arm on the chair and rested his chin on his fist.

"Well, I'll call Ham and tell him you're coming over. I saw him this morning, and I don't think he has court today. He'll work you in." He reached in his side drawer and pulled out a desk style checkbook. "Now, how much money do you need?"

"I hate to ask, Dad. I feel like such a jerk. I'm so ashamed that it has come to this." He stopped talking and tried to compose himself. He was glassy-eyed and more emotional than Charlie had ever seen him.

"Son, this money is yours. You've worked 60 hours a week for years with no extra compensation. You could have gotten a raise anytime in the past few years."

"It's not just the money, Dad. It's everything. I'm an embarrassment to my family. I've lost the best thing that ever happened to me because I was too busy trying to be what everyone else expected me to be. The truth is, I'd rather have worked 40 hours a week, have a few less things, and know what time my kids get out of football practice, or soccer practice, or whatever. Instead, I'm just a weekend Dad with a lot of toys and a burgeoning debt. I'm sorry I've disappointed you."

Charlie walked around his desk and put his hand on his son's shoulder. "You'll never be a disappointment to me. You've realized that you're not perfect and you've discovered what's important in life. Now you have to figure out how to fix it. I'm sure Lauren Reynolds will have Libby's case well built by this afternoon. You need to go see Ham Blankenship and get yourself in order. Meanwhile, see if you can't restrain that mouth."

He walked back to his desk and pulled out his checkbook. "Now, how much?"

Matt took the check from his father and headed straight for the bank. He made the deposit, paid off the loans for the four wheelers, the boat, and both vehicles. He walked across the street to Ham's office.

A large burgundy and gold sign proclaimed the offices of Blankenship Associates, Attorneys at Law. The sign proudly listed Hamilton Blankenship, Sr., Hamilton Blankenship, Jr., and Hamilton Blankenship, III in large letters. The sign should have read: Mr. Blankenship, Beau, and Ham. That's how everyone in town knew them. Another name had been added in smaller letters: Morgan Gray Peterson. Matt had never heard of him. He didn't know any Petersons from around the area either. They must have been recruiting for a new partner.

Nobody was sitting at the reception desk when Matt walked into the office. He continued through the door to the main office area and proceeded toward Ham's office. He stopped short of speaking when he got to the door. A nice, perfectly rounded bottom covered in the fine fabric of a gray business suit greeted him. The legs beneath the hem of her skirt were as well shaped as the rest. The owner was digging in a box in front of the desk.

Suddenly feeling like a lewd intruder, he cleared his throat to get her attention. "Excuse me."

She bolted upright and smacked her head on the edge of the desk. "Dammit!" She turned and grimaced at him, rubbing her head. "Who are you? And what is *wrong* with you? You scared the Bejesus out of me."

He just stood there, staring at the prettiest gray eyes he had ever seen. She had removed her jacket, leaving her white, silk shell to accentuate her luscious curves. Her creamy skin defied age, but something about her eyes led him to surmise that she was older than her tight derriere suggested. Late 30's, early 40's? He couldn't tell.

"Excuse me?" She sounded irritated and he realized he was gaping at her. "May I help you?"

"Um, I hope so. I'm looking for Ham. Is he around?"

"He's probably at lunch. I have no idea. He needs to be in here moving all his junk." She motioned to the boxes he had not noticed were stacked all over the office. Ham's favorite

Tennessee Volunteers prints had been taken down and were leaning against the wall by the door.

"Are you redecorating the office for him?" He assumed she was an interior designer.

His question was ludicrous and she was immediately rude and defensive. "I'm redecorating, but not for him," she snapped at him.

"Oh, I'm sorry." Matt was a little confused at what was going on and why she was so offended by his question. "I just assumed. I'll see if I can find him."

She caught his arm as he was walking out. "Sorry. I'm just a little frustrated at the mess. It's tough on a classic Type A personality to work in chaos. Let's start over." She put out her hand to shake his, flashing him a smile as she did. "Morgan Peterson. I'm the new partner."

He took her hand, surprised at how warm, soft and small it was. He was expecting cold and hard, like the way she had snapped at him. "Matt McDonald. I need to see Ham. My father was supposed to call."

"OH. Let me see." She started rummaging on her desk, finally pulling out a pink telephone note. "Ham dropped this off to me a few minutes ago. He said I should probably handle what you need today, and then he'll talk to you about the case later."

She pulled on a pair of tortoise shell half glasses and read the note. "Matt coming by to discuss divorce. Please help. Charlie Mc." She waved it at him. "Would that be your father?"

"Yeah. So, it sounds like Ham's pawning my problems off on you. Are you up to it? It looks like you have a way to go before you dig this out." He let his gaze survey the room. "I'm no Type A, but even I can't work in a mess."

"I'll manage."

"Why is Ham moving out of this office? He's been here since he graduated from law school."

"Mr. Blankenship is finally giving up his office, so Beau is moving in there, and Ham is moving into his father's office. I guess it's time to change the guard at Blankenship palace." She chuckled at her play on words.

He laughed with her. "I can't believe they've hired an outsider. There have been nothing but Blankenships in this office since Mr. Blankenship first hung his shingle. I suppose times change."

"Times change for all of us. I'm looking forward to working here. Everyone has been so nice. It's certainly a change from where I was." She started moving books and pictures off the chairs in front of the desk. She sat down and motioned him toward a chair. "Have a seat."

"So where did you come from?"

Morgan shifted uncomfortably in her chair. She had come here to escape the pressure of the practice she had left and the nightmare that had been her marriage. She wasn't ready to let all of that out yet. She had to think of Lindsey. Maybe she should just stick to the facts.

"I went to Harvard Law. I've been working for a large firm in New York. My specialty is family law. That's probably why Ham wants me to check out your case." She smoothed her skirt over her knees, unconsciously drawing his eye to them.

"We don't get too many Harvard grads around here. I'm impressed." He stared, spellbound at the smoothness of her silk stockings over her shapely calves. He realized he was gawking again and struggled to regain his composure. What in the world was wrong with him? He was acting like a horny teenager. "My wife is, at this moment, preparing to divorce me. Her mother is an attorney and will handle her case. I don't think it's going to be terrible or anything, but I want to be prepared. I *do not* want her to take the boys out of this county. I think she might want to move home to Nashville."

"Okay, let me get something to write on and we'll try to start from the beginning." She went to the other side of her desk, pulled out a legal pad, and sat down in her leather office chair. "I need the basics. How long have you been married, how many children, etc? Don't leave out anything you think I need to know. I'm sure everyone else in town could answer for you, but I'll need for you to tell me."

Matt outlined their courtship, marriage, kids, and the events of the past year. When he finished, he cocked his head at her and grinned. "So, do you think I'm an ass? Is this all my fault for not paying attention? Am I going to be screwed in this mess? Am I going to lose my kids, my house, and a large chunk of my paycheck?"

She took off her glasses and laid them on the desk, smiling back at him. "Don't get so worked up. I'm your attorney, and I'm not allowed to think you're an ass, or at least, I'm not allowed to say it. And I'll do my best to keep anyone else from thinking it, either. But just in case, you might want to stay away from the country club and…" she looked down at her notepad, then looked back at him with a mischievous grin, "Darlene. That's exactly the sort of thing that could contribute to your losing everything. You'll have to be saintliest man in Tennessee until we have this resolved."

"Great. I get to live like a eunuch while my wife does what she wants. That's really fair." He threw up his hands in frustration.

"You don't know the meaning of fair, yet." She shuffled in her desk until she pulled out a folder of papers. "This is the parenting plan and other information you'll need to complete." She explained the parenting plan to him, and gave him a flyer with registration information for the parenting classes.

He stood and started to pace around the office, looking at her things, occasionally pulling an item from a box and mindlessly looking at it. "I don't have any problem with most of that, I don't even have any problem with the child support issue. I just don't want her to move the boys away from here. That takes away all of my chances to be their Dad. That's important to me."

She was watching him prowl the office like a caged animal. He was so handsome and so masculine. She was impressed by his concern for his boys. Men like Matt McDonald were rare. Most men she represented were more concerned with how to get out of paying their child support. She was pleased that he was focusing on his children. "I'll need a schedule of when you are with them now. How much of their daily care you participate in, sports teams you coach, whatever you can give me."

He scratched his head and gave her a worried look. "I haven't done much of that lately. I've been busy at work and I don't have much time to chase them around. Libby has taken care of them for the last few years. She works one, maybe two nights a week; I work five or more ten hour days." He noticed the thin-lipped grimace on her face. "Remember, you're my attorney, you can't think I'm an ass."

She laughed. "I don't think you're an ass, Mr. McDonald."

"Matt."

"Matt. I do think, however, that you will need to get more involved. If you're going to make sure she can't leave, you have to be able to prove that it's in their best interest to stay. If she does everything for them, then what do they need you for?"

She rose from the chair and walked toward where he had stopped by the window. He was staring out into the main drag around the courthouse. He appeared to have stepped into another universe. "Are you okay?"

He turned and looked at her. In her heels, she was nearly as tall as he was. "Not really. As I explained, this has been a shock. Things weren't perfect, but I didn't know they were hopeless. I thought we would make it. I never imagined that I would be in an attorney's office bashing my wife so I could keep her from taking my children. I just don't see Libby as the type to drag them through all of this. She loves them as much as I do."

And Morgan was beginning to adore him. She was going to have a hard time being objective. He seemed like such a nice guy. What was wrong with his wife? She knew there were always two sides to every story, but he hadn't really told her anything bad about his wife. He had only outlined his deficiencies as a parent and husband. Was there another side to this?

She was anxious to get the paperwork from her opponent and find out.

"I can't tell you it will get better. It won't. It gets much worse. Sometimes it never gets past bearable. Divorces are always ugly. You show me a friendly divorce, and I show you a couple that was married in a drunken Vegas wedding. Yesterday. Anyone else is going to find something to argue about."

She pulled his arm and headed him toward the door. "I've seen everything. I guess the most common argument these days is who's going to pay for the boob job."

Matt chuckled. "You've got to be kidding me."

"No, really. She always says she did it for him, so he should pay. He says he shouldn't have to pay because he didn't get any enjoyment from them. They actually say that junk in court. If it weren't so funny, it would be pathetic."

They had arrived at the lobby, where the receptionist was eating a piece of pie. "Hey, Matt. I ran into Darlene over at the diner. She said you were out at the country club last night. She told me she wanted to take a bite out of you." She bellowed out a baudy laugh.

"How's Chuck?" Sandra Lawrence had carried a torch for Chuck since high school. She was smart, but had been too poor to go to college. She had taken secretarial courses at the vocational school and had landed a job in the Blankenship's office when she was barely twenty. Fourteen years later, she practically ran the place. She knew she would never be Chuck's type, but she always flirted with him and never failed to ask about him.

"He's fine. We're keeping him busy at work. I'll be living with him, so you can change my phone number on your Rolodex, just use my cell. I'm sure you have it. Don't give it to Darlene." He winked at her and turned to Morgan.

"I'll be in the office until about three. After that, you'll have to catch me on my cell. I'll be running the boys all over town since Libby is at her mother's for the night. I think she and my mother have conspired to punish me. I'm not sure for what, but I just get that feeling."

"You need to get that parenting plan filled out and arrange for that class. Drop the papers by when you have them completed. I'll let you know if I hear from her lawyer. By the way, what's her name?"

"Lauren Reynolds."

"*The* Lauren Reynolds? As in, Vanderbilt Law School? As in visiting lecturer my senior year at Harvard? I can't believe I'm going against *her*. You'd better be glad I'm good at what I do. She's tough." She gave him a quizzical look. "You married her daughter and got her to move here? Now *I'm* impressed."

"She's actually a nice lady. I've always liked her. She's a doting mother and a dedicated grandmother." He snickered. "She probably wouldn't appreciate my telling anyone that. She likes to maintain that fierce image."

"I can't imagine Lauren Reynolds baking cookies in a Santa apron, so I'll have to take your word for it. Meanwhile, you have to get that information to me so we can put together a case. I don't want her to blindside me with anything. And be on your best behavior. We can't afford any stupid mistakes."

"I hear you, I hear you. I'll see you later. Call me if you hear anything." He tipped his head toward both of them. "Ladies. Have a nice day."

He was gone. Her palms were sweating and her heart was racing. Lauren Reynolds. Now wouldn't they just freak over that in the fancy New York offices of Stearn, Franklin, and Peterson. She was living in the middle of nowhere and preparing to go head to head with a legend. What was it she heard Hattie Blankenship say? 'Who'd have thought it?'

Chapter 6

Mary Beth waited until everyone was settled for the morning before she made the call. She knew the number well. She had dialed it no less than twice a week for the last ten years. She and Lauren had been sneaking off to lunch and shopping at least once a month for most of that time. They had never shared their deep friendship with their children. Their husbands knew, of course. Neither of them would keep something like that a secret from their spouse. But their children might have been pressured or threatened to know that these women had formed a bond as close as sisters.

"Lauren? Can you talk?"

"Briefly. Libby's waiting in the car for me. What in the world is going on?"

"That's why I called. Can we meet tomorrow?"

"I think we should. How about the mall in Clarksville? We can have lunch and do some shopping."

"I'll meet you in the food court at 11:30."

"Bye."

"Goodbye"

Mary Beth sat in silence after she hung up the phone. She wasn't sure what to do about this situation, but she knew she was going to do something.

She went into the kitchen and started to prepare lunch. She had been making lunch like this for as long as she could remember. The boys were toddlers and Emily was a baby when she had decided to start working for Charlie. The company needed an accountant and she was ready to go back to work. They had remodeled the original office to include a kitchen and family room so the kids would have a place to play during the day. As they grew, they did homework, played video games, and watched television after school and during the summer. When they were old enough, they had learned to clean the office, take out the trash, answer the phones, and relay messages from the office to the shop. The boys had learned carpentry, masonry, and everything else needed to run this business before they could drive. They had literally grown up in the construction industry.

When the new office was being designed, she had insisted that they include a large, modern kitchen with a generous living area. She expected her grandchildren to use the area just as her children had. She wanted them to regard this place as much their home as it was hers.

Each day, one of them made lunch. Sometimes it was a hot meal, other times it was soup and sandwiches. Mary Beth had always believed that this family time was what differentiated their company from so many others. They were truly a family business. They came together each day, shared a meal with each other and any of their superintendents and laborers who were in the vicinity. Other associates, friends, and neighbors stopped by to snag a home cooked lunch whenever they could. Their hospitality and family values helped them build an organization that had become a formidable power in the regional construction market.

Charlie walked up behind her as she put the croutons on a salad. She had made a pot of spaghetti with sauce from a jar. Garlic bread was heating in the oven. "Mmm. Smells good in here." He nuzzled her neck as he wrapped his arms around her waist.

"That's the garlic. I hope you don't have a meeting this afternoon. I was distracted and got a little heavy-handed with it." She turned and wound her arms around his neck.

"Are you okay? You seem a little down." He planted light kisses on her neck and cheeks.

"I'm just upset about this stuff with Matt. I can't stand it. They're screwing up. I hate to see that." He ran his hand down her back and caressed her bottom. She moaned.

"I know, honey. I gave him some money this morning. At least I can fix that part of their problems. I don't know about the rest of it. I don't know what to do, except stay out of it." She nibbled his ear.

"I'm so scared for them. Marriage is hard." She slid her hand down to his crotch and massaged him, giggling at her double entendre. "They may need some interference to keep them from making a mistake they can't live with."

He took her hand and led her down the hall to his office. "I can't fix him right now, but I can fix you." He closed the door to his office, picked her up, and carried her over to the sofa. He made love to her, despite her protests that someone would hear or they would get mussed up before lunch.

"We haven't done that in a long time." She stretched and started pulling on her clothes. She walked into his bathroom to check her appearance.

"Too long." He hugged her from behind and looked at her in the mirror. "I'm glad we made it through when we had hard times. I can't fathom what life would have been like without you. I love you."

"I love you, too. I'm so worried about them. What are we going to do?" She turned, buried her head in his shoulder and started to cry.

"I didn't bring you in here and ravish you to make you cry." He pulled her head up and kissed her nose. "I know it's going to be okay. I'm sure you and Lauren will fix it."

"How did you know I had talked to her?" She flashed him a watery grin.

"You always call her when things are tough. I'm glad you have someone like her in your life." He added with a laugh, "It saves me a lot of grief and shopping."

"Now, wipe your face and come to lunch. Everyone will be there." He headed toward the kitchen, leaving her to regain her composure.

Everyone *was* there. Brad had stopped by to join Emily, Chuck had finished at a jobsite just in time to make it, and Matt strolled in as they were getting drinks.

"Get me a Coke," he barked at Chuck, who had his head in the refrigerator.

"Please!" Mary Beth added.

"Please!" Matt snapped and made a goofy face at Emily who was glaring at him. He looked at his mother. Her eyes were puffy and a little glassy. Had she been crying?

Chuck dropped a canned drink in front of Matt and took his place at the long table. It seated 14 comfortably. They had ordered it specifically for this room. It was made so that everyone could sit without straddling a leg. All of the seats were filled today. Spaghetti was almost as popular as chicken and dumplings, or Emily's fried chicken.

They chatted casually over lunch, and then gradually everyone got up and put their dishes in the dishwasher. Emily cleaned up the pots and pans and started the dishwasher. Matt and Chuck walked into Chuck's office.

"I need to talk to you." Matt fell into the chair in front of his brother's desk.

"Whatever it is, you know the answer is 'yes'."

"I know, but I still have to ask." He looked his brother in the eye. "It's really happening. We're getting a divorce. I talked to Ham's new partner today. She's getting my paperwork started. Libby's mom is handling hers, of course. I need a place to stay. I'm going to have to move out of the house." He collapsed back into the chair with a huge sigh.

"I'll help you move. You know you're always welcome at my house. It's certainly large enough for you and the boys. I'll be glad to have the company."

"We're supposed to tell them tomorrow night when she gets home. I guess I'll get some things together and bring over a load tonight. That would probably be less traumatic on the kids than seeing me moving out." He let out a miserable groan. "What in the hell am I going to do?"

"What do you want to do?"

"I want to wake up tomorrow and realize that this was all a bad dream. I want to know that my wife is coming home to my bed and that my kids are always going to sleep under the same roof as I am. Is that too much to ask?"

Chuck reclined in his chair, putting his feet on his desk and his hands behind his head. He napped that way for half an hour every afternoon after lunch. "I think you need to ask yourself what you want, and what you are willing to do to get it. You also need to think about everyone else and what this is going to do to them. I can tell Mom is torn up. Dad's worried to death, and Emily's freaking out over something. I'm sure it's you and the mess you've made. Libby's been a member of this family for a long time. We all like her. It'll be hard to have a family gathering without her. Do you think this will be easy on the rest of us?"

Matt fired back at him. "Why should I give a crap about what the rest of you think? She's my wife. I'll keep her or get rid of her because I want to, not because it's convenient for everyone else. That's crazy."

"Don't blow a blood vessel. You know I'm right. Divorce affects more than just the divorcing couple. People you've thought of as relatives no longer are. And who keeps your friends? How do you explain to Allysan and Meghan that Aunt Libby isn't their aunt anymore? Even if you don't care, this divorce is going to send ripples of heartache through this family. It's like collateral damage at a bombsite. This will hurt more people than you can imagine. Certainly more than just you or Libby. We're losing someone we love. You can't minimize our feelings for her. "

"Dammit, Chuck, *I* can't minimize *my* feelings for her. I don't expect everyone to pretend they don't know or like her. I hurt. My boys are going to hurt. How do I fix that? I don't want this divorce, but I'm not the one doing it. Right now, I can't figure out what to do about it. It's ripping me apart. I just have to do what the lawyers tell me."

"What did Ham say?"

"I didn't see him. He has a new partner, Morgan Peterson. I saw her."

"I had heard that he had a new lady lawyer over there. I also heard she's a looker." He sat up in his chair and leaned forward on his desk in one motion. "What's the verdict? Is she hot or not?"

"She's hot. She's also a Harvard grad. I sense a story in there somewhere. I can't quite put my finger on it, but there's definitely something. She knows who Lauren Reynolds is."

"Is she afraid of her?" He raised an eyebrow and cocked his head. Chuck knew Mrs. Reynolds' reputation. He had wondered if Ham would be comfortable taking her on himself.

"No, not really. She seemed excited. I think she'll be okay with it." Matt was sure she'd be okay with anything. Morgan didn't seem the type to shy away from a challenge.

"How old is she? Should I go pay her a visit?" He was tired of the local girls and could use a good diversion.

Matt rolled his eyes. "I would prefer that you stay away from my legal counsel, but she looks a little older than you are. Maybe closer to 40. Still, though, she looks good."

Chuck dismissed the idea, resumed his napping position and yawned. "What time do we need to move some of your stuff?"

"I don't know. I have to run the boys around town starting at 3 o'clock. I guess I can ask Mom to watch them while we do that. I hope she'll do it. I think she's mad at me." He stood and walked to the door. "Have a good nap."

"Yeah, I'll see you tonight." He mumbled as he drifted off. He was already late getting his nap.

Matt wandered down the hall to his mother's office. He needed to get some work done. He would have to leave in less than two hours to pick up the kids. His work was already suffering and they weren't even 24 hours into the divorce.

"Mom." He tapped on her door and walked in. She was sitting at her computer with a set of project documents spread out on her left; she appeared deep in thought.

She looked up at him. Her eyes were still puffy. He knew it was his fault she was so upset. He was sorry, but didn't know how to fix it. Right now, he just needed her help.

He looked tired. He usually did when he was worried or upset. He had been an insomniac as a child. Only his discipline kept him from getting up and wandering the house at night. He had been a good boy, staying in his bed in the wee hours making up stories and designing buildings in his head. She could see him now, in his cowboy pajamas, wide-eyed when she checked on him at 2 am. He had probably slept little the last few days.

"Hey, sweetie. Come on in. What can I do for you?" She was going to try to keep this businesslike. He didn't need for her to mother him right now. She was sure she would cry if she saw the least bit of distress in his demeanor. He would always be her baby boy.

"I need a favor. Can you keep the boys for a couple of hours tonight? I need to pack a few clothes and move some things to Chuck's. I think it will be easier on them if I do it while they aren't home. Libby will be home tomorrow, so I need to do it tonight." He raked his hands through his hair and sighed. He felt like a heel dragging her into this any more than necessary.

"I'm sorry to impose on you. I'm picking them up from school and handling their practices tonight. I don't want to drag you into this. I guess I could hire a sitter for a couple of hours."

"It's okay. I'll keep them. Just drop them off after dinner. You can pick them up when you're finished." He was at least thinking of his kids. That was a start. Maybe he would find a way to fix this without her interfering…too much.

"Sounds good. I appreciate it. I just don't want them to get upset. We're going to talk to them tomorrow."

"Just so you know, I'll be out most of the day tomorrow, so you'll need to make sure you know their schedules. I'm not sure what time Libby is coming home." She hoped he would have at least one more day of keeping up with the boys so he would understand what Libby's days were like. She doubted he had a clue.

"I've got it under control." He walked around the desk and leaned down to kiss her cheek. "Thanks, Mom. I know this is hard on you, and I'm sorry. I've made a royal mess of things. I'm going to do everything I can to make this okay for everyone. I just don't know how yet."

She put her hand on his face and looked at him, trying not to let her voice break. "I love you. I've always been proud of you. You will figure out what to do. Just hang in there and take care of those grandchildren of mine." She kissed him and turned back to her computer.

"Now get back to work." She swatted his bottom the same way she had a thousand times.

"I'm going, I'm going." He scooted out of her office and slipped into his own.

His desk was piled with messages, his message light was blinking madly on his phone, and a quick look at his e-mail showed a long list of incoming mail for the day. He needed to get busy.

First, he picked up his voice mail and answered a few of his e-mails. He made a list of all of the calls he could make while he was at practice with the boys. He made a note to call the computer shop in town and get a new laptop with a wireless modem. If he had to be out of the office, he needed to be able to take his work on the road.

"Excuse me, son, do you have a minute." Charlie walked into the office and stood across the desk from him.

"Sure."

"Have you called Mike Martin with Centennial? They need the interior submittals on the Oak Park Office Complex. Have you put those together yet?" He was concerned that his son would quickly get behind if he didn't stay on him.

"I have everything but the paint and paper samples. I called Peggy over at Southern Aesthetics. They had spec'd some paper that's discontinued, so we're waiting for some answers from the architect. Emily has the rest of the boards together. I'll call the architect and see what I can do."

"Let's get those out in the morning. We're set to break ground on Thursday. If we're to keep our time tight, we need to keep moving. Stay on your timeline." He walked out before Matt could respond. He didn't want to have to get tough with his son, but he would if necessary. He had a company to run, and he didn't have time for this divorce to have the entire operation in a shambles. Today had been nearly a wash for most of them already. He had to get everyone back on the team.

Charlie heard Matt walk out of the office at 2:45. Emily left shortly after to pick up her girls. She would be back and would stay until 5 or 5:30. Chuck was in his office on the phone arguing with another project manager. Mary Beth was tapping on her keyboard. Everything seemed normal, but he knew it was deceptive. An undercurrent of impending chaos swirled beneath them, threatening to drown them all.

He wanted so much to rescue his son from the mess he had made of his marriage. He wanted to shield his grandchildren from the hurt and anger they would soon experience. He and Mary Beth had lived through the pain and agony of a flagging marriage years ago. They had realized the damage they would do to the entire family and had put their lives back together. They both swallowed a lot of pride to get them back on track. It hadn't been easy, but it had been worth every effort.

He wasn't going to rescue his son. He assumed his wife would handle that anyway. He would do what he could for the boys. But the most important part of his family was his business. If they allowed it to slip or provided less than what their customers expected, they could lose more than a daughter-in-law. They could lose everything. He wasn't going to rescue anyone, but he was going to make damn sure this family fiasco didn't cost them a dime in business. He had to stay focused or they would all be in the poorhouse.

♥ ♥ ♥ ♥

Matt picked up the boys at school and went straight to football practice. At four, he ran Ben over to the soccer fields and stayed to watch him for about an hour. He ran back over to the football field and picked up Collin at five. They went immediately back to Ben's practice and picked him up at six. Most of the time, he was on the phone with customers, subcontractors, and vendors solving problems and putting out fires.

By the time they arrived at the house, he was exhausted and they were all starving. He found some frozen pizzas and threw them in the oven to cook while he supervised homework. They sucked down pizza and milk while finishing what seemed to him to be a ton of homework for the third and fifth grades. Some of it was even hard for him. It had been a long time since he had to underline the subject and verb in a sentence. Then he had to look up the information on predicate nouns and predicate adjectives. He hoped that Collin wouldn't fail his homework because his father was too stupid for the fifth grade.

The boys helped him clean up the kitchen, and then headed up to take their baths. By the time they had been bathed and settled into bed, it was after nine o'clock. He was tired, he needed a beer, and he wanted to talk to his wife. Maybe she would call to talk to the boys. He missed her, but he was not going to call her. He wasn't.

He was going to have to find another way to get some clothes over to Chuck's. He was supposed to have taken the boys to Mom's tonight, but there hadn't been time. It was too late to call her. He would just explain tomorrow.

After watching the first half of a boring game of Monday Night Football, he turned off the lights and went to his room. He turned the game on in the bedroom and went in to take a shower. Maybe a nice, hot shower would help him relax. He knew he wouldn't get much sleep. He rarely did, but since this mess had started, he hadn't slept more than two hours in a row. He would be dead in a month if this kept up.

♥ ♥ ♥ ♥

Matt and Chuck were sitting at the kitchen table when Emily arrived the next morning. She stormed in and stood before them with her hands on her hips. She was a younger version of Mary Beth. She wore her hair longer and usually twisted up into a clip with the ends fanned above her head. Today, she wore a pair of black tastefully low-riding pants and a white cotton blouse with three-quarter length sleeves. She was always well dressed in contemporary clothes. As the receptionist/secretary for McDonald Construction, she had to present a good image to the public. Daddy gave her a generous clothing allowance to make sure she did.

She glared at Matt. "What in the hell have you done?"

"Nice language. Do you kiss your mother with that mouth?" Chuck snickered at his wittiness this early in the day.

"Shut up. This has nothing to do with you." She looked back at Matt. "I asked you a question. I'll repeat it slowly so you'll understand me this time. What - in – the – hell – have – you - done?"

"I don't know what you mean."

"You damn sure do. Mother is torn up. She cried all afternoon yesterday. Daddy's pissed off about something, and you and Libby acted like strangers all weekend. Not to mention the fact that I heard at Meghan's cheerleading practice that you were groping Darlene at the Country Club Sunday night." She was flailing her arms and shouting by the time she finished.

She moved closer to him. "Now, what's going on? Please, Dear Lord, tell me you're not screwing that whore. I'll have to leave town." She threw her arms up and walked to the refrigerator where she pulled out a bagel and a container of cream cheese. She threw them on the table and walked back to the counter where she made herself a cup of coffee

"Did you teach her how to talk like that?" Matt looked at Chuck. "I don't think she got it from me. Since the boys were little, I've learned to leave some of the more colorful words out of my daily conversation."

"I guess she must have. Or maybe she learned it from the crew. We need to talk to Dad about that. She sounds like a sailor."

"Stop it! I mean it! Something's going on around here and I want to know what it is." She spun and stood between them, grabbing the lobe of each one's ear. They both flinched. "Speak, or I start pulling."

"God, quit it. You're vicious." Matt swatted at her hand, but she refused to let go, pulling gently as he struggled. "Okay, let go and I'll tell you. It's no secret anyway."

She let go and popped him on the back of the head. "Let's hear it. What have you done to upset Mother?" She grabbed her coffee and sat down at the table.

"Libby and I are getting a divorce."

"WHAT?" Her eyes bulged and her mouth gaped in disbelief. "You can't be serious."

"Close your mouth, you're letting in flies." Chuck continued to torment her, defying her to whack him as she had done Matt.

"I said for you to shut up. I want to hear this from Matt." She took a bite of her bagel and gathered her thoughts before she spoke again.

"Surely you two can work this out."

"I don't think so. I didn't know anything about it, really. I've seen my attorney and she's taking care of my interests. Libby's at her parents' house getting her papers ready." He took a long drink of coffee and waited for her response. It wasn't what he expected. Big tears were streaming down her face. Her lip was trembling and she was struggling to maintain control.

"Why are you all torn up? He's the one getting the divorce. You're all set with Bradley Dear."

She whacked Chuck's arm and turned to Matt. "I can't believe this. You have to be the most selfish, inconsiderate bastard I have ever known. Do you know what this is going to do to your kids? And what about the rest of us? She's the only sister I have." Her tears were flowing like rivers down her face and she had lost any semblance of control. She stood and put her hands on the back of her chair.

"She's the only reason I can tolerate you. I've grown up in the shadow of the McDonald boys all of my life. It makes me sick. I'll never be anything but the McDonald girl. Half the people in this town don't even know my name. And they don't care enough to find out. Libby is the only person who knows and loves me for me. Not because I'm your damn sister. Do you know what that means to me? She talks to me like I'm a human. She cares about something besides construction and football. She loves art and museums and music other than Led Zeppelin." She sniffed. Chuck handed her a clean napkin to wipe her nose.

She shouted at him, "If you divorce her, she's still my friend. I love her more than I do you."

Matt rolled his eyes up at her. "Maybe you should have told her that. One of the reasons she's leaving me is that she hates it here. She says nobody likes her. She feels all alone in this town." He looked up at his sister's red face. Her eyes were rapidly swelling and her makeup was smeared like a Picasso.

"I don't believe that," she sobbed and blew her nose in the napkin. "She's leaving because you're having an affair with Darlene. That's what I heard this afternoon."

He stood and looked at her. "I'm not having an affair with anyone, but if I were, it darn sure wouldn't be Darlene. Give me some credit." He wiped her makeup off her cheeks and hugged her to him.

"I'm sorry about all of this, Emily, but I didn't do it. She's leaving me, not vice versa. I'm doing everything I can, but I'm not sure it's going to help." He pushed her away and held her by the arms. "You might want to tell her how you feel. It can't hurt my cause. I can use all the help I can get." He kissed her nose and hugged her again.

"I'll talk to her. I'm sorry I jumped on you. Let me know if I can do anything." She wiped her eyes and watched him walk out of the room. She looked at Chuck. "What are we going to do?"

"I'm tired of everyone asking me that. Do I look like I can do anything? I'm single because I suck at relationships. All I know to do is to be there for him."

"You should probably keep him away from the club. I really did hear that about Darlene today. It'll be all over town by tomorrow. I hope Libby doesn't hear it. I'm sure that won't help."

They cleaned up the kitchen and made a new pot of coffee in silence. They were both suffering. Their hearts ached for the brother they loved and the sister they had made a part of this family. They agonized over the children. They didn't discuss the pain or the worry they both felt. They didn't have to. It was in the air. It permeated the office. If they weren't careful, it would consume them all.

Chapter 7

Mary Beth sat down at her desk. She had intended to get herself a cup of coffee, but had stopped short of the door when she heard her children fighting. She had listened to most of the conversation, then slinked back into her office before they knew she was there. She hated to hear them argue, but Matt needed to hear how Emily felt. This family was knitted together like a sweater. You couldn't pull one thread out without pulling the others. He needed to know, to understand that what was happening to him was happening to all of them.

She wondered where he had been last night. He said he would be by after dinner to drop off the boys so he could move some things to Chuck's. He must have been busy with the boys. She doubted he understood how much time and energy it took to complete one afternoon with them. She hoped he was finally learning to respect his wife and the contributions she made to their family and community.

She worked for a couple of hours and gathered her things around 10. She said goodbye to Charlie, checked out with Emily, and left the office. She drove out the highway, over the river, and on to Clarksville. She would drive for just under 90 minutes. So would Lauren. They had been meeting here for several years to shop.

Lauren and Mary Beth occasionally slipped into Clarksville, home of the United States Army's 101st Airborne Division, to do volunteer work when the troops were deployed. They recognized the tremendous need for childcare, home and auto repair, and legal and professional services for the families left behind. Quietly, and without the knowledge of their own families, they had rallied a group of colleagues who established a clearinghouse of other professionals who were willing to donate their services to those who made such a tremendous sacrifice. Nobody knew they had anything to do with it. They intended to keep it that way.

Mary Beth spotted Lauren's car as she pulled into the mall parking lot. She caught up with her at the main entrance. The two embraced and walked into the mall like giddy schoolgirls, happy to see each other despite the circumstances.

"Are you hungry?" Mary Beth asked Lauren as they came to the food court.

"Not really. If you aren't starving, I'd rather shop for a bit before we eat." She laughed before she continued; "You'd think I would have it out of my system. Libby and I spent a fortune yesterday."

"Is she okay? I've been worried sick." She stopped and turned to look at her friend. "Let's sit down and talk for a minute over a Coke, then we can stew over it while we shop."

"That sounds like a great idea." She kept talking as they found a bench. "We shopped, bought her some new clothes, and had a massage. I made her get her hair done. She looked like she hadn't done that in a while. What's going on there?"

"I don't know. Charlie gave Matt some money to pay off their bills yesterday. I think maybe they didn't talk much about it. She took care of the bills, and he just spent money. He thought they had it to spend. He wouldn't have been so careless if he had known. You do believe that, don't you?" She was concerned that they would think he had been irresponsible on purpose. It was important to her that they not blame either of their children.

"I know he's not like that. I also know my daughter didn't intentionally withhold their financial situation from him." She sighed, then laughed. "I suppose we're on the same page. They've neglected an important marital skill: communication. I'm afraid if we don't do something, they'll make this a bigger mess than it already is."

"Do you think she still loves him? She says he doesn't love her. She believes he never did. I think he believes she doesn't love him. That's what Charlie said. They've been arguing a lot, evidently, and saying terrible things to each other. I'm hoping some time and distance will help them gain some perspective." She stood and took Lauren's hand. "Let's shop while we finish this discussion. I think we're okay. I was worried that we wouldn't be able to talk about this."

Lauren hugged her friend, who had become her secret sister. In her life, her fierce image had kept many women from becoming close to her, she didn't want to lose someone who meant so much. "I agree. I was worried too. I'm concerned about my child and my grandchildren, but I don't want to lose my friend, either."

They walked toward the first store as they continued to talk. Lauren answered Mary Beth's question, "I know she loves him. She says he doesn't love her. She says he only married her because he had to. I don't believe that, but what I believe is not important at this point."

"I wonder where they've gotten so off track? It doesn't make any sense. Has Libby said anything to you about how unhappy she is in Ainsley? I didn't know that, either. I overheard Matt telling Emily this morning that it's one of the reasons she is leaving." She picked up a Christmas sweater and held it up to her front. "Is this not the cutest thing? I think I need this!" It was green cotton covered in Santas and elves. The Santas had fuzzy beards and the elves' hats had little balls that dangled off the sweater.

"I love it! It looks like you. I think the whole town would die if I showed up in that." Lauren chuckled as she picked up an identical sweater and held it up to herself. "Do you think I could sway a jury if I wore this to court?"

"Stop it!" Mary Beth was laughing so hard tears were rolling down her cheeks. "You're going to make me wet my pants"

"I think I'll buy it and wear it to the Bar Association Christmas brunch. For crying out loud, I'm a grandmother; it's time I acted like one!" She broke out in infectious laughter as they both selected slacks to match their sweaters.

"Onward!" Mary Beth exclaimed as they finished paying for their purchases. "We have at least a hundred more shops to go."

They shopped for another hour before deciding it was time to stop and eat. They decided to leave the mall and find a nice restaurant where they could relax and have a good meal. They left Lauren's car at the mall and drove to a chain establishment that specialized in fajitas and margaritas.

"I'm ashamed to say that I'd love to have a nice, big drink. This whole business has me frazzled."

Mary Beth laughed. "Don't apologize, I'm all for a big, salty drink. I haven't had liquor for lunch in years. It would scandalize Ainsley."

"I think you're right." She turned to the waiter and ordered their drinks and a plate of nachos. "Let's live a little."

When the waiter walked away, Mary Beth leaned back and relaxed in her seat. "Now, what do we do? We have to do something."

"I know. I've thought about it. I think you're right when you say that a little time and distance may help them. I also think that it's important to make sure that neither of them does anything stupid." She paused while the waiter set their drinks on the table. She took a long sip of her margarita and looked at her friend. "I don't know how to put this delicately, but I don't think they need to, uh, date other people." She took another drink as she shifted in her chair.

"I think I understand exactly what you mean. I can probably get his attorney to tell him he can't, you know, see other women." She cleared her throat and took a drink. Then she giggled. "It's hard to talk about your child and sex no matter how long they've been married. How ridiculous."

Lauren laughed and wiped the corner of her mouth with her napkin. "We can't talk about them, but we can still do it." She put her head down in a coy gesture.

"Oh, you're doing it again. I can't take it." She burst into uncontrolled laughter. She picked up her drink and peered inside. "What do they put in these things? It must be pure alcohol."

"I think you're right. I also think I want another one." She waved at the waiter and held up two fingers. "Please bring two more, honey."

"Lauren Reynolds, I believe you're flirting with that cute waiter."

"I'm not flirting, but he does look good when he walks away." She took a drink, draining her glass. "Now, about the kids. I think we need to keep them away from each other as much as possible. We need to keep them away from other members of the opposite sex."

They laughed and chatted for more than an hour, ordering several more rounds of margaritas. Mary Beth told Lauren all about the boys and their latest activities. They shared stories about their gardens, their husbands, and their businesses before finally returning to the subject of their children.

"I'll have to work on keeping them apart. Both boys start playing this week. They will both be at the games." She took her drink from the waiter and giggled at the look on Lauren's face when he turned to leave. "I guess I can enlist Charlie or Chuck to keep him away from her. Emily or I will keep her away from him. I can help with the transfer for visitation."

"Speaking of that, we have to keep them from discussing the parenting plan and visitation. That always causes a fight. They need time to think about the good things, not stir up some new reasons to argue." She took a blob of nachos and dropped it on her plate. "Mmmm, these are delicious."

"Do we need to come up with some sort of visitation schedule and just give it to them? I think we can manage to come up with something between the two of us." She reached across to load more nachos on her plate. Lauren held down a clump while Mary Beth dug in the pile. They laughed when the blob barely made it to Mary Beth's plate.

Lauren recovered first. "I think her plan is really the best. Of course, she won't be working three days a week for two more weeks. Do you know she had a job interview in Nashville today?" She took a bite of nachos and a big gulp of her margarita.

Mary Beth pointed at her and burst into laughter. "You have sour cream on your face. And I think you're drunk."

Lauren wiped her face and pointed back at her friend. "I think you're drunk. We're going to have to stop drinking and eat something besides nachos before we can drive home."

"Maybe we can keep drinking and just get a hotel room tonight." She slurped her drink and snorted when she giggled.

"That'd be okay with me, but I have to be in court at nine o'clock in the morning. No rooms. We'll have to sober up."

They ordered coffee and sandwiches and continued their discussion. They settled on a plan for visitation and Mary Beth agreed to call Matt's attorney and let her in on the plan.

"I thought the attorney was a man." Lauren inquired over their last cup of coffee.

"Well, he would be, but he's a bit conflicted over the case and he has this new lady lawyer, Harvard grad in his office. He's asked her to handle this one. She specializes in family law."

"Really? What's her name?"

"Morgan Peterson."

"You're kidding!"

"No, do you know her?"

"Sure. Well, I know of her. She was actually in one of my classes at Harvard when I was visiting lecturer, but I didn't know her then. I know who she is now because she married in to one of the most prestigious firms in New York. Her ex-husband is a partner in Stearn, Franklin, and Peterson. They handle all of the high profile cases in the city."

"What's she doing in Ainsley?"

"Well, that's interesting. I know some of the story, but not enough to tell it right, so I'll have to do some investigating and get back to you on that one. I hate to gossip."

"Don't forget about it. Find out and let me know. I'm dying of curiosity." She put down her empty coffee cup and placed her napkin on the table. They signed their checks and left the waiter a generous tip. "Okay, we have a plan and we're sober. It's five o'clock. I guess I should head home. Are you good to drive?"

"I'm great. That was fun, but I'll have a headache when I get home. Clay will tease me,

I'm sure." She reached in her purse and pulled out her keys. "When he sees that sweater, he'll swear I was drunk when I bought it! I can't wait to see the look on his face."

"Hey! I love that sweater. If you say another word, I'll be forever offended." She hugged Lauren and dragged her to the car. "You still have to get your car."

They drove to the mall and hugged again before they parted for the night. Lauren felt much better. With all of them trying to get Libby and Matt back together, they had a better chance of success. All that remained was to enact their plan and make sure the kids stayed away from each other. She had a feeling that wouldn't be easy, but it was the key to success.

Chapter 8

Libby woke up in the bedroom of her childhood. The house was cool from the air conditioning and she was snuggled deep in the quilts. The familiar warmth comforted her. She rolled over and checked the time. Just after nine. She barely had time to get dressed and get in to Nashville for her interview.

She rose and dressed frantically. Velda snuck in while she was in the shower and left her a breakfast tray of biscuits, jelly, and coffee. She wolfed it down while she dressed. She dragged her suitcase downstairs and searched for Velda to tell her she was leaving.

Velda hugged her and teared up. "I miss you so much. You have to come see us more often. I think I'm coming with your parents Thursday. I want to see the boys, too."

"Oh, Velda, I'm so glad to hear that. They'll be happy to see all of you and I have plenty of room in the house." She was panicked at the thought of cleaning it all before they came, but she was happy they were coming.

"You take care, honey. And you let me know if you need anything. I'll bake some cookies before I come."

"Thanks. I love you. See you Thursday."

Libby threw her suitcase in the back seat of the SUV and drove toward the city. She was nervous. It had been years since she had interviewed for a job. She didn't think it would be a big deal – nurses were in such demand she practically had the job based on her phone interview – but she was still apprehensive.

It turned out to be more of a hassle than it was difficult. She was offered a position immediately and sent to Employee Health to get her physical and drug screen. They wanted to schedule her to begin right away, but she agreed only to work one day a week after her orientation until the first of November, when she would start working weekends on their Baylor plan. She had to work four days of orientation two weeks from now. She wasn't looking forward to that. She would either have to stay with her parents or drive the two-hour trip from Ainsley back and forth each day. She would decide how to do that sometime next week.

She had the job she set out to get. It was what she wanted, but it didn't feel fight. She would be making plenty of money to support herself and the boys. She would work Friday, Saturday, and Sunday evenings, so Matt could have the boys every weekend. She would have the best of both worlds, a career and her children. Her only concern was that she might miss Ben's soccer games on Saturdays in the spring. She would figure that out when she got to it.

She didn't know what she had expected, but this empty, lonely feeling wasn't it. Somehow, this was supposed to be the start of her new life. Her own "Independence Day". Hardly. She felt...what? What was this feeling? Sadness, loneliness, depression? No, it was something else. Like a child who has just realized she can't find her mother, she felt a sickening panic rolling through her, radiating from the center of her body into ever fiber of her being. She was lost. She had wandered away from the life that had become so familiar and she had no idea where to go or how she was going to get there. And she had no one to show her the way.

She pulled into town around five and called Matt's cell phone. She went straight to voicemail, an indication that he was on the phone. She left him a message to call her so she could help with pick ups this afternoon. Since he should be at the football field picking up Collin, she went to the soccer field so she could pick up Ben. She hoped he would call her so she could save him the trip.

She saw him pull into the parking lot as she sat down on the bleachers. She got up and walked toward the truck. Collin ran up and hugged her before running across to greet his buddies. Matt met her half way.

"When did you get here?" His greeting was less than cordial.

"Just a few minutes ago. Didn't you get my message? I tried to call you so you could save yourself the trip over here." Why was he being such a snit?

"Oh. I saw where you called, but I was driving down the road on the phone. I was going to call you back when we got here. Collin got out a few minutes early. Their game is at 4:00 Thursday." He handed her a copy of the schedule.

"I have one, thanks. It's on the refrigerator. My parents and Velda are coming Thursday afternoon. They'll likely stay the weekend so they can see Ben play soccer Saturday. I have that schedule, too. It's also on the refrigerator. I'll make you a copy." She was rambling, and being a little snippy with him, but he was all of a sudden acting like he had a clue what the boys were doing. Where did he think she had been all of these months they had been practicing?

"I see." He pulled off his ball cap, scratched his head, and replaced his cap. "Look, I need to pack a bag and get some things moved to Chuck's when the boys aren't there. Do you think now would be a good time, since you're here? They're going to be upset as it is, I just think seeing me actually moving my stuff will be too traumatic for them."

She should have been prepared for that. She had told him to leave. She had started this. Why was she suddenly unable to breathe?

"I guess that's okay." She tried to gather her thoughts. "I'll get some supper together for them and make sure they have their homework and baths. Then we'll sit down and talk to them. I don't think we need to tell them about the divorce just yet. I think they'll do better in stages."

"Whatever. It's going to be hell on them. It's hell on me. I still don't get it." He closed his eyes and put a hand over them trying to regroup. "You're right. We'll just tell them we're having some problems and I'm going to go stay with Uncle Chuck. They won't be happy, but they'll think it's cool to go stay at his house."

"Um, okay. That settles it. We'll be finished here at six. Are you planning to eat with us or what?" She shifted her feet and fidgeted with her purse. "I don't care either way. I just need to know so I can be prepared."

"I'll just get something while I'm out. It'll be easier that way, since I don't know how long I'll be." He turned to walk toward the truck. "Thanks for asking, though."

"I guess I need to get their stuff out of your truck."

"Oh, I almost forgot about that. I'll just throw their bags in your backseat, okay? It'll save you the walk."

"Thanks."

"No problem." He nodded at her as he walked back to the truck. He was wearing a yellow polo and starched blue cotton slacks with loafers. His hair poked out and curled slightly beneath his cap. He looked like he belonged on the cover of a men's magazine. He had been polite, even helpful. He didn't seem at all like the man she had been fighting with for the past year.

He pulled into the driveway of the house he had worked so hard to design and build. It was everything he had ever wanted. The home he wanted for his family. Now, it was to be the home for his ex-wife and kids. That wasn't what he'd had in mind when he built it.

He had been involved in every phase, doing as much of the labor as he could do himself. He and Libby had mulled over every detail. Unlike so many couples who built homes together, they had rarely argued. It was, for him, the culmination of years of hard work., both in their careers and their marriage. He didn't really want to give it up, but he didn't know how much of a fight he would have if he made Libby move. No matter what they did, the kids would still live somewhere else half of the week. They would get used to it. Lots of kids did. He just didn't want to give up his house.

He went into the house and started packing his clothes into a suitcase. He gathered his toiletries into a grocery bag and took a load to the truck. He carried his hanging clothes to the truck in armloads, stacking them in the backseat. Shoes were thrown into boxes and tossed into the bed of the truck.

On an afterthought, he grabbed his golf clubs, his guns, his softball bag, and any other gear he could find. He had heard horror stories about what crazed ex-wives did to their ex's stuff. He couldn't stomach the thought of finding his Ping irons or his prized Great Big Bertha driver chopped into little pieces on the lawn because he was late bringing the boys home. You couldn't be too careful in times like these.

He looked around the house to see if there was anything else he needed to rescue. Nothing came to mind. He couldn't believe he was moving out of his home. It was surreal. He kept hoping he would wake up and it would all have been a bad dream. It would get worse. They still had to talk to the boys.

His cell phone rang. "Hello."

"Hey, sweetie. It's Mom. What happened to you last night?" She sounded syrupy sweet. More so than usual.

"I got busy with the boys and didn't have time to do anything. I'm actually finishing up now. I'm on my way to Chuck's to drop off my junk." He tried to sound upbeat.

"I'll just meet you over there. I'm about 30 minutes from town. Have you eaten?"

"No, I was just going to grab something. I have to go back to the house for a little while tonight. Libby and I are going to talk to the boys."

"I'll get us some chicken. Is that okay with you?"

"That's fine, Mom. I'll see you in a little while." He hung up and climbed into the truck. Something was going on or she wouldn't be bringing him dinner at Chuck's.

She hung up and dialed Ham Blankenship's home number. He gave her

Morgan's number at home. She added it to her phone's address book and dialed. Morgan answered on the first ring.

"Ms. Peterson? This is Mary Beth McDonald. I need to talk to you about my son's case."

"You know I really can't discuss what he's told me." Why was his mother calling? How strange. She piled her dinner dishes into the sink and finished clearing her counter of leftovers.

"I understand. I just need to let you know a few things." She had planned to do this in person, where it wouldn't be so awkward, but she needed to talk to her before she talked to Matt.

"Um, okay. I'm all ears." This conversation was getting weirder by the minute.

"First, let me explain the most important thing. This divorce will never go through. Do you understand me?" She wanted this point to be completely clear. She probably sounded a bit sterner than she intended, but Morgan's participation was vital.

"I don't think that's your decision to make." She was instantly defensive. Whatever this lady was up to, it was more than Morgan was prepared for.

"I don't mean to sound bossy. Try to understand. They don't know what they're doing. I've talked to both of them. I wouldn't interfere, but they need some help. Short of just telling them they're not getting a divorce, her mother and I are going to try to guide them through this mess and toward a reconciliation. Am I making sense?"

"Sort of. Isn't her mother her lawyer? Lauren Reynolds?" Small town law was going to be more complicated than she had imagined.

"Yes. Lauren and I have talked about this at length. We feel like they need to step back from their marriage and get a better look. A great deal of their problems have come from a lack of communication. We just want to give them a chance to mend this like adults." She hoped she was getting through.

"I see. What does all of this have to do with me?" She curled up on her couch and pulled an afghan over her legs. She turned down her television set and picked up a pad and pencil. Somehow, she knew this was going to be good.

"We want them to stay away from each other. That's going to be hard, given the boys' schedules, but my family and I will do what we can. We also don't want them to discuss the visitation or living arrangements with each other."

"I still don't understand what you want from me."

"I want you to call Matt and tell him to avoid contact and not discuss details with her. They'll fight over that for sure. We need to get them to spend a few weeks without arguing. They need to see what they can have, not what they have made." Her cell phone blanked out and she lost the connection. "Damn." She redialed.

"Sorry, I lost you. Where was I? Oh, did you hear the part about keeping them apart?"

"Yes, I got that. No contact. No discussion of the parenting plan and living arrangements." She made notes on her pad. "Do I contact Mrs. Reynolds for that? Who is going to make those decisions?"

"Well, Lauren and I have already made them for the time being. I know that's a little sticky for you, but you have to know that I would never do anything to hurt my own son. He's my baby. You're going to have to trust me. If you have any questions about my motives, maybe we need to let Ham take care of this. He's as torn up as the rest of us, you know." She was beginning to sound like a desperate old woman. Well, she was.

"I guess it's not out of the ordinary. I will have to get Matt to agree. I assume you'll take care of that end?"

"Yes. I'm on my way to talk to him now. I need for you to call him and tell him about the contact and discussion issues. He's moving out tonight and they plan to tell the kids. We don't want them to tie up over that. If you call him, and Lauren calls Libby, maybe we can avoid a fight tonight."

"Okay. I'll do this, but I'm still going to proceed as if this is going to happen. We can't afford not to. If your plan goes sour and this goes to court, we could lose too much if I'm not prepared. Do you understand what I'm saying?"

"I think so. I'll keep that in mind. And, oh, don't say anything to them about my talking with Lauren. They don't know how close we are, and they surely don't know we've met and discussed their problems."

"This is so unusual, but I'll do what I can. I'll help as long as it is in my client's best interest."

"I guess that's all I can ask. Please come by for lunch one day this week. I would love to meet you in person. Lauren will be in on Thursday and Friday if you feel you need to meet with her. Just call my office and let us know. We'll arrange a meeting." She hung up her phone as she pulled into the drive-thru at the chicken place.

Morgan looked at her notes. She had handled hundreds of divorces in her career. She had lived through her own. But she had never dealt with a mother and an opposing attorney who were on the same side. And whose side were they on? It was very unclear. She knew Matt didn't seem very anxious to divorce his wife, but she didn't expect to be told that she was going to participate in their reconciliation. Wasn't that for clergymen and counselors?

♥ ♥ ♥ ♥

Libby's house phone rang as she was setting dinner on the table. Her caller ID said it was her mother.

"Hey, Mother. I made it home just fine." She laughed.

"I wasn't calling to check up on you. I've been working on your papers and I need to talk to you." A little white lie wouldn't hurt anyone. She was just getting home from her shopping trip.

"Okay, hang on just a minute. I need to get the boys settled with their dinner."

"It won't take that long. I just need to give you the speech I give most of my clients. I forgot about it yesterday."

"What's that? I've probably heard it already." Libby dished out food to the boys while she held the phone with her shoulder.

"You and Matt need to stay away from each other. You'll have to work something out for transportation and visitation, but it shouldn't be too hard to avoid discussing it with him as long as I can talk to his attorney. We'll handle negotiations. You just need to work on keeping your life in order and maintaining some sort of consistency for the boys."

"How can we stay away from each other? We're both their parents! That's impossible. We have football, soccer, and Lord-knows-what-else this week."

"You'll have to get Mary Beth or someone to help with transportation. I mean it. No discussions and as little contact as possible. And you keep your mouth shut." She grinned at the firmness she managed to keep in her voice.

"Fine. But he had better watch his mouth, too. I'm not going to listen to his crap anymore. I've had enough. Are you going to meet with his attorney when you're here?"

"I plan to. I'll call her office tomorrow and make arrangements for Friday. Is that okay with you?"

"That's fine. I'll have to work Wednesday and Friday nights. Just so you know. I picked up tomorrow night so I'll have some money."

"Sounds good. I'll be in touch. We're planning to leave around lunch on Thursday so we'll be there in plenty of time for Collin's game. I love you, sweetheart. Hang in there."

"I love you, too, Mother. Thanks for everything." Libby's heart was in her throat when she hung up. This was getting so complicated. And what did she mean "her" when she was talking about his attorney? Last time she checked, Ham was still a man.

♥ ♥ ♥ ♥

Chuck's phone was ringing when he came back in the house with a load of Matt's clothes. He dropped the clothes on his sofa and ran to answer it before it went to voice mail. The female voice asked for Matt.

"Hang on. He's just coming back into the house." He walked out to the kitchen and handed Matt the cordless. "It's some lady for you."

"Hello. This is Matt McDonald." Who was calling him here? He hadn't been here for 15 minutes.

"Matt, this is Morgan Peterson. I'm glad I caught you. I was so rattled with all the details of our meeting, that I forgot to mention a few things to you. Do you have a minute?"

"Sure. Whatever." He opened the refrigerator and found a can of beer. He desperately needed a tall, cold beer.

"You need to make sure that you have as little contact as possible with your wife. I know you've got ballgames and school events, but you need to be careful. Don't say or do anything to provoke her. Don't discuss visitation or the parenting plan. Just stay away. In the early stages of a divorce, it's just best for everyone." It was good advice, but she felt foolish being a part of this plan. She had never become so involved with a client's family. After her conversation with Mary Beth, she knew it was going to get worse. She really needed to talk to Ham.

"Are you serious? That's nuts. We have children for crying out loud. How am I supposed to avoid her at a football game? And we're going to sit down and talk with the boys tonight. Do I just bow out of that so I won't make her uncomfortable? No way."

"I don't mean you have to act like she's a leper, you just need to avoid discussing anything that could start a fight. The last thing I need is to go to court and have her produce a tape of you acting like an idiot. From what you told me this afternoon, you can't hold your tongue." She was thinking on her feet pretty well. It sounded good to her, anyway.

"Okay! I'll keep my mouth shut. But I'm still going over there tonight to talk to my kids. They deserve to hear this from both of us. It's going to be a mess." It made him sick to think of it.

"I understand. Just watch it. I mean it. You need to keep that mouth under control." Now she was sounding like a mother.

"I get it. No mouth. Thanks for calling."

"No problem. I'll call you later this week when I get the paperwork ready for you to look at. I'll probably see Mrs. Reynolds when she's in town. We'll work out some details then."

"Fine. That's fine. I'll see you later." He hung up the phone and finished off his beer in one gulp. How did she know Lauren was coming to town?

"What's the deal? Who was that?" Chuck had a feeling it was the fancy lady lawyer, but he wanted to hear what was going on.

"That was my lawyer. She told me to stay away from Libby. We aren't supposed to discuss any of the details of the parenting plan or visitation. She said I have to keep my mouth under control." He reached in the fridge and pulled out another beer.

"Get me one."

He threw his brother a beer just as Mary Beth walked in the back door carrying two sacks of fried chicken with all the trimmings. "Help me. I'm going to drop your fixins'. She was giggling as she staggered in.

"Wow, Mom. That smells great. What's the occasion?"

"I forgot to tell you she was coming and bringing dinner." He looked at his mother. "You did bring enough for Chuck, didn't you?"

"Of course. I figured he'd eat it even if he had already eaten." She started unloading boxes and Styrofoam containers from the bags. "This ain't my first rodeo."

"I'm impressed, brother. I should have let you move in a long time ago. I don't eat like this very often." Chuck grabbed a chicken leg and started eating it with his hands while he retrieved plates from the cabinet.

"I don't think this is a social call." He glanced at his mother. "Am I right, Mom? Are you here just to visit, or is there a point to all of this?"

"I do want to talk to you, but let's get some food in our bellies first. You must be starved." She laid out their plates and seated herself at the table. "Can I get one of those?" She pointed at his beer.

"Oh, God. Is someone dying? You never drink beer." Chuck looked at his brother. "I get it. This is your doing. Now what?"

"It's not bad. Y'all just get worked up over nothing. I can have a beer if I want to."

"But this is about the divorce, right? Just get on with it. I can't stand the suspense."

"Well, I think you need to work on a few things. You know from the past couple of days how much the boys are into now. You'll need to be involved." She spooned potatoes and gravy on her plate and passed the containers to Chuck.

"I've already started working on that. What else?" He was piling food on his plate while he talked.

126

"You need to stay away from Libby and every other woman on Earth."

"My lawyer already told me that. Or I guess she's my lawyer. I went to see Ham, but I got her instead. She's bossing me around like she's in charge."

"You need to think about visitation. Since Libby works mostly weekends, you need to agree to have the boys then, or during the week if she's working. I'll help work that out if necessary. I just don't want any more fighting. It's going to be hard enough on the kids. The last thing they need is the two of you fighting over them."

"I don't want to fight over them. I do want to keep my house, though. I haven't talked to Morgan about it, but I'm going to request it in the divorce. I'm sure it won't go over well."

"You're right, but I do understand why you want it. I'll see what I can do to help with that." She hoped they wouldn't get that far in the negotiations, but she knew he wouldn't let the house go.

"You should probably just let her stay there for now, just to make it easier on everyone. She really doesn't have anywhere to go. You can at least stay here."

"I can appreciate that. The last thing I want to do is push her to move back to Nashville and take my kids with her. I'd play hell getting them back here if she did that. Now hand me the biscuits before someone gets hurt."

They carried on a neutral conversation over dinner. Both boys tried to keep it light and make their mother happy. Emily's comments from the morning had bothered them. The last thing anyone wanted was to upset Mom. She was everything to them. She had never failed to be there when they needed her.

Chuck got up to get another beer. "Where did you go all day today?"

"I just spent the day shopping. You know how I hate to Christmas shop at the last minute." It wasn't a lie; it just wasn't the truth.

"You can't be serious. Did you get me something good? You know my list will be at Baker's Sporting Goods real soon." Matt had been leaving his "wish list" with Mr. Baker since he was seven. Mr. Baker faithfully held it for his parents each year. Even when he was in Knoxville at school, he had managed to get his list to the store. Everyone teased him, but he always got what he wanted.

"You need to grow up, little brother. Don't you think you're too old to send letters to Santa?"

"It's not a letter to Santa; it's my Christmas List. It just makes Mom's job easier. It takes her weeks to figure out what you need. It's hard to find gift certificates for golf, beer, and loose women." He laughed as he stood up and started clearing the table.

"Matthew! That's unnecessary." She looked at them both with an evil gleam in her eye. "Your brother is not hard to buy for. As long as the department store still carries socks and underwear, he'll have something under the tree."

"Mom! You always side with Matt. I don't need any socks and underwear."

"Then maybe you should make me a list." She stood up and kissed his cheek, laughing at the stricken expression on his face.

"I need to get home. Daddy will think I've left the country or spent all of his money."

"No, you can't spend all of his money. I've already done that." Matt lowered his head at his self-deprecating remark.

"It's okay, baby. That was your money. There's plenty more for me to spend." She hugged him and kissed his nose.

"You two take care of each other. I'll see you in the morning." She walked out the door and reached her car before the tears started. For all of his joviality, she could tell her son was hurting. He was ashamed to have taken money from his father, and he had no idea what to do about his marriage. She knew he wouldn't sleep tonight. She doubted if she would either.

Charlie was sitting in the kitchen eating a ham sandwich and some chips when she walked into the house. They had built their home when Emily was in first grade. It was large and homey, filled with almost 25 years of memories. Mary Beth faithfully painted and redecorated every few years, but all of the school pictures, trophies, and mementos remained integral parts of the décor. This was a family home – well loved and well lived in.

"How was your trip?" He finished his sandwich and turned up his glass of milk before he stood to help her bring in her bags.

"It was fine. Lauren and I seem to be on the same page. We think they're jumping into this too quickly." She dropped a handful of bags and headed back out to the garage. Charlie followed her.

"I think you're right, but I don't know what you think you can do about it. They're adults, Mary Beth. You can't just interfere in someone's life. I'm having a hard enough time keeping him focused on his job." He took the last few bags from the car and headed back inside.

"Well, I don't think they'll make it without help. I've just left him over at Chuck's. He's putting up a good front, but he's a mess. I plan to do whatever I can to stop this divorce."

"I hope you know what you're doing. Nobody ever appreciates the interfering party."

"I'm only going to do a few, simple things. We'll need your help, too."

"Oh, no. You're not getting me involved in your crazy scheme."

"Oh, yes, I am. We have to keep them apart as much as possible. That means at all of these football and soccer games and practices, someone will need to sit with Matt and someone with Libby. We'll divide and conquer. I think a little distance will help them put things in perspective."

"I hope you're right, but I think you're nuts to get involved." He took her hand and pulled her into his arms. "I love you, anyway."

"I love you, too, but you don't have any faith in me. I'm not going to do anything crazy. I just want them to have a break from the stress they've put on their marriage and see what super people they both are. I would also like them to stop fighting. The last thing they need, or the boys need, is a hostile environment."

"You're right about that. I'm already tired of it, and I've only been around them for one weekend of it." He kissed her cheek.

She put her arms around his neck and kissed and nuzzled him. "Are you trying to seduce me, Charlie McDonald?"

"Not really." He snickered. "I just want you to sit down here and watch this movie with me. I've been waiting all night for it to start. I've had a helluva day and I just want to relax for a little while. How about it?"

"Oh, fine. Let me change clothes and I'll come in and watch it with you. Then maybe I'll seduce you." She threw her head back and flounced to the bedroom.

Chapter 9

Libby had fed the boys and cleaned up the kitchen by the time Matt walked in the back door. Collin had bathed and was finishing his homework in the kitchen. Ben was upstairs getting his bath. All of their clothes for the next day had been laid out and their bags were packed for practice. She had managed to sneak their school clothes for Thursday into their sports bags. They would be staying with Matt at Chuck's house while she worked on Wednesday night.

"Hey, bud. How's the homework? Did we do okay on the grammar the other night?" He sat down at the kitchen table with barely a nod to Libby. She tried to ignore him, too.

"Yeah. We made an A. I think we missed one sentence. Are you going to help me tonight?" He looked up at his dad with hopeful eyes.

"For a minute. How much more do you have?" He shuffled through the papers to see what his assignment was.

"I'm almost finished for the night. It's hard."

"Let's get to it so we can spend some time together before bedtime." He pointed to the next sentence and guided Collin through the rest of the assignment. Libby went to the laundry room and folded a load after she started another one.

If he had been helping with homework all along, she might have been able to keep up with things better. It was just like him to waltz in here on the eve of their divorce and start acting like a father. Well, he wasn't going to get away with it. He was still a jackass and he didn't have the first clue what it was like to raise two boys. She guessed he would be figuring it out soon enough, but only because she was forcing him to.

She heard Ben's bare feet on the stairs as she folded the last pair of little underwear. How were they going to make it through this? They were about to crush their children. Maybe this was a mistake. They could make this marriage work. Nothing was worth hurting those boys. She could survive living with Matt better than they could survive without both of their parents.

Clutching a stack of folded towels to her chest, she fought back the urge to run to Matt and tell him to call it all off. It wasn't right for them to live with the pressure of an unhappy household, either. They had to do this. It was best for all of them. Matt was already showing more interest in them. That would be good for the boys and their dad. It would be okay. They just had to get through the hard part first.

She put down the towels, took a deep breath, and walked back into the kitchen. "Let's all go sit in the living room for a few minutes. We can have a family meeting."

"Great timing. We just finished Collin's homework." Matt looked at her from his place at the table. His bruised eyes showed her how little sleep he was getting. The sun-etched lines around his eyes and mouth were turned down in an uncharacteristic sadness she had never seen.

She sat on the couch next to Collin. Matt sat in his recliner and pulled Ben into his lap. They looked at each other. Neither of them was ready to start this. Someone had to. Matt cleared his throat.

"Boys, Mom and I need to talk to you for a minute. We both love you very much. We want what's best for you."

"That's right." She took his lead. "We want you to be happy. Sometimes when grownups have problems, they make everyone else unhappy. Daddy and I have been making each other unhappy. We have some things we need to work out that don't have anything to do with you."

"Do you understand what Mommy's saying? We have some problems and we don't want them to make you unhappy." Matt hugged Ben closer to him as he looked over at the confused frown on Collin's face.

"What are you saying, Daddy? Are you and Mom getting a divorce? You said you'd always be here for us."

"Right now, we're just going to spend some time apart and think about our problems. It's sort of like grownup time out. I'm going to go stay at Uncle Chuck's while we try to fix things."

"You boys will still live here. I'll be here with you; then you'll stay with Daddy at Uncle Chuck's whenever I'm working. That'll be fun, won't it?"

Ben turned to his father and held Matt's face in his little hands, "Daddy, why can't you stay here and be in time out? I have time out in my room when I'm bad."

"It's not that easy, sweetie. Daddy and I have been arguing a lot. You know that. We just want to keep you from having to listen to that all the time. Don't you want to be happy?"

"Collin, are you okay? Do you understand?" Matt could see that he was angry and struggling to control it.

"I'm fine. Can I just go to bed now?" Collin stood and walked toward the stairs.

Libby looked at his back moving away from her. "I'll be up in a minute, sweetie."

"Don't bother. I'll see you in the morning. Daddy, can you come up before you leave. I assume you're leaving." He had adopted a short, clipped tone. His eyes were hard and emotionless, his voice flat.

"I'll be up." He turned to Libby. "I'll just take Ben up and say goodnight to them before I leave."

Ben jumped into Libby's arms. "Goodnight, Mommy." He was regressing to calling her "Mommy". It didn't seem to her to be a good sign.

"Goodnight, baby. I'll see you in the morning." She kissed him and hugged him tightly.

Matt picked up the eight-year-old, who clung to him like an infant. They climbed the stairs and Matt deposited him into his bed with a big show.

"I love you, Daddy. I don't want you to live somewhere else."

"I don't want to, either, son, but sometimes we have to do things we don't like. It'll be okay. I'll still see you all of the time. Just some days you'll live with Mom and some days you'll live with me."

"I'll try, Daddy, but if I don't like it, will you come home? I'll be good all of the time."

"I'm not moving because of anything you did, buddy. I'm moving because Mom and I have some problems. I'll still be here, okay."

"Okay, Daddy."

"Now, get some sleep." He leaned down and kissed his son. He wanted so much to be grown up, but he was still very much a little boy. Eight wasn't very old when your whole world was tilting.

Matt walked into Collin's room to find his son face down on the bed with his head on his arms. He was sobbing. He sat on the bed and placed his hand on his son's back.

"It's okay, bud. Get it all out."

"You lied to me. You said you'd always be here. You said you'd always be my daddy."

"I will always be your daddy. And I will always be here for you. Where I live has nothing to do with that."

"But I don't want you to leave. It'll be all messed up. Like when Hunter's daddy moved out. They got a divorce and his mother got a new husband. His dad got a new wife and now they have a stepsister and a new baby. Hunter doesn't like his stepdad, either. I don't want any of that. I like things just like they are."

"You're getting ahead of yourself. Nobody's getting a new husband or wife. We're just working some things out. Besides, it's already all messed up. Mom and I can't keep from fighting. You don't want to live like that, do you?" He rolled the boy over and picked him up. He held him close and rubbed his back. Collin continued to sob into Matt's shoulder. His heart was broken. His life was changing without his consent. Matt understood his son's distress. He felt it, too.

"Please don't go, Daddy. I need you. I have a game on Thursday and I don't want you to miss it. Hunter's daddy never comes to his games anymore."

"I'll be there, I promise." Matt couldn't stop the tears from filling his own eyes as he held his son. "It's okay."

They stayed that way for several minutes. Both of their hearts aching with staggering intensity. Libby watched from the door, afraid to move or say anything. She longed to go to her child, but she didn't know how to make it right.

"Time to go to sleep, son," Matt said as he reached over to pull the covers back. "Hop in." He was trying desperately to pull himself together for the sake of his son.

"No, Daddy. Please, Please. You can't leave me!" He wrapped his arms around Matt's neck and sobbed loudly. Libby walked in to comfort him.

"It's okay, son. You can stay with Daddy tomorrow." She reached out to touch him.

"Don't touch me. This is all your fault. Daddy wouldn't leave if you weren't making him. I hate you." He buried his wet face in Matt's shoulder.

Libby clutched her hand to her chest and looked at him in shock. He had never spoken to her that way.

"Don't talk to your mother like that. This is not her fault. It isn't anyone's fault." Matt's voice was firm and distant. He didn't look at Libby.

"Don't leave, Daddy."

"I have to go. You need to get some sleep for school tomorrow." He laid his son in the bed and pulled the covers up to his neck.

"Please, Daddy," he sobbed.

"You need to calm down and apologize to your mother. You don't hate her."

Collin looked over his father's shoulder where his mother stood, still and silent in shock. "I'm sorry, Mom. I didn't mean it. I do love you."

Matt backed away from the bed and moved to the door. She leaned over Collin and hugged him, her own tears falling on his pillow.

137

"It's okay. I know you do. This is hard for all of us. We'll all be okay."

She kissed him and left the room, numbly finding her way down the stairs into the living room. Matt followed her.

"You'd better be glad my lawyer told me to keep my mouth shut." He shot her a look of pure contempt and unbridled hatred. "You'll be hearing from her tomorrow regarding the parenting plan. We aren't going to keep putting him through this."

"Whatever." She fought to keep from verbally retaliating.

He slammed the door as he walked out. His heart drummed a staccato beat against his chest. He struggled to breathe as he stumbled to his truck. He managed to climb in and start it. He laid his head back on the seat and tried to calm himself before he pulled out of the driveway. He paused in the street and looked back at his home. From the outside it looked as it always did. Inside, it was no longer his home. He had abandoned his child in the hour of his greatest need. And he had never felt worse. She was going to pay for this.

Chapter 10

Libby left the hospital Thursday morning feeling dog-tired and emotionally spent. They hadn't been very busy, and she had rehashed the last few days with Jessica. Amanda wasn't there, but Libby knew Jessica would call her as soon as she could and let her know. At least she felt like she would have some emotional support from her friends at work.

Jessica watched her friend stagger to her car. She was honestly surprised that they were getting a divorce. She could understand Libby's frustration, but had a hard time believing that Matt had become the man her friend described. She had wanted to believe that it was a stage he would come out of once his business wasn't demanding so much of his time. She had known him forever and wanted to think the best of him. It wasn't easy. She knew Libby well enough to know she didn't take her marriage lightly and would never resort to divorce without a good reason.

Collin and her son, Jake, played on the same football team. Jessica had seen Matt picking Collin up after practice this week. She hoped to catch him at the game Thursday so she could ask him what was going on. As long as they had known each other, she felt she owed it to him to get his side of the story.

Libby arrived home to an empty house. Normally, the boys would be getting their breakfast and Matt would be waiting for her to come in so he could leave for the gym. She wondered what they were eating for breakfast this morning. Did Chuck keep their favorite cereals? Would Matt let them eat something inappropriate? She stopped herself from picking up the phone to call them. Surely they would remember their gear for the game and practice this afternoon.

What time was her mother coming? She assumed it would be sometime after lunch. She picked up the phone and called her mother to confirm. She needed human contact before she went to bed. The stillness in the big house was spooky.

Lauren was in court, but her secretary confirmed that the group was leaving around noon. They would be here before school was out. Libby picked up her purse and the canvas bag she carried to work and walked to her bedroom. She was going to have to learn to be alone in the house. She drifted off trying to remember whether she had packed socks for the boys.

Her alarm sounded at 1:00 and she reached blindly for the sleep button. Had she slept all day? How strange. She must have been more tired than she thought. She never slept that well during the day.

She felt refreshed after her shower and carefully chose her clothes for the day. She didn't want her mother freaking out over the way she looked again. She was determined to pay more attention to her health and appearance. She knew how easy it would be to let herself get rundown and end up sick. That was the last thing she needed.

By the time she had dressed and straightened her house, it was time to go pick up the boys at school. She quickly phoned Matt to make sure she was supposed to pick them up. As usual, Emily answered the office phone.

"Hey, Em. Is Matt around? I need to find out if I'm picking up the boys." She loaded canvas folding chairs and a cooler of drinks into the back of the SUV while she waited for a response.

"I'm so glad you called. I have to talk to you. What are you doing for lunch tomorrow?" Emily was determined to have her say with Libby before this situation went any further.

"My parents will be here this afternoon, so I guess I'll be with them. Velda's coming, too." Why did Matt's sister want to talk to her?

"Damn. I really need a few minutes of your time. I guess we can talk this afternoon. Let me ask Matt about the boys. He's right here." She hit the hold button and hailed Matt who was walking from his office to the kitchen.

"Libby's on the phone. She wants to make sure she's picking up the boys this afternoon."

"Yeah. I expected that she would. I have their bags in my truck. I'll give her their stuff at the game." He kept walking to the kitchen.

"He said, yes. You're picking them up. He'll give you their stuff at the game."

"Thanks. I guess I'll see you in a little while. You haven't seen my parents, have you? They should be here by now and I haven't heard from them."

"Nope, they haven't been here."

"Okay. See ya later." She hung up and dialed her mother's cell number. Lauren answered on the first ring. "Where are you?"

"We're pulling into town. Where should we go? Do you want us to pick the boys up and meet you at the football field? We're right here at the school."

"I guess that's okay. Do you know which line to get in? You pick them both up at the third grade door."

"We've got it. Daddy's pulling into the school now. We're so excited to be here. Do they know we're coming?

Libby hadn't thought about that. She couldn't remember mentioning Grandma's visit to them. "I don't think so. I've been so frazzled I forgot to tell them. I think they'll be pleasantly surprised. They need something. The last couple of days have been awful for them."

"Grandma will take care of them for you. I assume Collin can tell us how to get to the field?"

"Of course. He'll know. He'll need a snack and a sports drink. I usually have some fruit in the car for the boys. Can you stop at the store and get something on your way to the field? He'll be in a big hurry." How could she let someone else take care of this? They had a routine. Poor Collin would be unglued by the changes. She was beginning to wonder if she should let her parents handle the afternoon shift.

"It'll be okay, honey. We'll figure it out. He won't starve. We'll see you at the field in about an hour. We love you."

"I love y'all, too. Be careful. Call me if you have any problems. I'll have my cell on me." She hung up and walked back into the house. What would she do for the next hour? She couldn't remember having an hour to herself in years. She slouched on the sofa and absently turned on the television.

Ham had arrived at the office early and was trying to get all of his things moved out of Morgan's office. His father and grandfather had taken forever to move their things and he knew she was running short on patience with him. He was determined to accomplish this today if he did nothing else.

She found him dragging a box down the hall. "What are you doing? Wouldn't it be easier to just pick it up?"

He stood, grabbed his lower back and leaned into his hands. "It's full of books and weighs a ton. I'm not about to pick that up." He pushed his glasses back up his nose.

He was not what most women considered handsome, but he had a quality that attracted many of them to him. He had more women "friends" than many men had ever known. He wasn't tall, was a little heavy around the middle, and was hopelessly farsighted. Lasiks surgery had helped his vision, but he still wore glasses most of the time. His hair was a glossy dark brown, and receded a little more each year.

An only child, born when his parents were nearly 40, he had grown up cherished and spoiled. His parents' happy marriage had created a child who was easygoing and well liked. His boyish charm was the magnet that drew people to him. It also helped him maintain and grow the legal practice of his father and grandfather.

Morgan had liked him from the minute she met him. He was very much the successful attorney she expected, but he had a quality that immediately set those around him at ease. She almost believed he cared about his clients. She wasn't used to that. The pompous lawyers she had known in New York and Boston were ruthless, uncaring shells of humanity. They had no souls, no scruples, and no time for anyone who did.

Ham dragged the box into his office and abandoned it at the door. She followed him in.

"I need to talk to you about the McDonald divorce." She still wasn't sure if it was to be her case or his.

"Yeah, I guess you need an explanation." He walked back to her office and picked up the stack of prints leaning against the wall. She followed him down the hall and back to his office, waiting for her explanation.

"I'll just tell you, first of all, that I won't handle this case." He gently leaned the prints against his wall and looked up at her. "I would have if you hadn't been here, but I'm glad you are."

"What's the problem? The McDonalds are regular clients of yours." She cleared a spot on the corner of his desk and propped her hip on it. She crossed her arms and waited. She could tell this was going to be good. Who said rural law offered no challenges?

"They are. I've known them all of my life. I played football with the boys. Matt and I lived together in the frat house at school. For all that's worth, I feel compelled to stand behind Libby, too." He was laying prints on the floor in front of where he planned to hang them.

"I'm not sure I understand. She's not from here. How did you even know her?"

"We met our freshman year. She was a little sister in our fraternity. As a matter of fact, she was *my* little sister." He looked at her as if that would be explanation enough.

"What does that mean? I'm not sure that would be a conflict of interest."

"That's not so much the issue, although it probably would have been enough to give me some problems." He placed the last picture and walked over to his desk and sat down. She turned, still perched on the corner of his desk, and caught his eye.

"So. What's the big deal?"

"Well, I had some, um, difficulties our senior year." He looked down at his desk, avoiding her penetrating stare. "She helped me get through them. I can never forget what she did for me."

"I suppose I'll have to take your word for that. I don't mind handling it; it's just become a challenge figuring out what's going on. I've never had such an interesting cast of characters."

"What? I mean, what do you mean? They're all pretty normal people."

"I'm sure they are, but I'm not so sure what's going on." She outlined her meeting with Matt and the phone call from Mary Beth. "Every time I pick up the phone, I expect to hear from someone else who will tell me what to do next. This isn't so much a divorce proceeding, as a community intervention."

Ham chuckled. "You're probably right. I'm glad to hear that someone is trying to help. No matter what has happened, I can't believe they will go through with it. They're not like that. Neither of them. Libby's no quitter."

"Well, she seems determined to quit this marriage. Matt's distraught. He's afraid she'll take his kids and move to Nashville." She stood and faced the desk. "What do you think of her mother?"

"She's a tough one. I'm glad I don't have to try this case. I assume from your question that you know about her." He gave her a crooked smile.

"Oh, yeah. She was a visiting professor when I was at Harvard. I've never seen her in action, but I've heard. I'll be prepared. It won't be easy, given the circumstances, but I refuse to be caught off guard while the rest of this town tries to play peacemaker between them."

"I agree. I wouldn't expect you to do anything else. But the rest of the town won't be playing peacemaker. A lot of people have never liked Libby. They decided what she was like before she ever moved here, and they've never given her a chance. It's a shame, really. A bunch of folks have missed the chance to know a very special lady. I've been fortunate to call her a friend. I just hope she's okay."

"Matt seems like a good man, too." She felt obligated to defend him.

"I'm not saying he's not, but he's a hometown boy. When news of this hits the grapevine, most everyone will side with him. It doesn't matter what the divorce is about. Matt will be the wronged party. I hate that for her. She doesn't deserve it."

"I'm glad you're not handling this case. You really would be struggling. Lauren Reynolds would use that against you."

"Probably. That's what you're here for. I'll try to stay out of it."

"I'm leaving early this afternoon. I have some things to do. Is that okay?"

"Sure. This is Ainsley. We don't keep a timecard. Let me know if I can help you."

"Thanks." She walked out and wandered into her office, more confused about this case than ever.

He knew he should have told her more. It wasn't fair to give her such a vague explanation, but he didn't want to lose her respect. He had kept his secret for a long time. Nobody knew.

Not his parents, or his friends. Nobody. Except Libby.

♥ ♥ ♥ ♥

It had been a typical Thursday before a long weekend. Monday was President's Day and they would not have class. Most of them would be skipping class on Friday. Ham and a couple of frat brothers had spent the day at the fraternity house drinking beer. As evening approached, several went to pick up their dates, including Matt. Ham and three others had decided to go up to the Volunteer Grill and shoot some pool. They had run into some other friends and launched into a long night of barhopping.

That was the last thing Ham remembered until he woke up to Libby beating on his car window. Something smelled awful. Where was he? What time was it? What was Libby doing?

As he regained consciousness, he realized that he stunk. He had puked on himself. Everything was blurry. He fished around the seat of the car and found his glasses. It took forever to find a clean place to wipe them off. Disgusting. Libby was still beating on the window demanding that he open the door.

It was dark. He opened the door to the car. He was parked in the grass. Well, maybe not parked. He was off the road, a few yards from the entrance to the parking lot of her apartment complex. A small tree had evidently impeded his forward progress.

She held her hand over her nose and mouth. "Oh my God, Ham. Are you okay? What happened? What is that smell?" She looked around the door at where he was sitting in the car.

He followed her gaze. "I guess I got sick. I don't know."

"What do you mean, you don't know? How can you not know? Where have you been?" She was looking for a clean place to grab him and pull him out of the car. "Get out!"

"I'm getting, I'm getting. What's your problem?" He staggered out of the car, obviously still plastered.

"My problem is that you could have been killed, or worse, killed someone else." She looked him over to see if he had been hurt.

"I'm all right. I'm just a little sick."

"Yeah, I bet. Why are you driving? You're too drunk to walk, much less drive." She was getting herself worked up.

"I'm okay, I said. I just need to get home."

"I'll get you home, but you can't go on like this. How many times have you passed out lately?" She knew it was becoming a problem. Even Matt had commented that Ham's drinking was getting bad. He had missed several classes already this semester.

"A couple, maybe. Get off my ass." He pushed her away and opened the back door, fishing around in the backseat.

"I'm not getting off your ass. I'm worried about you. Something's wrong. Why are you drinking so much? It's not like you."

He pulled out a blanket and laid it over the front seat of the car. "You can sit on this while you drive me home. I need to lay down." He staggered around to the passenger side of the car and climbed in.

"Gross. Why do you want to live this way? You're screwing up, Ham." She eased herself into the car, trying not to touch anything that he'd puked on.

"I'm not a screw up, I'm just having some fun."

"No, you're not. This is not fun. What would your parents think if I'd had to call them and tell them you were dead? Do you want to do that to them?"

He looked at her thoughtfully. "That's not going to happen. I'm just enjoying my college years. Living it up. I'm not going to die from having a good time."

"Famous last words, Ham. You've got a problem. You need to get some help." She pulled into a parking space near the frat house. "Can you make it?"

"Yeah, I'll make it. I always do." He hesitated before he opened the door. "You aren't going to tell anyone about this, are you? I didn't hit anyone or damage any property. I'll just tell my parents someone hit me in a parking lot."

"I won't tell if you'll promise to think about getting some help. I really think you need it."

"Yeah, whatever, Libby. I'll think about it." He turned to her before he walked off.

"Are you okay to walk back to your apartment? It's cold out."

"I've got my coat on. I was walking home when I found you."

"Right. Um, thanks for helping me. You're the best." It sounded insincere. For the most part, it was. He hadn't asked for her help.

"I need to get to bed. I have an early class." She turned and walked away, shaking her head as she headed for home.

Ham had found his way to his room and crawled into bed. When Matt woke him up the next morning, he growled a few colorful expletives at his friend and covered his head with a pillow. He felt like hell. No way was he going to class today.

Matt had packed his bags and was leaving for home when Ham woke up again. "I'm going home for the weekend. Are you going to be okay?"

"Yeah. I'm fine."

"Well, you reek. Get a bath. And get rid of the stench before I get back on Monday. It smells like puke in here."

"Get off me. I don't need a mother." Ham pulled the pillow back over his head. It hurt like hell. His mouth felt like a herd of elephants had pooped in it, and his stomach was on fire. When he looked out from under the pillow, Matt was gone.

He threw up so much that afternoon, that he couldn't get up and get himself anything to drink. He knew he would dehydrate without it. He yelled for help from his housemates, but nobody answered. He assumed they had all gone home for the weekend. He didn't know what to do. He needed help or he would die in his own vomit.

He picked up the phone and called Libby's number. She answered.

"Can you please come over here and bring me something to drink? I'm dying and there's nobody left in the house. I'm sorry about last night. I really do appreciate your help." He collapsed from the effort it had taken to call. Then he gagged, overcome by dry heaves.

"I'll be right there." She hung up and rushed to his side.

She had stayed with him all weekend. She nursed him through the hangover, lectured him, put cool cloths on his head, and made him promise to quit drinking. She went back to her dorm only long enough to clean up and change. She made him shower and put on clean clothes. She changed his bed and washed his sheets and soiled laundry.

She slept in Matt's bed. They had watched movies, eaten junk food, and spent the weekend fighting off Ham's urge to drink and the physical effects of his deprivation. He was a wreck. He had tossed and turned, waking from his fitful sleep to find her by his side each time.

By the time Monday rolled around, he had made it through the worst weekend of his life and she had been there for him. Tuesday morning, she walked with him to the counseling office and waited for him to finish his first session.

The rest of the semester, she had kept a discreet eye on him. He never drank again. He stayed in counseling until graduation. He went to his professors, begged for forgiveness, and got his grades back up. To his knowledge, she had never told a soul. Not even Matt. She helped him out of the pit he had dug himself into and had kept his demise a secret. He owed her his life. He would never betray her, not even for Matt.

Libby arrived at the football field to find her parents huddled up with Mary Beth and Charlie. Chuck and Matt were standing on the sidelines with a group of dads. Ben was hopping back and forth between Mary Beth's lap and Lauren's lap, occasionally landing on Clayton or Velda. He was giving and receiving a generous amount of kisses.

She unloaded a chair and the cooler of drinks and headed for the group. She avoided looking at Matt. She would not have a confrontation with him today. This was Collin's big day. She searched the crowd of boys in green uniforms and found him throwing a football on the sidelines. They still had 30 minutes until game time.

"Hey, everybody. Got a spot for me in here?" She dropped her chair and hugged her family as they all stood to greet her. Clay picked up the chair and unfolded it beside his.

"I want you to sit right here with me so I can talk to you. We haven't spent ten minutes together in six months." He patted the seat for her to sit down.

Ben crawled into her lap, kissing her cheeks. "I missed you this morning, Mommy."

"I missed you, too. Did you have fun at Uncle Chuck's?" She kissed him back and smoothed his hair.

"It was cool. He bought us a Wii and some games. We all played video games until bedtime. Uncle Chuck's pretty good, too."

"I'm glad you had a good time." She was sincere. She wanted this to go well for them.

"I did. But mostly, I just missed you." He sighed as he leaned back into her and crossed her arms over the front of his body, like wearing a Mommy coat.

She kissed his cheek. "I'm glad you missed me, but we'll get used to it. I've always worked at night, so that won't be different. You'll just stay with Daddy on those nights."

"I know. It's okay." He squirmed out of her lap and jumped into her mother's.

Clay reached over and took her hand. "It really will be okay. It won't be easy, but eventually, you'll all adapt. I've seen too many divorces in my day. Some of them turn out ugly, most of them involving children have horrible moments, but over time, things smooth out. If you try, you and Matt can make this work for yourselves and the boys. Just remember that you have a family to support you, too. Don't sit over here and assume you're all alone. You never will be."

"Thanks, Daddy. This is getting so hard already and it hasn't even been a week. I can't imagine what it's going to be like in a month or two. I hope we get the bad stuff out of the way in a hurry. I'm ashamed to be hurting my kids this way." She held his hand to her cheek.

Emily walked up and put her hand out to Libby. "Come with me. I need to go to the restroom and I refuse to go in that place alone. Something might get me."

Libby laughed and followed.

"I know this is awkward for you, but I've got something to say."

"Say whatever you want, Em. We're friends."

"Well, that's kind of what I want to say. I've already told Matt that you will always be my friend. I want you to know that, too."

"That's sweet, I appreciate it."

"I don't think you understand what I'm saying. I'm not doing this right." She stopped outside the door to the ancient restroom facilities.

"I've always thought of you as my sister. I've always felt overpowered by my brothers. The day Matt brought you home to us was the greatest day of my life. I thought you were fantastic. I wanted to be like you. I wanted to be close to you. You were my link to the rest of the world. I guess I should have said something. I thought maybe you didn't want to be close to me. Nobody else in this town ever has."

"I never knew that." Libby was looking at Emily's damp eyes. She didn't know what to think about what she was saying.

"Let me finish. I love you. You're the only member of this family who listens to me like I have some sense. You know that I want to go back to school when the girls are older and you don't condemn me for it. I'm sorry I never told you before. Maybe we could have been closer. Maybe you would have been happier here. Maybe you wouldn't be leaving Matt. I'm sorry."

"It's not your fault. I'm sorry I never knew. When all of this is over and calms down, maybe we can be better friends. I would like that. Right now, though, Matt needs his family. This is going to be awful for everyone."

"He has Mother and Daddy and Chuck. I don't care what he needs. Whatever has happened between y'all is taking you away from our family. I don't like it, and I'm siding with you. He's already been told. He said he didn't care. I'm keeping you in the divorce."

Libby laughed hysterically. "That's the nicest thing anyone has ever said to me!"

They hugged and Libby looked apprehensively at the restroom building. "Do you really need to go in there?"

"No, thank goodness. I think I'd rather go up to the Mini Market." They linked arms and headed back to where the game was about to start.

As they approached the field, Libby could see Matt standing next to the bleachers talking to a woman. She was very pretty. Libby had never seen her before. Who was she?

Emily gasped as she saw him. "Who in the hell is that? And what is he doing talking to her in public? I know he's been told he can't do that."

"I don't know who that is, or what you're talking about, but you'd think he'd be a bit more discreet than to be flirting in public. I'm doing everything I can not to embarrass my kids or your family any more than necessary, but he's dragging us through the mud as quickly as he can."

Jessica strolled up to them in a huff. "Who's the bimbo? I want to know, right now."

"We don't know. I don't want to talk about it. This is ridiculous." Libby walked toward her chair next to her father. She held her head high and tried to keep her legs steady. She would be damned if she let him see that he had upset her.

Daddy took her hand when she sat down. "It's okay, baby. Don't let it bother you. You don't know who that is. It could be anybody."

"I know. I'm fine. Just drop it." She leaned toward where her mother was carrying on a conversation with Mary Beth and Velda and feigned interest until the game started.

Matt stayed huddled up with the strange woman until nearly halftime. Emily and Jessica worked their way through the crowd, visiting with everyone they knew. She saw Emily stop next to Matt where he introduced her to the unknown woman. Emily smiled and slowly made her way back to Libby.

"Thank goodness. I've found out the identity of the mystery woman."

Lauren overheard her. "That's Morgan Peterson, his attorney."

"How did you know that? And why didn't you say something sooner?" Libby was torn between relief and embarrassment.

Emily was astounded. "You let us sit here all this time thinking my brother was flirting with some bimbo when he's been over there talking to his lawyer?"

"I didn't know who she was, either." Mary Beth laughed. "You've had us all going. You should have said something."

"I thought you all knew. You live here...not me!" She joined in as they all laughed at the foolishness of the situation.

"What's she doing here? Is this what they call 'field work?'" Libby laughed at herself.

"Oh, the third cheerleader from the left is hers. I didn't know that until now. Her name is Lindsey, and she's in Meghan's class." They all followed Emily's directions to look at the child. She reminded Mary Beth of the conversation she and Lauren had had over lunch.

"Lauren, don't you have some information for me?"

"I do. I almost forgot. I'll tell you later."

They settled in to watch the cheerleaders perform their halftime routine. Collin had a great game in his debut as quarterback. After the game, the family gathered around to congratulate him. Libby had to hustle Ben off to the last hour of soccer practice. Matt and the rest of the family, including hers, took Collin out to dinner to celebrate. She was instructed to meet them all there when Ben was finished at practice.

Ben's practice was long, since it was their last practice before the season opener on Saturday. By the time they were finished, everyone had gone home. She took Ben to get a burger and rushed home. Collin was bathed and sitting at the table doing homework when she walked in. She hustled Ben to the table and set out his dinner.

She bent down to hug and kiss Collin, hoping that he would no longer harbor the animosity he had shown toward her. He gave her a cool kiss back.

"Congratulations, buddy. You had a great game. I'm proud of you."

He beamed. "Thanks, Mom. It was fun."

"Did you have fun at Uncle Chuck's house last night?" She wanted him to be able to talk to her about it.

"Yeah, it was okay. We played PS2." No matter how hard he tried, she was still the mother who loved him and took care of him. He couldn't be mad at her forever.

"Ben told me you had fun. I'm glad." She hugged him again and walked into the living room where her parents and Velda were having coffee.

She visited with them for the rest of the evening, tucked the boys in and went to her room. For the second time in ten years, she went to bed alone. Horribly, sickeningly alone.

Chapter 11

They made it through the weekend without an incident. They were both trying hard to stay away from each other. It showed. Matt still had the boys while she worked Friday night, despite her parents being there. He let them go back to her house after Ben's soccer match Saturday morning.

Libby and her mother sat down and listed her work schedule for the next few weeks. Her mother suggested that she stay with them when she was doing her orientation in Nashville. She agreed. Matt would have the boys during that time. She would be working Wednesday and Friday in Ainsley for the next two weeks, then spend four days in Nashville. The next week she was working Wednesday in Nashville and Friday and Saturday in Ainsley. Working two places was complicated, but necessary.

The next week was uneventful. Mary Beth helped them make smooth transitions for visitation. Libby worked Wednesday and Friday. Mac kept the boys all weekend so he could take them to the Vols game. They stayed away from each other.

Sunday night, Jessica called and asked her to lunch on Monday. A bunch of other night shifters from the hospital were getting together. She gladly accepted. She hadn't had a lunch with grownups in ages. It was past time for her to enjoy herself.

She met the group from the hospital at the Pretty Plate Diner. It sat a block off Court Square and advertised the best home cooking in the county. It was clean and had great food, but it hadn't been decorated in 40 years. Football calendars from years past still hung on the walls next to ancient deer and fish trophies. Nobody knew whose they were.

Every morning a gang of folks met for breakfast at a table in the back affectionately known as the "Liars Table". The State Representative from their district, a couple of judges and attorneys, businessmen, doctors, and high school coaches hashed out the problems of the town. It was often said that more decisions were made there than in any session of any government assembly from the city commission to Congress. Nobody doubted that.

Libby spotted her group immediately. They had been placed in the back at a long table running the length of the room. She sat next to Bart Ross, the night pharmacist. He was younger than she, but she had always liked talking to him when he did his rounds. He was funny and she needed a good laugh.

Bart was friendly and attentive. Libby enjoyed visiting with him and the rest of the night staff. They tried to get together periodically, but she had rarely made time to join them. She vowed to change that. They were nice people who were nice to her. That counted for something.

She was talking to Jessica when it happened or she would never have known. The difference in Jessica's behavior was so slight, it would have been imperceptible to anyone else. But she knew Jessica, and something was definitely amiss. She tried to discern from Jessica's expression what it might be, but her friend was trying to cover it up.

Libby gave in to temptation and turned to look behind her. Matt was standing a few tables away, staring at her with the meanest, most hateful look she had ever seen. She sucked in a breath of surprise. She looked at the lady whose chair he was holding. The lady lawyer. Well, people in glass houses...

It was none of his business what she did and where she did it. They were separated. They were getting a divorce. She could have lunch with the Tennessee Titans if she wanted to. She flashed him a flat smile and turned back to the table. The silent stares gradually morphed into quiet conversation again. She was relieved. Her heart was beating so fast she was sure everyone could hear.

How dare he act like she was doing something wrong. He was the one having lunch with the hot lady lawyer. She was here with friends. He had no right to act the way he had. She was humiliated. No wonder she never went out with friends. With a husband like that, who would want to be her friend?

Her cell phone rang when she got in the car. It was Matt. He must've been waiting for her to leave.

"What?"

"What was that all about?"

"What do you mean? I was having lunch with friends. Not that it's any of your business."

"Whatever, Libby. You've embarrassed us enough. Can't you behave in some reasonable fashion until we get this over with?"

"I've embarrassed us? I'm not the one who was out groping Darlene at the Country Club before the papers were even started. And you weren't exactly dining alone today."

"I told you that was nothing with Darlene. And I can have lunch with my attorney anytime I want."

"And I'm telling you I was having lunch with friends. I don't know what your problem is."

"I don't have a problem. I just wanted to know what was going on before I find out from someone else. Kind of like I found out about our problems."

"Now what are you talking about?" She had no idea.

"I'm talking about being told through the grapevine that we're getting a divorce before I ever heard a thing from you. I've never been so humiliated in my life."

"I can't imagine where that would have come from. I only talked to Jessica and Amanda about our problems. I didn't tell anyone we were getting a divorce. I didn't know myself until the weekend before I went to Mother's."

"Whatever, Libby. Are you picking the boys up and bringing them to the office, or am I? We haven't discussed it and I need to know what to plan for the afternoon."

"I'll pick them up and take them to the office. They don't have practice today, so it'll be early. Then I'll leave for Nashville. I have their bags already packed."

"What time do you plan to be back Thursday? Do you want them then, or on Friday afternoon?" He didn't care; he just wanted to yank her chain. He still wasn't over seeing her at lunch with someone else.

"I'll be finished around 4:00, so I'll just pick them up from Chuck's after Collin's game, if that's okay with you. It should be around 6:00."

"That's fine, I just need to know."

He hung up, not feeling much better than he had when he called. She was turning into a real witch. He hadn't thought he would ever feel that way about her. However it had happened,

she was turning into the wicked ex. He didn't
like it, but he couldn't do much about it.

♥ ♥ ♥ ♥

"Collin, where's your uniform? Your mom
said she packed it." He had torn up both of their
bags looking for it. It was nowhere to be found.
"She did. I had to get something out of
my bag Sunday night. Maybe I pulled it out.
Isn't it in there with my pads and stuff?"
"No, it's not in there with your pads and
stuff. You must have left it at home. We'll have
to go over there and get it. Hurry up. Let's go.
You'll be late."
They loaded up and rushed to the house.
Matt ran around to the back door, retrieved the
spare key from under the mat and let himself in.
The mess floored him. The couch was piled with
laundry, the furniture was dusty, and he could
see dirty dishes in the sink. If he didn't know
better, he'd swear she'd been robbed.
Shaking his head, he went upstairs to
Collin's room where he found the uniform exactly
where the boy must have put it when he was
rifling the bag. The room was as big a disaster
as the rest of the house. She probably hadn't
even been up there in weeks. He looked out the
window at the pool. It was worse than it had
been when they had started this mess weeks
ago. Evidently, it wasn't high on her list of
priorities.
He ran out the door, replaced the key,
and rushed them to the game. The more he
thought about the house, the madder he
became. How could she neglect their home that
way? She obviously hadn't cleaned a thing
since her parents left almost two weeks ago. It

had been dirty before that. He just didn't get it.

When she got to his house to pick up the boys, he was livid. He knew he was supposed to avoid a confrontation, but he was tired of walking on eggshells. He walked out the door and met her in the driveway.

"When do you plan to clean the house and pool?"

"What are you talking about?"

"I had to go by the house and get Collin's uniform. He took it out of his bag. I was more than shocked at the state of the house. The Health Department would declare it uninhabitable."

"You had no business being in my house. It's not yours."

"It will be soon enough. I'm going to ask for it in the divorce."

"You can't do that. I don't have anywhere else to go."

"I don't give a damn what you have or don't have. I won't sit by and watch you destroy something I worked my tail off to get. I want the house."

"Then have the damn house. I'll move to Nashville and take the boys with me. You don't think for one minute my mother can't beat that fancy assed city lawyer you've hired."

"You aren't taking them anywhere."

"You just watch and see. I'll have them everyday and you can have them every other weekend. Don't push me, Matt. I've got the best damn lawyer in the state and you know it."

He reached over and grabbed her arm. "You try it. You'll find out just how good my fancy assed city lawyer is. If you don't believe me, ask your mother. Morgan was a student of hers at Harvard. She learned from the best. I won't lose."

She slapped at his hand until he moved it off her arm. "Believe what you want, you know I'm their mother and you'll have to prove I'm an ax murderer to keep me from taking them with me. It'll be a cold day in hell when I give you the house or my children."

"Get out your parka, baby, 'cause hell's about to freeze over."

"That's rich, Matt. Really classy." She threw her hands up in defeat. "Where are the boys? I need to get them home."

"I'll send them out. Don't bother coming in."

He turned and went back into the house, sending the boys out to her car as promised. She was shaking so badly from the encounter that she found it difficult to drive home. She tried to maintain a modicum of sense so she could converse with the boys, but it was hard. She didn't want this to end up in a huge court battle. Collin and Ben would undoubtedly suffer the most.

She didn't even care about the house. It was his house. He designed it and built it. She had always found it too large and too much to keep up. Living there alone was making it impossible for her to manage. She should just let him have it. What difference did it make? She could afford to find herself a new house somewhere else in town. Did she really want to move to Nashville now? No. She hadn't planned to do that for a while. She wanted the boys adjusted to the divorce first. The entire argument had been ridiculous, but she wasn't about to admit that to him.

♥ ♥ ♥ ♥

She and the boys spent the weekend cleaning house. The fall rains had set in, making it impossible for her to work on the yard or the pool, but they managed to get the house back in order. The boys even helped clean their rooms and fold laundry.

While the boys were upstairs cleaning their rooms, she took down some family portraits that hung in the living room. She didn't want them on the wall anymore, but she didn't want the boys to see her take them down. She replaced them with some pictures of the boys when they were little. She hoped they wouldn't notice. She just couldn't stand to look at them anymore.

Ben's soccer match was called because of the rain, so they didn't leave the house until Saturday afternoon when they decided to buy groceries. The list was long. She hadn't been to the store since Matt left. The boys were wound up from being in the house all day. They all acted silly the entire afternoon.

Saturday night, after a movie marathon, she tucked the kids in and went to her office to pull the parenting plan papers. Her mother had tired of waiting for her to do them and had completed them and sent them to her for her review. How like her to take things into her own hands. Libby appreciated it. She couldn't even bring herself to look at them now.

She had thought it would be so simple. She and Matt would divorce, the kids would be shuttled back and forth and everyone would be much happier. Her father had warned her that it wouldn't be as easy as all that. She should have listened to Daddy. The whole affair was getting worse by the minute.

♥ ♥ ♥ ♥

The call didn't come until Wednesday of the next week. She had just finished dressing so she could do her volunteer run for Meals on Wheels. It was the Principal at the boys' school.

"Mrs. McDonald? This is Mr. Cawthon at Ainsley Elementary. There's been an incident."

"Oh my. Are the boys okay?" She went into full-blown mother panic.

"Yes, they're fine, but Ben's had some trouble. I'll need you to come in immediately."

"I'll be right there."

She hung up and instantly grabbed her cell to call Matt as she ran out of the house.

"Ben's in trouble at school. Can you meet me there?"

"I'm on my way." He hung up and rushed out of the building.

They arrived at the same time and walked into the building together.

"What happened?" He was worried, but furious with her for turning their children into heathens.

"I don't know. The principal said there had been an 'incident'. Whatever that means."

"I guess we'll know soon enough." He opened the door to the school and held it for her while she entered. He did the same at the office door.

Ben was sitting on a chair in the sick room. She could barely see him from the counter. She scooted around the counter and went to him. His shirt was torn and spotted with blood, his face was tear stained, and he was still sobbing.

"What's wrong baby? What happened?" She pushed a lock of hair off his forehead and smoothed it back.

"He's been in a fight." Mr. Cawthon stepped out of his office and leaned on the counter. He was in his mid to late forties, balding, wearing a short-sleeved shirt and a tie that ended in the middle of his paunchy belly. She was certain it was a clip-on. She normally liked him, but for now, she viewed him as the enemy.

"If y'all will just step into my office, we can discuss this in private." He held the door open and indicated with a sweep of his hand that they should all enter.

"What's going on, Mr. Cawthon? Ben's never been in any kind of trouble before." Matt opened the conversation, knowing that Libby wouldn't be able to. She was still fussing over her son.

"I'll let Ben explain it to you. There's no sense in my paraphrasing the incident. He was there." He looked at Ben, who had been seated between his parents.

"Okay, sweetie, just tell us what happened to get you so upset. Who tore your shirt?" Libby looked at him, then looked at the principal with an animosity usually reserved for serial killers and child molesters.

Ben wiped his eyes on the back of his hands and tried to compose himself before telling his story. "It all started this morning in gym class. We were playing dodge ball. John Mark Wilkes threw the ball and hit me really hard in the side of the head. You aren't supposed to hit in the head." He looked at Mr. Cawthon.

"Go on." Matt patted the boy's knee.

"Well, it hurt. I started to cry, 'cuz it was stinging. John Mark started laughing at me. Then he had everyone laughing at me. I was embarrassed." He sniffed back new tears.

"Where was your teacher?" Libby was getting more upset by the minute.

"He was on the girl's side of the curtain, talking to Miss Adams. He came over when he heard all of the laughing. Then my nose started bleeding. You know how it just does that sometimes. Well, it was bleeding real bad. It was gross. He let me go to the locker room to stop it."

"Okay, then what happened?" Matt looked over Ben's head at Libby who was obviously going to blow a blood vessel if they didn't get this over with.

"Gym was over, so we went to lunch. John Mark kept saying things about me, making everyone laugh at me. I couldn't hear him, I just knew he was talking about me, 'cuz everyone was looking at me. It made me mad." He sniffed and Libby handed him a tissue.

"I told him to stop talking about me. Then he said he could say whatever he wanted and there wasn't nothing I could do."

"*Anything.* There wasn't *anything* you could do." Matt corrected him.

"Well, I said if he didn't stop, I'd punch his lights out. Then he said I was nothing. That his momma said my momma was just a snooty old bitch and she didn't belong here. Then he said that my daddy was divorcing my momma and she was going to get run out of town. That's when I punched his lights out."

Matt had put his hand over his eyes and was leaning on the arm of his chair. Libby had gathered up Ben and had him sitting in her lap. He was sobbing anew.

"I know this is highly unusual for Ben to be in trouble, and the Wilkes boy was wrong, but I can't let my students fight. We have zero tolerance for violence."

"What about zero tolerance for bullies? Where were the teachers when all of this was happening? If the gym teacher had been doing his job, this could have been avoided." She was hot and on a roll. Matt had to think of a way to diffuse the situation before she got them all thrown out.

"What is his punishment?"

"Well, under the circumstances, I think he'll just be suspended for the rest of the week."

"What?" Libby had risen and pushed Ben into Matt's lap. She was leaning on he edge of the principal's desk. "You have to be out of your mind. How in the world can you suspend my child for two and a half days when he was defending himself? I won't stand for it."

"Now, calm down, Mrs. McDonald. The other boy will be suspended as well, but Ben's behavior was unacceptable. He didn't just punch the other boy; he kept punching until a teacher pulled him off. He was out of control. I suggest that you take this time to get him some counseling. Maybe some family counseling. You obviously have some sort of family situation going on. It does affect your children."

"Excuse me. I hate to interrupt." Matt was standing now. He had plopped Ben into his chair. "I don't think it's any of your business what our family situation is. From what I've heard, this whole thing started because someone stuck their nose in someone else's business."

"It is my business when your child is disruptive in my school."

"Perhaps, but let me remind you of the contribution my family makes to this school district, and the time my wife spends volunteering here. I don't think you want to do anything rash." He had never used his family name for anything before, but he was going to do it now.

"I don't think this is rash. I'm sorry you do, but the suspension will stand. He may come back to school on Monday." He stood. "I believe this meeting is now over."

"This meeting may be over, but you can rest assured you haven't heard the end of this. You have overstepped your boundaries this time."

"You can remove me from your volunteer list. I won't have time to spend up here if I have to keep my child at home." Libby took Ben's hand and turned toward the door. Matt followed her.

"I'll be right behind you. We need to talk to him about fighting. I'll be at the house in a minute."

She nodded and loaded Ben into the backseat. She drove home, shaking from anger and humiliation. How could someone say something like that about her in front of a child? How could any child be so cruel to another? It was unbelievable. And who in the hell was John Mark Wilkes that his mother was talking about her?

They settled in the kitchen around the table for their talk. She made Ben a glass of milk and a sandwich since he had spent his lunch period in the office. She brewed a pot of coffee and fixed a cup for Matt and herself. She sat down at the table with them.

"What made you think it was okay to hit someone, baby?"

"I don't know, Mom, he was just being so mean to me. Everyone was laughing. I was embarrassed. I didn't know how to make him stop."

"But you know you can't hit people. We don't do that. There are other ways to settle a problem. You should have gone to a teacher." Matt sipped his coffee and patted Ben's hand.

"I tried. Mr. Simmons, the gym teacher, just told us to go to lunch. He said to let it go. I tried to let it go, but John Mark just kept on making fun of me."

"Who is he?" Libby looked at Matt.

Matt looked back sheepishly. "He's Darlene's son by her first husband, Mark Wilkes. I guess she's up to her old tricks."

"Unbelievable."

"Yeah, well, we need to get back to the problem at hand. Son, do you understand that they won't let you go back to school until Monday?"

"Yeah, I've been spended."

"*Suspended*. It means you'll get zeros on all of the work your class does for the next two days. Your grades might be bad on your report card because of this." Matt looked at Libby for help.

"You know you can't play soccer if your grades aren't good. You'll also be getting a bad conduct grade. We'll have to stick by our rules about grades and sports. I know you were embarrassed and upset, but you can't solve anything the way you did. You've just gotten yourself into trouble."

"I'm sorry. I just didn't know what to do. Nobody's ever made fun of me before. And he was talking about you. I don't want you to leave town." He put his face in his hands and started crying again.

"I'm not leaving town." She looked at Matt. "Mommy's not leaving you. I love you. And I'm not worried about what anyone else says. As long as you and Collin love me, I'll be okay."

"I do love you, Mommy." He threw his arms around her neck and hugged her. He turned to Matt. "I love you, too, Daddy. I just want us all to be happy like we used to be."

"We'll all be happy again, buddy, I promise. Sometimes these things just take time." He glared at Libby over Ben's head.

"Why don't you go up to your room, clean up, and take a little nap? We'll have to leave to pick up Collin in a little while, then I have to go to work. You'll get to see Daddy later. I need to talk to him right now."

"Okay. See ya later, Daddy."

"Bye, bud." He listened for his son to get up the stairs before he addressed Libby.

"I hope you're happy. This is all your fault."

"How can you blame me? It was your 'friend', Darlene, who started this. She can't seem to keep her mouth shut about me. Why is that? What have I ever done to her? She's exactly the reason I hate living here. I've put up with this for my children. Now it seems I've made the wrong decision. They don't deserve to have to live somewhere like this. It's insane."

"So you think that moving will solve this problem? You just told him that fighting is not the answer. Running away isn't the answer, either. Unless you really are a snooty old bitch who thinks she's too good for us. What is it, Libby?"

"You're just an ass. I can't believe you said that. Who and what I am has never seemed to bother you before. Why does it matter all of a sudden? Am I ruining your reputation?"

Their voices got louder as the conversation progressed. They were both standing, facing each other across the table in red-faced rage.

"I didn't want to move. I didn't want to have to uproot the boys in the midst of the turmoil over the divorce, but I can see that maybe I've made a mistake. This town won't allow us to make this easy on them. They'll be forced to suffer no matter what we do to stop it. I won't allow that."

"Well, I won't allow you to move away and take them with you. You've got another thing coming if you think that's going to happen. I'm tired of this. They need more. They need a home that's stable and happy, not this pigpen you've created here."

"Get real, Matt. You're the one who's got another thing coming. I already have a job in Nashville. All I have to do is pack them up and go. We'll be gone before you and 'Hot Pants' know what hit you."

"I'll see you in hell first."

"Leave. Now. I've had enough."

"I'm not finished with you," he shouted as he slammed the back door.

"Me, either."

Chapter 12

Matt drove back to the office in a fury. He wanted to drive straight to Morgan's office, but he knew it wouldn't do any good today. He would have to wait until tomorrow. But he was definitely going to do something before she did. He was not losing his children.

He didn't want to spend a year fighting her in court. Things like this had a way of dragging out until everyone was completely miserable, not to mention broke. Attorneys like Lauren Reynolds and Morgan Peterson made their fortunes off long, nasty divorce cases. He did not intend to be a statistic. Somehow, this was going to have to be resolved before it tormented his children anymore.

His mother's car was still in the parking lot. He was relieved. He needed to talk to her before he did anything. She always knew what to say to make him feel better. She was in her office when he tapped on the door facing.

"May I come in? I need to chat for a minute."

"Sure, baby, have a seat." It scared him how much she sounded like Libby talking to Collin or Ben. Did all mothers talk like that?

"I've got problems, Mom. Real problems." He dropped into a chair in front of her desk and sighed loudly.

"Get it out. You'll feel better. You look like you haven't slept in weeks."

"I haven't, but that's not my problem. I'm getting used to that. My problem is Libby and this stupid divorce."

"What's happened now?"

He told her about Ben's incident at school and the things he and Libby had said to each other.

"I thought you were supposed to avoid each other. I particularly recall telling you to watch your mouth."

"I didn't start it, Mom, I swear. She just gets going and I can't stop myself from responding."

"It really doesn't matter who started it. What matters is that now you've opened up a big, fat can of worms. What do you intend to do about it?"

"I don't know. I'm going to talk to Morgan tomorrow. I want the boys and the house. Now. I know she can do something. That's what I'm paying her for."

"Do you honestly believe that's the answer? That you need to stir up something this complex so early? I'm afraid you're going to make a bigger mess than you already have."

He rose and started pacing the room. "How can this be any worse? My son is being harassed at school. My wife is threatening to take them and move to Nashville, and to top it all off, she's turning my house into a hovel. My kids are living in squalor. I can't do this any longer. If I stand by and watch the way this is hurting them, I might as well be a participant. No. I won't stand for it."

Mary Beth rubbed her forehead. How was she going to fix this? He seemed so determined to make an issue of this latest incident. What could she do? She did the only thing she could think of at the time.

"I'm telling you right now, as your mother, as your boss, and as the person who writes your paycheck: You will not do anything foolish until I have had a chance to discuss this with your father."

He slapped the top of her desk. "You can't tell me what to do!"

She straightened in her chair, folded her hands in front of her, and pulled out her most severe CFO persona. "I can, and I am. You were told not to provoke any sort of argument with her, and you have deliberately defied that order. You will do as you're told, or you will go this alone. You have done enough."

"That's ridiculous. You're saying I'm supposed to let her do whatever she pleases. She can just continue to threaten to take them and move and I can't do anything about it. Bullshit, Mother. If that's your solution to this problem, I guess I'll have to do this alone." He walked to the door as if to leave.

"You come right back in here, young man. And you watch your language."

Charlie turned the corner and nearly ran into Matt standing in the door. "What is going on in here? I can hear you down the hall."

"Mother's trying to tell my how I'm going to handle my divorce. She's threatened to cut me off if I don't do what she says."

"I'm sure she means it. She's threatened to cut me off a dozen times. I suggest you listen to her. She has the checkbook." He chuckled nervously and took his son by the arm, leading him back into the room.

"Come on, y'all. I'm not ten years old. You can't tell me what to do. I'm a grown man in the middle of the worst nightmare of my life. You can either wake me up, or help me get out of it. Telling me I have to sit back and let her screw up my life is not helpful." He leaned his arms on the back of a chair and hung his head. Charlie put his arm around his son's shoulder.

"We don't want to need to tell you what to do, but sometimes it is necessary to keep you from making an enormous mistake. We've always tried to let you boys make your own way in life, and I'm proud of the choices you've made so far. At this time, though, I'm with your mother. I think you need to let your attorney handle things. You're making a royal mess of this."

"How do you even know what we're talking about? I just told Mom a minute ago."

"I received a phone call from John Northington, the school superintendent. I can only imagine what you and Libby said to each other after you terrorized the principal at Ben's school. I also heard why Ben got in that fight. I don't think Darlene's son making comments about Libby is her fault. Sounds more like some crap you stirred up when you were out at the country club. You should have known better."

"You can't blame that on me. That woman has always been trouble. If Libby hadn't started this divorce business to begin with, there wouldn't be any gossip for people to be passing around."

"All the same, you've made your bed. Now you're going to listen to your mother. You'll do nothing for the moment. I mean it."

"Fine. I'll wait this out, but if she does anything crazy, I'm calling my lawyer and proceeding with this immediately. I'm still not sure why this is taking so long to begin with. Shouldn't we have already filed something?" He looked at his mother for a response.

"It depends. You have a good deal of property, and you do have to consider the children. Sometimes it just takes a bit of time to get things going." She was making it up as she went. He didn't need any reasons to suspect that she was already interfering. He would really be upset about that.

"I don't buy that, but I guess I don't have a choice. I need to get back to work. She's bringing them here after she picks up Collin at school. I assume that's okay?"

"That's wonderful. I look forward to seeing them. They need some Grandma loving and spoiling. Why don't I take them home with me and y'all can have dinner at the house tonight? I'll even let Chuck come so he won't feel left out. He's getting a little sensitive about my attention lately."

"That sounds fine. I'll tell him when I go by his office. Thanks, Mom." He walked around to her chair and leaned down, giving her a big hug and kiss. "I mean it."

"You're welcome. And I mean it, too. Dinner will be around six thirty."

"I'll be there. Make sure they get their homework started or we'll be up all night."

He stopped by his brother's office and told him about dinner, then proceeded into his own, closing the door behind him. He needed a few minutes of privacy. This whole business was going to kill him. He was having enough trouble keeping up with work, the last thing he needed were these ongoing complications from the divorce.

He leaned back in his chair, closed his eyes, and drifted off to sleep. The sound of his sons banging on his door woke him. He called them in. They ran around his desk and fought for places in his lap. He hugged them both and fought back the urge to cry. They would soon be all he had left to show for so many years of marriage. He wouldn't trade them for anything, and he certainly wouldn't let them be taken away.

He would do as his mother asked and wait out the next step in their divorce proceedings, but the minute Libby pulled some crazy stunt, he was making a move. He didn't care whose checkbook his mother was holding.

♥ ♥ ♥ ♥

October mornings in Tennessee were always cool. No matter how warm the day would eventually be, Saturday morning soccer matches were guaranteed to be chilly affairs. This morning was no exception.

Libby left the hospital and drove straight to the field. Ben's game was scheduled for 8:00. Whoever scheduled the stupid games so early was some sort of masochist. Nobody needed to be up and about so early on a Saturday. Eight-year-olds needed to be having cereal and watching cartoons, not traipsing around a damp field at dawn. It was crazy.

When she arrived at the field, she retrieved a sweatshirt from the back of her SUV and pulled it over her scrub top. She grabbed a blanket and her chair and headed for the field. The usual groups of parents had formed. She found a spot apart from them and set her chair out. She didn't know many of the parents from Ben's team, and Matt was holding court in the middle of them. After Wednesday, she was determined to stay as far away from him as possible.

Sitting alone, watching the rest of the parents chatting over steaming cups of coffee, made her melancholy. She was already tired and depressed. She didn't need this.

Emily and Mary Beth arrived just before the game started. They sat with her. She felt foolish, sitting there feeling sorry for herself. She knew they were just sitting with her because she was so pathetic. She supposed his family must think she was going to run off with the boys at the first sign of trouble. She wanted to. She knew it wasn't the right thing to do. That didn't keep her from wishing.

"This field is a mess. All the rain has made one big mud hole out there. You'll never get Ben's uniform clean." Emily shuddered at the thought.

"Oh, Emily, you obviously don't have boys. I can get mud out of anything. A little stain fighter, a little bleach and that uniform will be like new. Don't you agree, Mary Beth? You raised two boys."

"No kidding. Those boys could get anything dirty. Emily never got as dirty in her entire childhood as they could get in one afternoon. It's uncanny."

"Yeah, I'm sooo lucky. You try telling a nine-year-old girl she can't wear makeup. Where do they get this stuff? I couldn't wear makeup until high school. Now I wish I'd never started. I would love to spend my life au natural. My skin's never been good enough. Not like yours, Libby. You've got the greatest skin."

"Thanks. I didn't do anything to get it. It's hereditary. Just look at my mother."

A commotion on the field drew their attention away from their conversation and back to the game. Ben had the ball and was dribbling quickly down the field. He had pulled ahead of the other players. The goalie was set and waiting for him. He ran straight for the defender, faked right, dribbled left, and kicked the ball past the goalie.

The crowd went wild. Matt was standing, clapping madly. Libby was screaming and jumping up and down with the others. She and Matt locked eyes across the crowd of cheering parents. They smiled at each other. The one thing they had left, the only thing they hadn't forsaken, was their love for their children.

Mary Beth saw the exchange. She knew it wouldn't be enough to heal their wounds, but she hoped it would be a bridge. They needed a catalyst. So far, the only thing she had been able to do was to keep them from actually divorcing. She had to find a way to get them back together. Soon.

Chapter 13

Chuck sat at a table by his pool and looked at his younger brother. Chuck and Matt had built this house five years ago when his parents finally shamed him into moving out of theirs. At 34-years old, he was a self-proclaimed bachelor. He dated as much as possible and thus far had managed to dodge the numerous women who longed to latch onto the eldest McDonald son. He was glad Matt had moved in. He was able to see his nephews more. They were great kids.

He was sorry Matt and Libby were having problems. He had always liked Libby and had actually been jealous of Matt's marriage and family. The few times he had attempted to discuss the divorce, Matt had shut him out and refused to talk about it. It just didn't make any sense.

The cool Saturday morning had turned into an 80-degree afternoon. The boys were staying here for the rest of the weekend so Libby could work. She had picked up an extra shift at the hospital in Ainsley and was working through the weekend. He didn't care; he was just enjoying the boys. They were having a big time in the pool.

"Hey, Uncle Chuck, watch this. I can hold my breath all the way to the bottom of the pool."

"Show me Big Ben. Get this quarter off the bottom and you can keep it!" He tossed a quarter into the pool and watched Ben catch his breath and dive to the bottom.

He clapped and shouted encouragement to the boys, then turned back to his brother. "Now what's the matter with you? You're just so quiet. What's going on? Can't you score with the Harvard lady? What's her name? Morgan something. She is a hottie. I finally got a chance to see her in the diner the other day! I'd sure like to get a look at her briefs."

"Who? Oh, Morgan Peterson. This isn't about her. It's about Libby. Oh, I don't know what I'm saying. I think she's lost her mind." Matt swigged his beer and looked out at the kids playing in the pool. "I don't even know how to explain it."

"I doubt it's as bad as all that. She's about the most together woman I've ever known. I've been jealous of you since the day you brought the girl home from Knoxville to meet the family." He cocked his head at Matt and wiggled his eyebrows. "Now *she's* a hottie."

"You're sick. She's your sister-in-law."

"EX sister-in-law."

"You know what I mean. She's family anyway." Matt shook his head as if to get rid of the cobwebs. "She's just so different from what she used to be. I didn't expect her to turn out like this." Matt started telling Chuck about their arguments, Ben's fight, and the house. "I hate to see my house run down like it is. We worked so hard to make it nice and now it's just a pigpen. And the boys act like savages around her."

"They're boys, Matt. They act like savages whenever they think they can get away with it. Look at them now."

They watched Collin and Ben throwing colorful kooshie balls at each other as hard as they could. The water in the pool was white-capped from their sloshing around. They were surely hurting each other, but they were laughing and shouting with each hit.

"Okay. I'll give you that. I guess we pulled a stunt or two when we were their age. But what about the house and the pool and the yard? Why can't she keep up with all of that? She managed before. I saw her at lunch with that pharmacist kid at the hospital. I think he's about twelve. I think she's too busy playing with her 'boy toy' to take care of her responsibilities like a grown up."

"How can you say that? The 'boy's' name is Bart Ross and he's 28. You know his brother, Bryan. He graduated a year after you did. I can't see Libby being interested in a kid anyway. I think you're making things up."

"Maybe, but my house is a wreck. You should see the pool. I doubt she'll ever get it clean. It'll have to be drained at the rate she's going. She needs to just pay someone to do the yard and the pool. She might even need a housekeeper."

Chuck noticed how Matt was referring to the house as 'his'. "Give her a break. I'm sure she has a lot to do with work and the kids. You know how much Mom complains about all of their practices and lessons she has to drive them to when she's keeping them for you. And that house note is going to be draining her paycheck. You have it made here splitting expenses with me, but she's paying for that house and the enormous utilities you used to complain about. I'm sure she can't afford to hire someone or she would have done that already. Why don't you offer to help her with the yard and the pool? Be part of the solution, not part of the problem." Chuck clutched his chest and started laughing uncontrollably. "I don't know where that came from, but I hope it isn't starting a trend. 'Confirmed bachelor offers advice to the lovelorn.'"

"Ha, ha. We'll just change your name to "Dear Chuck." Matt was obviously not receptive to his brother's interference. "I'm not lovelorn. I'm protecting my investment. I did build that house, if you remember. I designed it, built it, and made it my home. The least she can do is try to preserve it for the boys. If she can't handle it, she needs to let me have it."

"Are you sure you aren't afraid someone else will come in a make it his home instead of yours? That's what it sounds like to me." Chuck walked back into the house to get another beer. "You do realize she's not your wife and it's not your house anymore."

Matt felt like he had been punched in the gut. "It is my house," he mumbled to himself, "and she may not be my wife, but she's not going to be anyone else's wife, either."

Later, after the boys were bathed and put to bed, Matt sat on the deck and contemplated his brother's outrageous suggestion. Should he offer to help her? Did she really need help? Whatever the case, if he volunteered to help with the yard and the pool, he would be around to watch out for her. He could make sure she didn't get involved with the wrong people.

A month after their separation, he wasn't sure why it was suddenly important to him who she dated or who was around her. But it was.

♥ ♥ ♥ ♥

Matt waited until noon on Saturday to make his first move. He dropped the boys off at his parents' house and drove to Libby's. He knew she'd be well asleep by then and wouldn't plan to get up before 3:30. He had plenty of time to take care of her yard and the pool before she woke up and realized what he was doing. Chuck had made him feel bad for fighting with her and for complaining about the house and yard. He had decided to take his brother's advice. That was new.

First, he backwashed the pool and treated it with the proper amount of chemicals. He raked the leaves and burned them in a gully behind the house. Then he gassed up the mower and trimmer. He mowed, edged, weeded, and trimmed. The yard looked great when he was finished. By three o'clock, he had put everything away and was headed back to his parents' to join the family for a small cookout. For some reason, he wasn't really in the mood for a bunch of company, but the boys would have a ball with their cousins. He could tolerate it for them.

His mother was waiting at the door when he pulled in the driveway. She had two sons, a daughter, and a husband who was little more than an overgrown child. They adored her. And feared her wrath. She managed them all with a soft heart and an iron hand. He could tell something was wrong and he was in trouble. He was instantly afraid.

"What is wrong with Ben? He's withdrawn and won't say why. Collin says he thinks he blames himself for some fight you had with Libby." She stood in front of him with her hands on her hips defying him to go past her without answering.

"It was nothing, really. After our meeting with the principal, we had a fight. I told you about it. I guess Ben must have heard us. We said a lot of hateful things to each other. We argued about her moving. I don't know what all we said. We were mad. It was a fight." He raked his fingers through his hair and sighed. "I'll talk to Ben and fix this. First, though, I need to get a shower."

"No. First, you need to make your son feel better. You can get a shower later. You definitely need one. You stink."

"Gee, thanks, Mom."

"Where have you been, anyway?" She cocked her head and gave him that scary, squinty look only mothers have.

"I, uh..." His conspicuous hesitation earned a smack on his arm.

"Out with it."

"Okay! I went to Libby's to clean the pool and do some yard work. I felt bad for complaining so much about the house and yard. I couldn't keep up with it when I lived there. That, and Chuck gave me hell for not helping her more. It was nothing. She's probably going to be pissed off when she finds out I did it."

He flinched when she smacked him again. "Don't use that sort of language around your mother."

She smiled at him and pulled her son to her in a big hug. "I'm proud of you. She does work hard and you've never really appreciated that. Now go work on the baby. He's hurting and confused, too. Make it right."

Chuck and Matt passed each other as Matt went outside to find Ben. Chuck looked at his mother still standing in the kitchen door with her hands on her hips. "Now what? You scare me when you look like that. That's your 'someone's about to get it' look."

"Don't get smart with me." She chuckled as she walked to the counter and started chopping vegetables for dinner.

"Well, what's going on? I know you've got something rattling around in that mind of yours."

"I think Matt loves his wife."

"Ex-wife."

"Whatever." She turned to him, using the knife to point at him when she spoke. "I think those kids never had a bit of passion in their marriage. They never fought in the beginning; then when they did start fighting, they never learned to fight and make up. Nothing spices up a bedroom like a good old fashioned fight."

"MOM! I could have lived forever without hearing that! Yuck!"

"You know it's true. You can't love or hate or feel or fight without passion. Maybe good make up sex is what those two need to put some spark in their lives. Lord knows they could use a little. I don't think either of them is pushing to get this divorce finalized. Subconsciously, I think they're both waiting for some miracle to happen. They want to wake up tomorrow and find out this was all a very bad dream. I'm sure of it. That gives me hope."

"You need to be careful. You're meddling and that never works out well."

"*I'm* meddling? Matt told me that you're the reason he went over there to work in her yard today."

"He did that? How funny! I was just yanking his chain. She really does need the help, though. I don't think they've thought through this whole thing much. That house is a lot to take care of." He reached over her shoulder and grabbed a slice of bell pepper.

She turned and hugged him. "You're a good man. I'm a lucky woman to have raised two rowdy boys into such wonderful men."

"Thanks, Mom, but I think we're the lucky ones. You're the best." He hugged her back and picked up the veggie tray she had finished. "I'll take this outside. The crowd is getting hungry and Dad's going to torment us all by cooking those chickens as slowly as he can."

Aunts, uncles, and cousins were spread out along the patio, around the pool, and were spilling out of the game room. Charlie and Mary Beth McDonald were both from Ainsley and had numerous relatives living near them. They kept in touch with nearly all of them. A "small" family gathering could mean anything from 20 to 100 relatives. This one looked to be in the range of 50 guests.

Matt searched the crowd for his youngest son; finally finding him seated alone on a swing. He was swinging slightly with his head held down, dragging his feet in the dirt. Matt felt like a jerk. He walked over and sat down in the swing next to him.

"What's up little guy?"

"Nothing."

"I know you're upset with me for fighting with your mom. I'm sorry. I didn't mean to. Sometimes grownups just do stupid things and hurt each other."

"It's all my fault because I punched out John Mark. You said Mom couldn't take care of us. Does that mean we have to go away and can't see her anymore?" His little heart poured out an endless stream of worries as tears streaked his face. "That's what happened to Ashley Sammons. Her mom was bad and couldn't take care of her and now she lives in a faster home. Do we have to go to a faster home? I don't want to be sent away. I love Mommy. She's a good Mommy. And I love you, Daddy. I'm sorry I was bad. It was all my fault."

"Ashley lives in a *foster* home. You haven't done anything and neither has your mom. She's a good mother and she loves you very much. We both do. Whatever happens between your mother and me is not your fault. And NOBODY is EVER going to take you and Collin away from us. Ever. I mean it." He got up and knelt on the ground in front of his son. Matt held out his arms and Ben folded himself into his father's hug, crying uncontrollably on his shirt.

"You promise, Daddy? Promise we'll always be a family? I know we can't all live together like we used to, but I'm scared. I don't want to miss you." He sniffed and wiped his nose on his shirt.

"You don't have to worry about that. I don't want to miss you either. Mommy and Daddy will always be here. You and Collin are everything to us. Okay?"

"Okay." He broke away from his father and looked around to see who might have witnessed his moment of weakness. "Can I have a Coke?"

"Yeah, you can have a Coke. Just don't spray it on your brother." He laughed and patted his son on the back then watched him walk away. What a mess.

Meghan greeted him as he walked back to the house. "Hey, Uncle Matt. Where's Aunt Libby?"

"She's working."

"Did she send my strawberry gelatin salad with you? I didn't see it in the fridge."

"No. She didn't send it."

"But she always makes it for me. She makes it so I can eat it. I can't have the other desserts." Meghan's diabetes forced her to watch her diet. She had an external pancreas that helped maintain her blood sugar, but she had been taught early to choose the right foods for herself. Libby had been making Meghan's favorite salad with all the ingredients she could have: sugar free gelatin, nuts, sour cream, and fruit packed in its own juice. When Meghan got her pump, she and Aunt Libby had used a computer program to calculate the number of carbohydrates so she would always know. It was their special bond. Libby had helped the child adapt so that her disease interfered with her life as little as possible. Meghan worshipped her.

"Mom and Dad don't live together anymore." Collin had heard the conversation and walked over to join them.

"What do you mean? Where do they live?"

"Well, Daddy lives with Uncle Chuck and Mom lives in our house. They're separated." He told the tale in a matter-of-fact tone.

"Does that mean you're getting a divorce? When April's parents separated, they got a divorce and she had to spend her summers in St. Louis with her dad. She never got to play softball again. She hated it."

"I don't know what we're doing, yet. We're just working some things out."

"It's not fair. I love Aunt Libby. She makes my salad, fixes sugar free Kool-Aid for me, and knows how to calculate my carbs so my insulin pump works right. Nobody else cares." She put her hands on her face and started to cry. "I don't want to be separated from her."

"You can still see her. She and your mom will still be friends. You can still call her Aunt Libby if you'd like."

"What do you mean, I can still *call* her that? Won't she still *be* my Aunt Libby?"

This was getting way out of control. "No, she might not be your Aunt Libby really, but she'd love it if you'd still call her that. She loves you very much."

"Are you not going to be my Uncle Matt anymore?" Her curiosity over the familial ties involved outweighed her distress enough that she wiped her hands over her eyes and peered at him through tear-dampened lashes. She waited impatiently for his answer.

"I'll always be your Uncle Matt. Your mother is my sister. We can't change that."

"I don't understand. How can we make Aunt Libby not my aunt, but you'll always be my uncle? I would rather have Aunt Libby. You can just separate from the family." She waved him off with her hand and flounced off, ending up in the safety of Grandma's lap. He was sure she was telling his mother how awful he was.

Why did everyone want to keep Libby and not him? He didn't realize even his own niece thought more of her than of him. Did his kids feel that way? He couldn't be that big of a jerk. Could he?

Libby lay in bed Saturday morning trying desperately to sleep. She was upset about the fight she had with Matt. She knew she should just tell him he could have the house. She couldn't keep up with it anyway. She could probably find a nice three-bedroom ranch in a good neighborhood for less than half of what she would have to pay for this house. With a smaller yard and no pool, she would be able to keep everything clean and tidy and have plenty of time to spend with the boys on her days off. They might miss the pool, but everyone else in their lives had a pool, so they would be able to swim most of the time, anyway.

She drifted off to sleep and didn't wake up until her alarm went off at 3 o'clock. She felt groggy and ragged. She stared at the ceiling and again pondered the more technical aspects of the divorce. She was willing to give up the house. She would stay in Ainsley, if only for the boys. She would find some way to be happy. She made a note to call her mother and give her all of that information to pass on to Matt's attorney. She would not tell him herself. They couldn't be in the same place without starting an argument.

She rolled over and turned on the TV. She didn't feel like getting up yet. She watched a movie and put off getting up until the last minute. In a frenzy, she showered, dressed, fixed a bowl of cereal to eat and took off for the hospital. Maybe they would have a quiet night. Saturdays in Labor and Delivery were either slow or rowdy. Her stomach was churning and her head was aching. She would appreciate a slow floor tonight.

She should have known better. The patients seemed to come two at a time. They had several outpatients, but they were nothing compared to the true labor patients who kept coming in.

"Has someone posted a neon sign on the street?" Amanda handed a chart to Libby. "You're up next. Melissa and I both have a labor patient and two outpatients. This one is yours. She's 30 weeks and thinks her water broke at Wal-Mart. Good luck with that."

"Well, if she's truly ruptured, she'll have to go to Vanderbilt, so we'll need the call person." Libby looked at the line up board and chuckled. "Looks like Jessica may get to ride to Vandy tonight. I'll go do the assessment and see what's up. How's the rest of the floor?"

Melissa walked up behind her and tossed her chart on the desk. "I'll tell you how it is – it's hell. Pure hell. I don't know who wished this night on us, but I hope you've learned your lesson! If I have one more family member ask me for a pillow or a warm blanket,

I'm going to smother them with the pillow and throw the body in the dumpster."

"Yeah, some of these folks think the sign out there says "Holiday Inn" not "Hospital". Libby snickered and headed down the hall to her newest patient.

And so the night went. Jessica came in and rode in the ambulance to take the preterm patient to Vanderbilt University Hospital in Nashville. Outpatients came and went and babies were born throughout the night. By seven o'clock the next morning, they had delivered 4 babies, performed one stat cesarean section, and treated 12 outpatients. The staff was exhausted.

Libby could barely remember the drive home. She collapsed into bed and fell asleep instantly. Her near comatose state was interrupted by strange sounds coming from her garage. She rolled over and looked at the clock. It was just after one. Had she left the garage door open in her near unconscious state when she got home? Maybe someone's pet was rummaging through her garbage. That's what it sounded like. Banging and rummaging.

She dragged herself out of bed and started down the hall. She opened a hall closet and looked about for a weapon. She grabbed Collin's baseball bat and cautiously proceeded toward the kitchen and the source of the strange sounds. The sounds seemed to have stopped. Maybe she had imagined them. She stepped from the hallway into the den just as Matt turned around. He was standing in the corner of the room holding one of the family portraits she had taken off the wall. He must have picked it up from behind a table where she had stashed it.

They stared at each other in an uncomfortable silence. He didn't know what to say. He and the boys had come by to pick up their bikes so they could go riding in the park, but he no longer had a garage door opener. He had taken her spare key from under the mat and let himself into the house by the door off the den. He had opened the garage door and told the boys to haul their bikes to the truck. He had closed the door and was heading back out the way he came in when he spotted the picture peaking out from behind its hiding place.

Just looking at it confused him. The family in the photo looked happy and secure. Libby was so sure that their marriage was unsalvageable. He had gotten caught up in her certainty. He hadn't wanted this divorce from the beginning. Had they really been so unhappy? He looked on the table in front of him and saw several snapshots of their trips to Disney World and Destin the two summers before they split up. His memories of those trips were good. The people in the picture looked happy. They looked like a family. What were they now? They were nothing. Two kids, two parents, two houses, a visitation schedule, and a lot more work than the marriage had been. They had fought more in the past month than they ever had. Was this what they both wanted?

He was shocked at his own reaction when she came into the room. She was slightly tousled from sleep and oh-so-sexy in a pair of little cotton shorts and the tiniest tank he had ever seen. And she wasn't wearing a bra. Good grief, he felt like a randy schoolboy. He didn't remember ever wanting her this much when they were married. If the boys weren't outside waiting, he could think of a few ways they could spend the afternoon. He would love to get his hands on her.

"What are you doing?" She finally managed to blurt out. He was looking at her so strangely she didn't quite know what to say. After their last encounter, she was afraid he was inspecting her house for dust and cockroaches. What a jerk.

"Um, nothing." He felt ridiculous. "The boys want to go riding in the park, so we came by to get their bikes. I had to use your spare key to get in. I'm sorry we woke you up. I had hoped to get in and out without disturbing you."

"The bikes aren't in here. Why are you holding that portrait?" She was defensive. He didn't belong in her house anymore. She suddenly realized she was wearing her pajamas. And she was wielding a baseball bat like a claymore.

He must have taken the boys to church with his parents. He was dressed in a gorgeous conservative gray suit. She had always loved the way he could look sexy in a starched shirt and expensive suit or a t-shirt and shorts. He looked like something out of a catalog no matter what he was wearing. And she looked like an idiot. Please don't let me have toothpaste on the front of this shirt, she thought. Oh-my-gosh. She looked briefly at her reflection in the television set, trying to remember what she had put on when she got home. It was worse than she thought. Her shirt was tight and she was not wearing any underclothes. None. She crossed her arms in front of her.

"Oh, I'm sorry again, I suppose. I just saw this sticking out when I was getting ready to close the door. I haven't really looked at it in a long time. Funny how time changes your perspective, isn't it? I remember that day like it was yesterday."

"Yeah, me too. I was called in to work the night before and didn't get home until 7:30 that morning. Our appointment was at eleven. You had to get the boys bathed and get their clothes together so I could get enough sleep to banish the dark circles from under my eyes. I looked awful that day."

"No, you were beautiful." He said it so quietly she was not certain she heard him correctly. He put his head down and turned away from her to put the picture back behind the chair.

"I'd better get out there or they'll have my truck scratched up trying to load the bikes." He walked toward the back door.

"You can go out the front if you'd like." She felt a sadness overcome her. A lonely, aching sadness she hadn't felt until now. "And you can have that picture if you want it."

"Maybe I'll get it later. Now's not a good time." He walked out and quietly closed the door behind him.

Libby went into the den and pulled the portrait from behind the table. She put the picture on the floor and picked up a snapshot. Memories flooded her mind. A lifetime had slipped away with no more regard than an old shoe. She felt the crack in her heart become a giant, empty hole. She sat on the floor and for the first time since the separation, the tears came. Her broken heart grieved for the family they had torn apart.

Chapter 14

Matt loaded the bicycles into the truck and drove home. The boys were excited about their afternoon at the park and quickly changed clothes. Collin helped his dad make sandwiches while Ben gathered up fruit, chips, and cookies to load into the picnic basket. Matt put drinks into a cooler and hauled everything to his truck. The boys chattered endlessly about their bikes and the picnic they had planned.

When they arrived at the park, they found the perfect spot and laid out their meal. The boys ate their sandwiches and crammed down some cookies before they jumped on their bikes and rode off to find their friends. Matt cleaned up their mess and set out a canvas folding chair. He took off his shoes and stretched out in the chair. So much for spending the day at the park with the boys. He could see them riding up and down on the hills of the track around the park.

Finally relaxed, his mind wandered back to this afternoon. Had he noticed how pretty she was when they were married? Or had she suddenly started taking care of herself like so many divorced women did. He thought back to the portrait and realized that he had just never paid much attention. They had been friends before they dated and had dated for several months before Collin forced them to marry. They were both attractive, well educated, and personable. Their "shotgun" wedding hadn't seemed like much of a problem for either of them. They had both finished college and were ready for family and career. Their lives just seemed to drop into place. Everything had been too easy and they had fallen into a rut.

Was it too easy? They had always enjoyed a comfortable, if routine, love life. Their family backgrounds were similar enough, even though Libby had been raised in the city. They agreed on everything from finances to childrearing, creating an atmosphere of complacency in their home. Had they really agreed on everything or did they just not care enough to argue? As much as he had hated Ben to see them fight Wednesday, he had been amazed at how the fiery anger in the air had aroused him. Is that what made make-up sex so great? They'd never had it, so he didn't know.

Where was all of this deep thought and reflection heading? He wished he could figure that out. What did she think of their marriage and divorce? They hadn't even talked about it. Since they had been advised to stay away from each other, it was impossible to discuss much. After their fight Wednesday afternoon, it made sense that the lawyers had told them to stay away from each other. Would they ever be able to be in the same room again? Would they ever get out all of the problems and pain that had led them to divorce? He was glad his mother had stopped him from running to Morgan. He was sure what he was planning at the time wasn't the answer to their problems.

He could feel that he wanted her in a way he never had. When they dated in college, their sex drive was pure hormones. She had worked so hard on her degree and had dated very little before they met. In fact, he had been her first, and only he assumed, until recently. Had she been with anyone else? Had her mother given her the same ultimatum that his attorney had given him? The thought of her with another man made that sick feeling return to his gut. She was his. Every inch of her gorgeous body belonged to him.

When did she get to be such a saint? He had discovered more about her in the last few months than he had ever known. How long had she been volunteering at the school? And the church, and the hospital? And how could he not know about Meghan's salad? She was a remarkable woman. Everyone who knew her loved her. What a shame for those in this town who had refused to give her a chance. And what a jerk he was for letting her slip away.

Why had he not realized what their marriage could have been? Instead of spending his spare time with friends or fiddling with his CAD program, he could have been enjoying her body. Those long, boring nights could have been replaced with hot, sweaty sex. He imagined her long legs wrapped around him, their sweat-slicked bodies moving together in frantic need. He was aroused at the thought of her beneath him, her breasts pressed against his chest.

"Wake up, sleepy head. Aren't you supposed to be watching the kids?" He jolted up as the sound of her voice interrupted his daydream. She laughed and plopped down in the grass beside his chair.

"I couldn't go back to sleep, so I went outside to work on the yard. Funny, but the lawn fairy seems to have paid a visit. The pool is also clean. Well, as clean as it can be under the circumstances." She looked at him over the top of her sunglasses. "You wouldn't know anything about that, would you?"

"That all depends." He shot her an uncomfortable grin. "Are you mad because the fairy felt bad and tried to make it up to you?"

"I was at first, but I decided not to look a gift horse in the mouth." She picked up a stick and twirled it in her fingers. "Especially since I've been a little less than cordial to the fairy lately."

"Well, maybe I deserved it. You were right, I had no right to say some of the things I did." He bent over and slipped on his shoes, then stood up and held out his hand to her. "Let's take a walk and see what our guys have gotten themselves into."

She hesitated, then took his hand and let him help her up. He held her hand a little longer than necessary, forcing her to look up at him. He was looking at her in the same, strange way he had at the house earlier. Was it a sad face? Apologetic? Wistful? It was hard to tell. He had never looked at her that way before. She felt a warm, swirling feeling in her belly slide low and tingly as he bent to kiss her. Oh, no. Was he really going to kiss her? Why? Does it matter? Just do it, already.

She was so cute when she was surprised and unsure of herself. He couldn't help wanting to kiss her, especially with her mouth gaping as it was. He leaned in, anticipating her retreat, and reveled in her taste as she allowed him to kiss her. He pulled her to him, tasting her, feeling her body as it fit perfectly to his. She smelled like sugar cookies and tasted like heaven. He swept his tongue in her mouth and explored what he should already have known, but somehow didn't. It had never felt this good before.

What was she doing? She was letting him grope her in a public park. They were in the middle of a divorce! She couldn't make herself stop him. His face was warm from the sun and soft from his morning shave. His shirt was crisp under her hand. He smelled like shaving cream and cologne. He had his hands on her bottom and was holding her up against him. She shouldn't be aroused, couldn't be embarrassed – they had touched each other thousands of times during their marriage – but she was sinking. He was pulling her into a vortex and she was drowning in him. Her mutinous hands had taken on a life of their own. One had found his hair and was tangled in it, while the other caressed his perfectly muscled chest. She didn't want this to end. It was too good, too powerful; she had never felt this way before. She had to stop it.

She pulled her mouth from his and pushed him away with the hand she had been rubbing on his chest. She looked down at the ground, unable to control her uneven breathing and rapid pulse. Her heart was pounding in her ears.

He seemed to be struggling as much as she was, but managed to speak first. "I refuse to apologize for that."

"Yeah, I um..." What could she say to that? If he wasn't sorry, then she wouldn't be, either. "Let's go find the boys."

She shook her head when he reached for her hand. "I think we both might be sorry if we do that. Let's just move on." He noticed that she didn't suggest they forget what had happened. He doubted if they could.

They spent the rest of the afternoon at the park. The boys rode their bikes, chased their friends, and played on the playground. Libby and Matt chatted away the afternoon; running down the usual gossip and keeping up a light banter of small talk. They avoided any mention of the divorce, visitation, and living arrangements. It was the way they had spent their marriage – comfortable, unemotional, dodging the difficult issues. A kettle of need bubbled beneath their cool exteriors. They couldn't help but wonder what would happen when it blew.

Libby arrived at work to find only two patients on the floor. Both were scheduled to go home within the hour.

"You can downstaff if you want," Jessica said. "I know you've put in a bunch of hours lately. We can handle it. If we get in trouble and need you, we'll just call you in."

"Normally, I wouldn't care, but I would love to go home. I'm not even going to clock in. Just write me down as being on call. I'll phone Matt and see if he's put the boys to bed yet. Maybe I can take them home with me."

Chuck answered when she called Matt. "Hang on. He's upstairs supervising showers and making sure their stuff is packed to go back to your house tomorrow. Before I get him, I have to ask you something."

"Sure, Chuck. Ask away."

"Are you okay? Are you sure this is what you want?"

"I'm fine. As for the other question, I have no idea what I want. I doubt anyone in our situation does. What seems right one minute seems foolish the next. I guess we'll know for certain when it's over."

"Yeah, I guess. I just hate to see it. We had a get together at Mom's this weekend and it wasn't the same without you. We miss you."

"Thanks, Chuck. I appreciate that." The conversation was awkward. She didn't know what else to say to him. She felt like she was breaking up with him, not his brother.

He cleared his throat, a gesture she interpreted as confirmation of his mutual discomfort with the conversation. "No problem. I'll get Matt. He's coming down the stairs now."

Matt took the phone from Chuck and greeted her.

"I'm not working tonight. I've been downstaffed. Is there any way I can get the boys? I know you're supposed to have them, but I thought it would be fun to spend a few hours with them."

"Actually, they're bushed from this afternoon at the park. They've both had baths and they're upstairs watching a movie in bed. I doubt if either of them makes it for another hour. I can get them ready for you, though. I don't want you to think you can't come get them." He would do anything to avoid an argument.

"No, that's okay. I know they played hard this afternoon. They could probably use the rest. I'll just go home and have a bubble bath and read."

"Uh, do you think you could spare a few minutes to talk to me? We've been told not to talk, but I don't think we're getting anywhere this way. I promise to mind my manners if we can simply try to talk about this. If it gets out of hand, I'll leave. I promise."

"I don't know. Do you think we can have a civil conversation about all of this? We don't have a very good track record."

"I think we owe it to ourselves and our children to try. What do you say?"

"Fine. I'll be home in about 20 minutes. I'm sure I'll be up for awhile. Just come on when you can." She wasn't sure this was a good idea, but nothing they had done so far seemed to be working. He was right; it was time to try a new approach.

"I'll be there around eight. The boys will be out by then." He hung up the phone. For the first time in a month, he felt hope. He didn't know what he hoped for; but they could at least do better than they had.

He drove to the house, not sure what to say. He didn't want to start an argument, but they needed to talk about the divorce. How could they talk about it without fighting? They had to try.

She had left the garage door open for him, so he pulled his truck in like he did when he lived there. It felt good. Once again, he was hopeful.

She was standing at the coffeepot pouring two cups when he walked in. Her scrub top had pink and blue hand and footprints on it. She was barefoot, as she preferred to be, her pink painted toenails sweetly sexy poking out beneath the legs of her blue scrub pants. How could he have missed what a jewel she was? His stomach lurched in distress over their situation. What could he say to make this better instead of screwing it up even more?

"I made a cup for you, but if you would prefer something else, I think you still have some beer in the fridge. I also have some diet drinks."

"Coffee's fine, thanks." He took the cup from her and walked to the living room. He walked to the portrait hidden behind the table. He pulled it out and studied it.

"Where did these people go, Libby? This wasn't so long ago. I feel like the rug's been pulled from under me and I didn't even know I was standing on it."

"I know. I don't know what to say. I just can't live in a war zone. The fighting was suffocating me. I hated to see you coming home because I knew we would argue about something. I was constantly afraid of you. Not of what you would do, but of what you would say. Our arguments were becoming vicious."

"You're right. I don't even know how to explain what I was thinking. I know you've been overwhelmed with the boys and their schedules and with our finances. I wish you had told me. Instead, you just took it all on yourself and let it build up. I could have helped."

"I didn't think you wanted to help, or that you even had time to help me. I felt like it was all my responsibility. I know now that I can't be super mom. I've "un-volunteered" for several things. I can't do it all. I have learned to pick my battles. Right now, my children are my priority."

"Mine, too. Ben had a hard time over the fight we had Wednesday. He thought he would have to go to a foster home because I said you couldn't take care of them. I felt like a real ass."

"Oh, poor baby. He must have suffered over that. He never said anything to me. I can't believe it. What are we going to do?"

"I don't know. I don't want what we had, though. We either need to work out the details of the divorce and get it over with before we permanently damage our kids, or we need to decide to try again. Whatever we're going to do, we need to do it."

"I agree. I can't honestly say I'm drawn either way. I know we can do what's right, if we'll just do it together." How could they have a marriage if he didn't love her?

"Yeah, I can't stand to see you sitting on the other side of the universe when Collin throws a touchdown pass or Ben scores a goal. I want you there with me to celebrate their successes."

"And to soothe away their failures."

"That, too. Although, they are my sons. Failure won't come often or easy." He chuckled and took her hand. "Can we sit down and try to figure out what to do?"

She agreed and they sat at opposite ends of the couch. They looked at each other for a moment before she asked what he wanted to talk about.

"That's easy. I don't want this divorce. I never have. If you're determined to go through with it, then we need to make this as easy as possible on the kids and ourselves."

"So how do we do that? I've already decided to let you have the house, and I'll agree not to leave Ainsley. That's only fair."

"Why?"

"Why what?"

"Why are you giving me the house and agreeing not to leave? I thought you wanted the house or you were leaving?" This was too easy. There had to be a catch. Did she want him to build her a new house? Did she want a new car or part of his business? How could she be after his jugular one day and give him everything the next? She wasn't making sense.

"I was just mad. I've never wanted this house. It's yours. It always has been. I can't keep up with the house and the yard. I checked into getting a housekeeper, but they wanted to charge $150 per week. That's way more than I'm willing to spend. If you add in the cost of a lawn service and a pool cleaner, I'm way over $1500 a month in maintenance alone. Add in the house note and the utilities and I'm flat broke at the end of the month. I can't live that way."

"I paid off your car. You won't have to worry about that bill."

"You didn't have to do that. I've never wanted you to support me. I am more than capable of supporting myself."

"I realize that. I just paid off everything. Dad gave me the money, but I guess you already knew that. He said I had it coming for all the hours I've worked in the past few years."

"He's probably right."

"Maybe, but I'll tell you something this whole ordeal has taught me. I wish I had worked less and spent more time helping you with the kids. And I need to know how to make that damn strawberry salad for Meghan. She threw a fit because I didn't bring it. She said she wanted to separate from me, not you. It's sad when you don't even know your own family."

"I would have made it for her if I had known you were having a family gathering. I'll give you the recipe, or you can let me know and I'll put it together for her. She deserves a special treat. I've never known a child work harder to adapt to and overcome an obstacle like she has her diabetes. I'm proud of her."

"She knows that, and she adores you for it. I guess I do, too. I never knew you did so many things for so many people."

"Well, my lesson in all of this is that I've tried to make a place in this town by killing myself doing all of those things. In the long run, few people really appreciate it. My time would have been better spent cleaning my own home or working in the yard."

"I'm not sure that's true, but I'm proud of you, nonetheless." He paused and looked into her eyes. They were full of emotion. He knew his were, too. He wanted so much to hold her in his arms, to feel her against him like this afternoon. He couldn't resist the urge. He leaned toward her and gathered her in his arms.

She knew what he was thinking before he ever did it. She wanted it. She wanted to feel his strength, to glean some of it for herself. He felt so good. She felt good in his arms. She turned her head into his neck and brushed her lips against his skin. He responded with light kisses in her hair.

He moved his hand up to her neck and moved her head toward his mouth. He covered her mouth with his; kissing her with all of the emotion he had held inside for weeks. His mind went blank of everything except her. Her mouth, her body, her warmth, her scent, her taste. His world was nothing but her. He shifted and put his arms under her legs.

"I'm taking you to bed." He looked at her for some sort of argument. He didn't get one, so he rose from the couch and carried her to their room.

She didn't know what to think. She didn't want to think. All she knew was that this was the only man she had ever been with. The first, the only. And she had never felt the way she did now. She was melting in his arms and she felt powerless to stop it. It was the most exhilarating and frightening feeling she had ever experienced.

He stopped by their bed and eased her down. He sat beside her, drawing her into his arms again. "We can stop now, if you want. I don't want to push you into anything. Now's the time to say."

She pulled back from the embrace enough to slide her hands underneath his shirt and work it up his body. He raised his hands over his head so she could take it off. She put her hands on his chest, slowly touching, exploring, sensitizing them both.

He reached beneath her scrub top to touch her skin. She was warm and soft. He took her shirt off and reached around to unhook her bra. He wanted to touch all of her. He removed the final barrier and explored her body with innocent fascination. Every stroke of his hand, every feathery kiss, every nibble, sent waves

207

through her, increasing her craving for more of his body. They disposed of the rest of their clothing and attacked each other with youthful vigor. They had awakened in each other a passion so hot it threatened to incinerate them both.

They lay together in blissful silence, each staring at the ceiling. Libby couldn't understand what had happened. It had never been like this before. They had to forget this ever happened. They couldn't do this again. Why not? Because they were getting a divorce, that's why. He didn't love her. They hadn't exchanged soft words or words of love. What they had done was quench a thirst they both had, that over a month of separation had created.

He couldn't believe he had come over here to talk and they had ended up in bed. He wasn't complaining; he just couldn't believe it. Was it wrong? They were still married, and he hadn't been with anyone else. Had she? He didn't think so, but where had she picked up this sudden wild streak? She had never shown anything but proper interest in their love life before. Tonight she had been a tiger. He supposed he had too. Where had that come from? She was probably just using him. He assumed that she had been given the same moratorium on dating that Morgan had given him. Their sex life hadn't been great, but they had one. She had told him they couldn't have a marriage without love. Maybe that didn't apply to sex.

Why had she let him come over, and why had she let them do this? This wasn't going to solve anything. Well, it might solve a few minor problems she was having since the separation, but she had resolved herself to a life of celibacy. She certainly wasn't going to go running about town looking for partners in a world that included diseases you died from or couldn't get rid of. She probably wasn't the first woman on earth to sleep with her ex, but she was already prepared for the guilt and shame she was going to feel when she thought about this later. So much for the "no contact" order from their attorneys.

Matt rolled over and put his arm around her middle, snuggling up to her. She ran her fingers through his hair, then rubbed her hand down his back. "Don't get too comfortable, champ, you have to go back to Chuck's."

"Why? This is my bed," he mumbled sleepily.

"Not when our children are at Chuck's and have to be at school early in the morning. You have to be there to wake them up and take them to school."

"That's not fair. I was just getting comfortable." He groaned and put a fake pout on his face and feigned trying to convince her he should stay.

"You know I'm right. As much as I'd love to linger, you need to get up so I can get some sleep." She shifted the covers so most of them were on her, exposing his back and buttocks. She was tempted to let him stay.

"Fine, I'm getting up, but you haven't seen the last of me, young lady."

"You're probably right about that, but I still think you need to get moving." She laughed as he searched for all of his clothes and headed to the bathroom. "I feel like we're in college. I keep expecting the housemother to pop her head in and tell me that it is past curfew and I need to leave. That used to be so embarrassing."

He flashed a wicked grin over the memory of her infamous "walk of shame" to leave the frat house after spending the night with him. He dressed in the bathroom, splashing water on his face and combing his fingers through his hair. She had thrown on a t-shirt and panties when he walked back into the bedroom.

"I guess I'm leaving."

"I forgot to tell you that we're having Collin's birthday party Saturday afternoon. I've talked to your mother. Everyone's coming. We'll also have a bunch of his friends. I've turned the heater on for the pool. If it's warm enough, they can swim. If not, we'll just let them run wild in the yard while we cook burgers and hotdogs. I didn't think about that being your day to have them. Is it okay? The Vols are away."

"That's fine, Libby. You don't have to ask me something like that. Please stop acting like they're some sort of commodity we have to exchange. They're boys. They're *our* boys. We'll deal with them like they are." He sat down on the edge of the bed next to her.

"You're right. This is just so hard. But while we're on the subject, I do need some help tomorrow."

"Tell me what to do." He smiled so sweetly and sincerely she briefly couldn't remember why she wanted to divorce him.

"Collin has football from three to five. Then he has piano from five to six. Ben has piano from three to four, then soccer from four to six."

"Good grief, how in the hell do you keep that straight?"

"Practice." She chuckled and took his hand. "It's not usually quite that bad. They normally have piano at the same time on Wednesdays, but the teacher has other plans this week, so we've had to change it. If it's not convenient for you to help, I'll ask your mother."

"It's okay. I've reorganized myself so I can work while I'm sitting at practice. It helps." He kissed the hand he was holding and put it back down.

"I'll take care of Collin, you take Ben. Do you have to work tomorrow night? I can't keep up with that, either. I have it on my computer."

"Yeah, I do. I'll just bring Ben to Chuck's after I pick him up. I can go to work from there."

He rose with a reluctant sigh. "See you tomorrow."

"Yeah."

Chapter 15

Libby was anxious to get home Thursday morning. She gathered her things and headed for the elevator. Barbara Warner, the Vice President of Nursing for the hospital, hailed her from down the hall.

"Can you stay a few minutes? I need to talk to you." Barbara was in her early 50's, stocky, gray-haired, and grandmotherly. She was also an excellent manager. She kept the nurses happy and the unit running smoothly. Libby couldn't imagine what she had done to gain an audience with the boss.

"Sure. I can make it a little longer."

"Let's just step into the conference room. This won't take long."

Libby's heart was pounding in her ears. Had she done something wrong? She frantically searched her mind for any reason she would be in trouble. She couldn't think of anything.

"I know you're tired, I'll make this fast." She pulled out a chair at the long conference table and motioned to Libby to take the other one.

"What's going on?" Libby tried to sound casual, but she was nervous.

"You may have heard that Regina Adams, the Clinical Coordinator for Women's and Children's Services, is resigning. Her husband has been transferred."

"I heard that last night. I didn't know."

"I would like to formally offer you that position. I know you've been working PRN, but I've also been told that you have accepted a job in Nashville. I don't want to lose you. You're a good nurse with an excellent record here. We want to keep you. I think you'd be great at this job."

Libby was speechless. She couldn't formulate a question or make a comment. She was completely stunned. It took all of her power not to let her mouth gape as she stared at Barbara in disbelief.

"I know this is unexpected, but I'm determined to convince you to take this position. It pays well. The hours are 7:00 to 3:00. You'll be on administrative call for one week a month. I think you know the responsibilities. You're more than qualified. With your experience here and in the community, I know you can manage people. The rest you'll learn as you go. What do you think?"

"I'm not sure what to think. I hadn't considered something like this coming open. I'll have to think about it. You know I'm in the middle of a divorce. I'll have to talk to Matt about managing the boys' schedules." She rambled senselessly about the details she would have to address.

"You don't have to give me an answer today. Go home and sleep on it. Talk to Matt. I'm sure the compensation will be comparable to what you would have been making working in Nashville and here. The benefits are excellent, and you'll be home by 3:30 every day."

Libby picked up her bags and stared at Barbara for a moment. "Thanks for the offer. I'm stunned. I'll think about it and get back with you tomorrow."

"That's all I can ask for."

Libby was so tired when she got home that she couldn't think. She pulled off her scrubs and collapsed in the bed. She lapsed into a motionless coma until her alarm woke her at 1:30. She felt grainy and foggy. Her stomach was burning and her head was pounding. She dragged herself into the shower; trying desperately to make sense of the offer she'd been given.

The hours would be good, provided Matt or Mary Beth could help pick up the boys and shuttle them around until she could meet them at 3:30. What about summers? They wouldn't be old enough to stay alone for at least four years. Would they hate daycare? They had never been. She needed to check into summer day camps for boys their age before she made a decision. She would have to talk to Matt and Mary Beth before she could give the hospital an answer.

Matt and Emily were sitting with Mary Beth when Libby arrived at the football field with the boys. The shower and a sandwich had helped her feel better, but she was still distracted by the offer. With Matt's family sitting together, it was definitely a good time to talk about it. She unfolded her chair next to Emily and sat down. She leaned forward to address Mary Beth.

"I got a job offer from the hospital this morning. You won't believe it."

Matt leaned forward and looked down the row of chairs at her. "What kind of job offer? I thought you were going to work in Nashville."

"I don't know what I'm going to do, now. They asked me this morning."

Mary Beth looked from Matt to Libby. "What's the position? Do they have a Baylor position open? That would be great. No more driving."

"No, it's not that. They've offered me the Clinical Coordinator position. It's a 7 to 3 job. It has great pay and benefits, too. There are just a few things keeping me from taking it." She looked at Matt.

"Don't look at me." He put his hands up in surrender. "I'm not getting into your career plans. You need to do what you want."

"It's not that. I'll do what I want to, with or without your permission." She slumped back in her chair in defeat. "Never mind. I'm not going to start something today. It's not worth it." She just didn't have the energy to fight him anymore. She already had two jobs; she didn't really need to pursue anything else.

"Who's starting something? I just said you should do what you want. So what's the big problem?"

Why did she always have to get so worked up? He was sincere when he told her he would stay out of it. Besides, she might not be so grumpy if she kept the same hours as the rest of the world.

She leaned up and addressed Mary Beth. "I don't know what to do about the boys. Technically, I wouldn't get off until 3:15. I would also have to work in the summer. They've never been to daycare or day camp. I don't know how they would handle all of that."

"They don't have to go to camp. We built the new office so our grandkids could grow up there just like our kids did."

Emily chimed in, "Meghan and Allysan stay there all summer. We just enroll them in classes at the community center a couple of times a week. They also go to Vacation Bible School and sports camps. You'd be surprised what all we can find for them to do."

"I think it's a great idea. I'd love to have the boys with me. They can even start learning the business like we all did. I'm sure Chuck will give up his trash emptying duties so the boys can earn a little money." Matt stood and walked to her chair. Mary Beth held her breath. She wasn't sure what he was doing.

He knelt beside her and put his hand on her leg. Emily and Mary Beth exchanged confused looks. "You do what you think is best for you. We'll work this out. Every kid in this family has been raised in the office. They'll do fine."

She pushed his hand away from her leg and frowned. "I appreciate your cooperation, but I still don't know what I'm going to do. It just complicates things."

Mary Beth looked at both of them, confused at the exchange. "He's right, Libby. We'll work it out. That's how families operate."

"Thanks, y'all. It helps. I told Barbara I'd give them an answer tomorrow." She turned to the game, which was just starting, and ignored Matt, who had remained by her side. What was she supposed to do when he was being so damn cooperative? He wasn't supposed to be this way. She wanted to take the job, but he was being so agreeable she was afraid she might be making a mistake.

"Just remember, Libby, we're still a family. We'll make it work if that's what you want." He walked back to his chair and sat next to his mother. She touched his hand and smiled at him. He grinned back.

What was going on between them? Something was. She needed to talk to Chuck. If something had happened, he would know.

Matt wandered off at halftime to visit with the other daddies and some of his school buddies. He stopped and talked to his attorney. Libby still had not met her. She studied him as he made his rounds. He looked so tired. His eyes were droopy and bruised, and he seemed to lack his usual verve. For someone so normally full of life, he appeared almost sickly. She reached around Emily and touched Mary Beth on the leg.

"Is he okay? He looks so tired."

Mary Beth raised her eyebrows and gave Libby a thin-lipped grimace. "Helping you with the boys has been very good for him. He realizes how much work it takes, but he still has work to do for the company. He goes back to the office in the evenings unless he has the boys. When he has them, he takes work home. He's probably up until the wee hours trying to keep up."

"He looks like he's not sleeping." She said it quietly, and covered her eyes with her hands. This was hard. Too hard.

"You know him, sweetheart. He doesn't sleep much when things are going well. Imagine how little sleep he's getting now. He's coping the only way he knows how." She reached over and patted Libby on the knee, "He's a big boy. He'll be okay. You can't get yourself worked up because he's not sleeping. You don't look like you're sleeping much yourself."

"Gee, thanks." She lifted her head up and wiped her eyes. "Now you're saying I look like hell. That's great."

Libby grabbed a quick nap after work Saturday morning, then dressed quickly so she could prepare for the party. Her parents would be there, along with most of Matt's family and a dozen of Collin's friends from school. The house was straightened and decorated for fall. She added pumpkins, witches, and other goblins. The disadvantage to having an October birthday was that every birthday had a Halloween theme. Collin never seemed to mind.

The front yard was decorated with hay bales, corn stalks, and chrysanthemums. She added a "Happy Birthday Collin" banner to the mix. A skeleton sat in the porch swing holding a bunch of black and orange balloons. She moved to the backyard to finish decorating there.

The day had turned out to be warm, with temperatures expected to reach the mid 80's. The boys would be able to swim, so she didn't have to worry about entertainment. She arranged the patio furniture for the party and placed orange and black tablecloths on the tables. More balloons, Halloween decorations, and candy jars scattered about completed the festive atmosphere.

She was slicing tomatoes when her parents arrived with Velda in tow. The hugs and kisses took several minutes, as did retrieving the bags of gifts they had brought. Velda pushed Libby out of the way and insisted on finishing the food preparations.

"If I can't do this for you, my day'll be ruined. Now, you go on in the living room and visit with your Mother and Daddy. They're about to come unglued worrying about you. Your momma's been frantic over all of this. And if your Daddy says one more time that he's going to come over here and 'take care of that boy' I'm just going to die."

She kissed Libby's cheek and reached for an apron. "Go show them what you're made of."

"Thanks, Velda, but I didn't invite you here to work. You're family. You don't have to fix our dinner when you're here." She knew the argument was futile, but she wanted Velda's place in her home to be clear. She hugged her and walked to the living room as her parents returned from freshening up.

"How was the ride over? Are the leaves pretty?" She dropped into a chair and settled herself with her feet curled under her. She smiled as her mother and father looked her over.

"Do I pass muster? I don't think you've looked at me that closely since that night in high school when you thought I was drunk. I'm fine, y'all. I'm a little tired, but that's because I worked last night. I'm going to make it." She said it with such conviction that she was certain they'd never believe her.

"You look fine, dear. We're your parents. We have every right to worry about how you're coping. This sort of thing is never easy on anyone involved." Libby smiled at her mother's speech. She actually looked a little motherly today. She was wearing black cotton slacks, a crisp white blouse, and a black silk scarf with pumpkins and skeletons on it. It was pinned with a bright orange pumpkin.

It took her a minute to process her mother's attire. Since when did Lauren Reynolds wear scarves with seasonal motifs? And where did she get that pumpkin pin? Libby didn't realize how she must have been frowning until her mother spoke.

"What's the matter, dear? Why are you so wrinkled up? You need to stop that or you'll look old before your time." She knew exactly what Libby was staring at, but she was determined to make her ask.

217

Would it be rude to ask her mother about the scarf and pin? She didn't want to sound ridiculous, but she had never, ever seen her mother in something so, well, common. She was certain the scarf was not a Ralph Lauren or a Gucci. She couldn't stand it. If she didn't ask, she'd be doomed to stare for the rest of the night.

"Where did you get that scarf?" There. She had said it. Maybe Mother wouldn't be offended.

"Don't you just love it?" She ran her hand across it like it was the finest piece of clothing she owned. "I picked it up on a recent shopping trip. I think it's fabulous. It'll knock 'em dead in court next week." She flipped her head back in defiance.

Libby was shocked. "You're wearing *that* in court?" She looked at her father for support. "Daddy, *do* something. Has she lost her mind? Mother would *never* wear something like that."

She looked at them, both grinning from ear to ear. Were they just teasing her? Her father bent down and kissed her mother on the cheek. "I think it's cute. She's been a lawyer all of these years. Today, she can be a grandmother if she wants."

She had seen it all, now. Her father thought the silly scarf was cute. Whatever worked for them was okay with her, but she made a mental note to keep a closer eye on them. Maybe senility was beginning to set in.

Matt and the boys arrived, followed by the rest of Matt's family. Over the next half hour, a dozen boys descended on them, all wearing swimsuits and carrying bags with towels and dry clothes. They marched through the burgers, chips, and candy like Sherman through Atlanta, leaving behind wrappers, plastic cups, and paper plates like the ravages of war. By the time they left, every adult in the yard was exhausted and happy to see them go.

Collin, Ben, and Allysan were hopped up on candy and Cokes. Meghan was picking at her strawberry salad and asking cryptic questions about the number of carbohydrates in the various types of candy represented by the wrappers now blowing around the yard with the leaves. Emily instinctively reached over and adjusted her insulin pump. Libby dragged Meghan into her lap and coaxed the child into sitting there for a while by asking her questions about cheerleading. When they were all sure she was okay, they sent her out to play with the others.

They had used the ruse on her for years. She was probably on to them by now, but she went along, probably for the attention. Libby's throat closed over the emotion she felt as she watched Meghan playing. She loved these people. They were as much her family as her parents who sat with her. Sadness weighed on her heart like a sack of concrete.

Matt looked across the yard where Libby sat holding his niece. They had formed such a tight bond. As much as he loved his boys, he had always regretted not giving them a sister. Girls were so much different from boys. Sometimes he thought Libby must feel outnumbered in a house full of men, and he would love to have a sweet, dainty little girl who adored him as much as Brad's girls adored him.

The party started breaking up when the Reynolds' announced that they were returning home. Mary Beth grabbed Lauren and pulled her aside.

"Did you get all of the facts you were going to tell me? I'm dying of curiosity."

Lauren dragged her into the kitchen where they huddled on barstools while she told her the story of Morgan and Kyle Peterson. It seemed that Morgan had caught Kyle in the act of fooling around with his secretary. She changed the locks on their Manhattan apartment and filed for divorce. He went to the other partners and had her dismissed from the firm. She, in turn, filed a suit against the firm for wrongful termination, loss of income, and a half dozen other charges. She also filed for full custody of their daughter with the intention of moving her away from New York, using her dismissal and the subsequent bad press as grounds for the necessity to move her practice to another state.

She won. In the end, she had her daughter and millions of dollars in damages from the firm and a generous monthly check from good old Kyle. She stayed in New York for a short time for Lindsey to finish the school year and for her to get used to seeing her father infrequently. They both survived.

Morgan was barely looking for a job when she found the ad Ham had placed on the Internet. When she visited Ainsley, she knew it was where she wanted to raise her daughter. She looked forward to the slower pace, the wide-open spaces, the clean air, and the chance to have a life without the constant reminder of her public humiliation at the hands of her ex-husband. No matter how thoroughly she had beaten him in court, he had broken her spirit. She had no faith in people. She had been so completely screwed by the people she thought were her friends and trusted colleagues that she doubted she would ever allow more than a casual relationship with another human besides her daughter.

"So, she screwed them all and moved here." Mary Beth summed up Lauren's story for her.

"That just about says it all. I remember when it was all over the news. Most people wouldn't have noticed the stories if they didn't know the players, but I did. He was vile in his efforts to destroy her before she could divorce him. I was so proud of her for hanging in there and going after him. She was always a good student and seemed to be a nice girl."

"I'm happy to have her here. From what I've seen of her, she seems to be a little melancholy. But I like her. She's played our game well. I just hope she stays with us. It appears we may be doing some good." She looked out into the yard where Libby had joined Matt and the kids in a football game. Matt had just tackled her and they were rolling on the ground beneath a pile of rowdy, giggling children.

"I think you may be right. I sure hope so."

Chuck walked up behind them and grabbed them both in a huge embrace. "Just what are you two up to? I can feel the conspiracy in the air."

They emphatically denied his accusations.

"Y'all are up to something. I want to know what it is." He moved around the bar and pulled a stool up to face them.

Ben ran in from the backyard and swung open the refrigerator.

"Hey, Ben, did you and Collin have fun at the park last Sunday?" He knew what the answer was, but he wanted to let his nephew drop the bomb on the grandmothers.

"We rode our bikes on the trails and played on the big slide with our friends. It was pretty cool, then Mom got there and she and Dad started kissing. It was so gross. They were all mushy like in the movies. My friends saw it. I thought I would die." He took a Coke from the refrigerator and ran out the back door.

Mary Beth glared at him. "You knew and you didn't tell. That's not fair. What else do you know? If you don't tell, I'm going to let the attorney cross examine you."

"All I know is that she called Sunday and asked for Matt, then he left. He came back around 2, I think." He raised an eyebrow at both of them and waited for their response.

They were jubilant. Between the two of them, they must have hugged him and kissed him a dozen times. He hoped they weren't getting their hopes up for nothing. He suspected it was little more than a chance for both of them to exorcise a few demons, but he was willing to go along if it kept their mothers happy.

Clayton gathered Lauren and Velda and herded them to the car. Brad and Charlie seized the opportunity and dragged their respective families home as well. Chuck lingered long enough to gauge the situation before leaving Matt and Libby alone. He didn't want them to get into a fight and destroy the peace they had found.

He could tell Matt was anxious for him to leave. He wasn't sure if it was so he could be alone with his wife, or so he could be alone with his family. Who knew? He finally decided to give his brother a break and left. He had planned to play with the boys until they all collapsed, but, since his brother was obviously not going to come home tonight, he headed toward the country club. He could always find someone to play with out there.

Matt helped Libby get the boys bathed and ready for bed. Since it was still early in the evening, they begged to stay up and watch movies. They rented a good family film off pay-per-view and settled in with popcorn and Cokes. Matt and Ben snuggled up on the floor and Collin curled up with his mother on the couch. The boys made it through the whole movie, but both of them had to be carried to bed. It had been a long day for everyone. Matt was as content as he had ever been.

Matt tucked in both boys and wandered downstairs to find Libby. She was finishing the dishes. He silently started putting things away, drying her dishes and gathering the trash. He took the full bag to the outdoor bin and replaced it with a new one. He wiped off the table and rinsed the rag. He got a broom and swept the kitchen floor.

She stood at the sink, trying to wash dishes and observe him at the same time. What in the hell was he doing? In eleven years of marriage, she had never seen him pick up a broom unless it was to move it out of his garage. She didn't know he had any idea where the condiments went in the refrigerator. He put them all in the correct places. She was torn between amazement and fury. When had he become so handy? Was it just so she would put out for him? That was disgusting. How had they reached this point?

He put the broom in the closet and walked to her at the sink. He wrapped his arms around her and nuzzled her neck. He peppered her neck with light, sweet kisses. He nipped her lobe. He slid his hands down to her hips and ran them up and down her side in a slow, lazy motion. He pulled her gently against him, sharing the strength of his desire with her.

She turned in his arms. Could this be so bad? He had never stirred her like this before. She wanted him like she never had. She moved against him and pulled his head down to put her lips to his. They met in a light, tentative kiss. He groaned and pulled her closer, deepening the kiss and exploring her mouth with youthful abandon. He took her hand and led her toward the bedroom.

He stopped in the middle of the living room and put his hands on either side of her face. "What are we doing?" He was desperate to know she loved him and wanted him back.

She took his hand and headed for the bedroom. "I think that's fairly obvious."

He followed, although he wanted more to talk to her than to make love to her. Parts of him overrode the talking center in his brain and he dragged her onto the bed on top of him. He slid his hands up her shirt and proceeded to undress her. She fought his clothes to get them off, giggling and moaning like a sloppy teenager. She didn't care. She couldn't remember ever having this much fun.

They played and pleasured each other for hours. She was resting in the crook of his arm with her leg slung over his when the clock struck 1:00 am. She jumped up.

"You've got to get out of here. We're going to fall asleep and get caught."

"Get caught doing what? This is not the first time we've slept together."

"No, but I don't want the boys to see you here. They'll be confused."

"Dammit, Libby, they're already confused."

"I mean, we might get their hopes up. I don't want them to be disappointed."

"You sound awfully damn sure this situation is going to lead to their disappointment." His temper was flaring. She sounded so certain that they were not going to get back together. He thought they were doing so well.

"I'm trying to protect my children from any more heartache. This has been awful on them." She got up and threw on an old robe. She stood at the end of the bed, hair mussed, makeup smeared, and arms crossed in front of her staring at him with ferocious scowl. She looked like a fuzzy pink troll.

"No kidding? I had no idea." He was tired of her perpetual assumption that he didn't know or care what was best for his boys. His sarcasm made him feel better.

"I don't need your smart mouth. I just need you to leave." She pointed to the door.

"Is this how this is always going to go? I come over, service you, and then you get to insult me and send me home? It would be much better for me if you'd leave my payment in an envelope by the bed. At least I'd get a little something out of these liaisons." He stood by the bed, deliberately dressing in front of her, showing no modesty while he watched her desperately try to avert her eyes from him. Good, she needed to be uncomfortable.

She was furious. "How dare you make an accusation like that? You wanted this as much as I did. You're always so quick to blame everything on my character flaws. I guess it's easier to do that than to admit that you might have some yourself."

"Oh, please. I think I've had about as much of this garbage as I'm going to take. I thought we might actually have a chance, but I was wrong. Nobody deserves to have to live with you. You're crazy as hell."

He stomped to the bedroom door and turned to look at her. "This is it. We'll get those damn papers finished on Monday. I won't let you do this to me again. You'll hear from my lawyer."

Chapter 16

Ham was in his office Monday morning eating a sausage biscuit and drinking his coffee while he perused the Wall Street Journal. It was his only concession to the theory that there was life beyond Ainsley. He didn't have one, so he assumed there must not be one. Even so, his financial future depended on at least a rudimentary knowledge of the outside world and the economic status of the country. He read it every day and thanked God he didn't have to live in the world it represented.

Matt stormed in at 8:15. He demanded to see Morgan. She was in her office preparing a case for the following day. She hadn't expected to see any clients, so she was wearing blue jeans and a red t-shirt with a short navy blazer. She was absorbed in her case, so she was startled when he barged in unannounced.

"May I help you? Do you have an appointment?" She looked at him like an errant child.

He snapped back at her, "I don't have the luxury of having time to make an appointment." As an afterthought, he added, "Sorry, I need some help."

He started outlining what he expected her to file that day. Not next week or next month, he wanted the divorce filed that day. He wanted the boys, the house, and everything else, Libby be damned. Something had happened. She wished she knew what it was so she could diffuse this situation. As it stood, she had no choice but to do what he asked. She had explained to Mary Beth in the very beginning that Matt was the client and her loyalty was to him.

Ham heard the conversation. Or what might be misconstrued as a conversation. Matt's screaming and barking orders could scarcely be called that. He was furious and ranting like an angry bull. Ham listened intently to Matt's demands. He hesitated briefly, and then picked up the phone.

"You've got problems."

"I could have told you that. Is there something specific?"

"I could be disbarred for making this call, but I owe you."

"You don't owe me anything."

"Yes I do. I'm going to tell you this and then I'm hanging up. You need to call your mother and get her here right now."

"I'm sure she's busy. I can't call her and demand that she drop everything and come here. That's ludicrous."

"I'm hanging up. Get her here now."

Libby stared at the phone before she pressed the hang up button and dialed her mother's number. Within five minutes, Lauren and Clayton had dropped everything and were driving toward Ainsley. Velda, left behind at the house, was frantic.

Lauren called Mary Beth to find out what was going on. She wasn't sure, but she explained to her that Chuck had come in and eaten breakfast alone that morning. Where was Matt? With Lauren summoned by some cryptic caller, she was certain she knew where he was. She walked into Charlie's office and closed the door. He called Ham Blankenship and found out what had transpired earlier that morning.

They spent the next half hour trying to decide what to do. Every alternative they discussed came back to one thing: Libby and Matt had to be forced to talk about their feelings for one another. Somehow, the truth had passed them both. The biggest problem was going to be keeping Morgan from filing any papers until Lauren could get to Ainsley and they could sit down and talk. How could they do that?

An hour later, Matt finally walked into the building and went into his office. He didn't speak, he didn't get his breakfast, he didn't get coffee, and he didn't even check his messages. He just went into his office and sat at his desk staring blindly into space. Mary Beth peeked at him as she walked by his office on the way out.

She walked the two blocks to court square and went straight to the Blankenship offices. She nodded a curt good morning to Sandra and told the receptionist she would see herself back. She barged into Morgan's office and closed the door behind her. Nearly forty years of running a business had given her the ability to take command of a situation. Her stance in front of Morgan's desk left no question as to who was in charge here. Morgan resented the interference, although she was certain she knew what this was about. The atmosphere was immediately hostile.

"You're the second member of your family I've had barge in here today. I'll have you know, your retainer doesn't cover rudeness." She stood and faced Mary Beth across the desk.

"You'll have to excuse my manners," Mary Beth said sarcastically, "I'm a little preoccupied with keeping my son from destroying this family."

"I do believe *he* is the injured party here. He did not originally seek to file for divorce." The younger woman had fewer years on Mary Beth, but she was not without her own cache of fortitude. They were squared off like rabid dogs.

"I know precisely what is going on here. I also know who pays your bill. I'll tell you now, that you are not to file anything official in court until after noon today."

"How dare you come into my office and make ridiculous threats like that. I assume that is some sort of threat?" She squared her shoulders and stuck her chin out in defiance.

Mary Beth laid her hands on the edge of the desk and leaned in to get closer to Morgan's face. "You can take it as whatever you'd like. I'd prefer to say that your client has asked you not to file anything yet. There are other matters to be considered and I'll not have this blown out of proportion by my hothead son and a gung ho lawyer."

Morgan leaned closer to Mary Beth's face. "This meeting is over. You need to leave."

"Gladly, but you'll heed my words, or suffer the consequences." She turned on her heels and walked out as abruptly as she had walked in.

Ham heard it all. He sat staring out the window with his chair spun around, the back toward the door to his office. He should never have gotten involved. He was about to lose a damn good partner and probably be disbarred in the process. He hoped he hadn't made a huge mistake.

Morgan was banging on the keys of her computer as if punishing them for some vile offense. He was afraid she would spring them if she beat them any harder. He walked in and closed the door behind him. He leaned back against it, already regretting every word of what he was about to say.

"You're going to find this most unusual, and I'm certain you're going to want to report me to the Bar Association, but I'm afraid I'm going to ask you to do something very difficult."

"I'm sure you are. This has been one of those days." She rested her chin in her hands and looked across the room at him.

"It's going to get worse, I'm sure. I want you to wait until after lunch to file those divorce papers for Matt." He crossed his arms in front of him and stood up straight.

Morgan shook her head. "You've got to be kidding me. How can I represent my client's best interests if I have so much interference from his *mother* and my partner?" She sarcastically stressed the word 'mother' to underscore the absurdity of the situation.

"I'm sure, from a legal standpoint, you'll represent his interests just fine. From a personal standpoint, though, his interests need to be addressed a little differently." He walked over to her desk and sat down in one of her chairs.

"I don't know what in the world Libby has on you, but it must be good. I just don't see how one person can inspire such loyalty in so many people." She leaned back in her chair and threw her arms up in defeat.

"It's not just loyalty. If you knew her, you'd understand. She is a very special lady. Matt's a great guy, too. Don't get me wrong. I know you've surmised that everyone is on Libby's side, but that's not true. We're all on *their* side."

"I don't see how you can practice law and be on both sides."

"I don't see how you can't. Honestly, my father and grandfather have been doing it for years. This town is so tediously interwoven that it's nearly impossible not to know both parties in any issue. This isn't the big city where you can have a client you know nothing about."

"I'm coming to that conclusion myself."

"It creates a different standard of practice. Our primary goal isn't just to rake in the dough, although it's certainly one of them. The main objective here is to be a catalyst for maintaining justice and a sense of fairness in the community. We achieve that by being part of the community, by understanding when you need to pull out the big guns, and when you need to pull out the tissues."

"I never thought of it that way, but I think I might like it." She walked around the desk and perched on the edge, smiling at him. "So what do I do about this paperwork?"

"Just sit on it. If you hear from Matt, just tell him you've been too busy to get it over to the courthouse, but it's on your priority list. I'm sure you can handle him." He stood and walked to the door. "Besides, in about an hour, it won't matter any longer. You might want to plan on lunch at McDonald Construction. Your client is probably going to need you."

"Great." Every new day in this town was more interesting than the last.

♥ ♥ ♥ ♥

Lauren called Mary Beth from her cell around ten thirty. "We're almost to town. Where do we need to go? Have you found out what's going on?"

"Yes, I have. It's a mess. They've had some sort of falling out and Matt's demanding that Morgan file the papers immediately. Additionally, he's asking for full custody and the house."

"I sure hope we can stop this, because you know I'll never allow that to happen."

"I know. I also know what that sort of battle would do to our friendship. We have to do what we can."

"Can you get everyone to your office? I think it would be better than trying to meet at Morgan's. That's instantly a hostile environment."

"I'll call Libby and tell her I need to see her here." She paused, "I feel sick."

"Me, too. You'd think I could handle this better, but so much is at stake. I want to come in there as her mother, not her attorney. It's going to be hard, but Clayton's with me, and Charlie will be there. Maybe they can temper us a little."

"I hope we're doing the right thing." She looked at her husband who was shaking his head back and forth in disapproval.

"I know we are. I just hope it works." Mary Beth hung up and took a deep breath before she picked up the phone.

She summoned Morgan, who alerted Ham to the impending showdown. Morgan wasn't sure what they wanted from her. Mary Beth had made it clear that she was in charge of this operation. The woman was so domineering. Morgan couldn't understand how her family could live that way.

Her own parents had been comfortably distant since she had graduated from law school. She loved them, and they loved her, but they had never even commented on the choices she made, much less attempted to change them. She was happy with their relationship, still, they had never seen Lindsey play ball or cheer. They had never been around to baby sit or attend a birthday party. Perhaps there was some middle ground where families could be close, but not interfering.

She walked up the street to the McDonald Construction building. Emily was on the phone when she walked in. She waved at Morgan to have a seat. Morgan wandered around the lobby, looking at the various photos on the wall. Some of the homes in them were spectacular. She wondered which ones belonged to members of the family. Most of the photos of office buildings, churches, and schools were labeled with names, locations, and dates. All of them were fabulous.

Emily hung up the phone. "Sorry. I couldn't get them to let me go. Everyone has a problem today."

She stood and walked around to the reception area where Morgan was looking at the photos. She pointed at the various homes. "That's mine. This one is Chuck's, and that one is Mother and Daddy's." She pointed to the last photo in the row. "That's Matt's."

"They're all beautiful. I'm sure you're proud." She was polite, but sincere.

"We all are. We've all worked hard here. Whatever this business accomplishes is because we all work together. It's the way we look at everything, including family."

"I'm beginning to see that." She turned from looking at the photos to look at Emily.

"I'm sure you think my mother is just being a nosy old woman, but she's not. She's agonized over how much to get involved in Matt's personal life. If she didn't think this was the right thing, she would stay out of it. I would expect her to do the same if I were in his shoes." She took Morgan's arm and led her down the hall to the kitchen.

"This is fantastic." She walked around the room, touching the countertops and admiring the furniture. "This table is so long." She looked underneath at the twin pedestals on which it sat. "That's great! Nobody has to sit on a leg."

"Mother found the craftsman who made that. She had seen another one in an old home she toured once. She never forgot it. When they built the new office, she had this one made. We all eat together everyday." She walked to the coffeemaker and started another pot.

"Everyone? Do you cook every day?" She looked at Emily with a new respect. It was short lived.

"Hell, no!" She laughed. "The only thing they let me cook is fried chicken. It's my specialty. I usually cook it on Wednesdays. Someone else cooks each day. We take turns. The boys and I eat breakfast here each morning. We have since we were children. I guess that's why we're so close." She pointed to the roaster sitting on the counter. "Today's menu includes pot roast with onions, carrots, potatoes, and biscuits. It's Chuck's day. That's the easiest thing he knows how to fix."

"I couldn't cook that if I wanted to. What's the living area for?" She motioned toward the sofa, loveseat and television on the other end of the room.

"That's for the grandkids. My girls do their homework here when we're not running around. They stay here all summer when they're not at a camp or workshop. We all grew up in this office."

"I'm impressed. I knew your mother was unique, but I never imagined someone could actually 'have it all.' I guess that was great for you guys."

"Yeah, we loved it. I grew up answering the phone. Some of our customers still treat me like a little girl. It's irritating, except at Christmas when they bring me boxes of candy!" She giggled and poured two cups of coffee. "How do you take yours?"

"I'll get that, but thanks." She moved over to Emily's side and put sweetener and creamer in her coffee.

A bell 'dinged' and Emily set her cup down and walked toward the front of the office. "That would probably be some of the rest of this party."

Lauren and Clay unceremoniously entered the front door and walked toward Mary Beth's office. She spotted Emily coming out of the kitchen and waved her off. "We know where we're going. We'll see you in a minute."

They stepped into Mary Beth's office and closed the door behind them. Emily walked back into the kitchen. She felt obligated to entertain Morgan. Nobody else would be on her side. Chuck walked in on her heels.

"What's going on? Was that Lauren and Clay?" He noticed Morgan standing in the kitchen as he rounded the corner. "What're you doing here?"

"I was summoned." She shrugged her shoulders and seated herself near the middle of the long table. "You probably know more than I do."

"I doubt that. They don't tell me anything these days." He filled his cup and sat down across from her.

Emily grabbed her coffee and moved toward the door. "I need to go back to the front in case anyone else comes in." She gave Chuck a knowing look and headed to her desk.

Libby arrived minutes later, huffing and puffing from rushing in. "Where is everyone? Let's get the show on the road."

"I'll let Mother know you're here."

Lauren and Clay came out of her office and hugged Libby. Mary Beth slipped into Matt's office where Charlie had been with him behind closed doors. Libby was led into the kitchen and introduced to Morgan.

Morgan extended her hand. "I'm sorry we've never met before. I've seen you several times when Lindsey's cheering."

"Sure, I've seen you around a time or two," Libby answered flatly. "We could have met under better circumstances."

Mary Beth, Charlie, and Matt entered the kitchen. Matt stopped short when he saw the rest of the group. "What in the hell is going on?"

"We thought it would be best if we sat down and discussed this situation before it goes any further." Mary Beth pulled him into the room and pushed him into the chair across from Libby.

"You don't understand, Mom. You don't know what you're doing." He kept his eyes on her, refusing to acknowledge anyone else in the room.

"No, you don't understand. You two are going to talk about this. I think you owe it to yourselves." She sat next to him and motioned the rest of the group to be seated. She gave Chuck a look that indicated he should leave, but he stubbornly remained in his chair.

"We've discussed this to death. It's time to get it over with. I'm filing for divorce and I want custody of the boys. I also want my house." He turned on his last words and looked at Libby. She was standing.

"Like hell. I told you you'll never take my children from me! I can't believe you'd even try that. As for the house, you can forget that, too. And you'll be paying the note for me!" She turned to her mother,

235

"Aren't you going to say something?"

"I'll jump in when I need to. First, you need to tell him why you want this divorce." She pushed Libby back into her seat.

"He knows why."

"Humor me. Tell him."

Mary Beth reached across the table and held Libby's hand. "Please tell him. He needs to know."

"Marriage can't survive without love." She snapped out the words in a quick cadence and looked down at the table.

"No shit."

"Watch you language, Matthew," Mary Beth admonished him. "Libby, you'll need to elaborate."

"Why? It's embarrassing to discuss this in front of the entire world. I don't really want to talk about it." She crossed her arms and kept her head down. Hot tears were dropping onto her lap.

"Go ahead, Libby, tell me. I can take it." He was hateful. Why were they doing this? His own mother was going to humiliate him in front of the whole room.

"You don't love me!" She stood and stared at him across the table. "You never did! You married me because of Collin, but you merely tolerated the 'city girl'. You've never cared how I felt or how anyone treated me because you don't love me." She plopped back into her seat, defeated. "There, I said it."

He looked at her, his face twisted in pain and disbelief. "You've got it all wrong. You can't actually believe that."

"How can I not; it's true." She kept her head down in shame.

He walked around the table, still stunned by her announcement. He pulled her chair back from the table and knelt beside her.

"You're wrong. If that's what you think, you've got this all wrong." He turned her face to him and forced her to look at him. "I've loved you since the day

I met you. I thought you were the most amazing girl I had ever known. I still do. When you got pregnant with Collin, I felt guilt because I was so happy. I knew you would marry me. That's what I had wanted all along. I almost felt like I had trapped you into marriage. I was afraid you'd never want to move here and be my wife because our lives were so different. I've always been afraid you didn't love me. When you started talking about divorce and marriage without love, I figured you had finally had enough of living with a man you didn't love."

She launched herself into his arms. "Oh, Matt, we're both so stubborn. You're all I've ever wanted. I love you so much, but I couldn't stand to live with you anymore if you didn't love me. I thought you were tired of me."

He pulled her away from him and put his hands on either side of her face. "I will never be tired of you. When we're old and gray and don't have any teeth, you'll still be the most beautiful woman in the world to me. You make life worth living. I know I've said some really mean things to you in the past few months, but I just said those things because I was mad. Honestly, I think you're the most wonderful wife and mother in the world. I couldn't be any luckier."

They held each other, all of the pain and heartache flowing from both of them in waves of uncontrollable sobs. Everyone slipped out of the kitchen to give them some privacy.

Mary Beth turned to Lauren and hugged her. Both were glassy eyed. Chuck was sitting at Emily's desk filling her in on the events of the last few minutes. Charlie and Clayton were uncomfortably mumbling to each other, trying not to lose control of precariously maintained emotions.

Morgan found the entire scene surreal. She replayed the morning in her head over and over. How had their mothers known what was going on? They must have spoken to Libby and Matt and compared notes. She had never seen anything like it before. Did everyone around here talk to their parents about their problems? She couldn't imagine such an exchange with her parents. When she divorced Kyle, they had read about it in the papers like the rest of the world, never asking her about her feelings or how she was faring through it all.

She didn't realize she had tears running down her cheeks until Chuck walked over to her and handed her a tissue. "Are you okay?"

"Yes, thanks. I've just never seen people who care about each other as much as your family. How did they know? How could they have known what those two were thinking?" She sniffed and wiped her eyes.

"That's what families are for. They both talked to their mothers, and Libby had even talked to Mom. She and Lauren just refused to believe that the divorce was really what either of them wanted. They thought it would work itself out, but when it came to a head today, they decided it was time to quit monkeying around and straighten it out themselves."

"I still can't believe it. I would have sworn he thought she was the spawn of Satan. You should have seen the way he stormed into my office today." She looked past him to the front door where Ham Blankenship had walked in and was surveying the scene.

"I assume y'all have managed to get this mess worked out?"

"Yes, we did." Lauren answered him from across the room where she was holding her husband's arm. "I need to see you if you have a minute."

"I thought you might." He walked toward her and followed her into Mary Beth's office.

"I realize I could be disbarred for what I did today. I'll understand if you feel like you should report me. I won't try to deny that I called Libby. I would do it again."

"I'm sure you would. As her mother, I'm grateful for what you did. You sacrificed a great deal for her happiness."

"I sense a 'but' in there somewhere." He cocked his head and waited for the ax to fall.

"Yes. But, as her attorney, I could report you. I understand that you felt obligated to help her, but you should be sanctioned, maybe even disbarred for violating attorney – client privilege." She gave him a reproving look.

"I understand." He put his head down in shame.

"But I won't turn you in. My daughter would never forgive me, and I would never forgive myself. I don't recommend what you did as a general practice, but you've saved my baby's marriage, and I can't forget that. I'll keep our little secret, just don't do it again."

He looked up at her, seeing a side of her he was sure few had. "Thanks. I knew it was wrong when I did it, but it would have been worth it, even if I had lost my practice."

"I know that. I'm proud of my daughter for having such good friends. She doesn't think she has any here. I wonder if she's ever really thought about what she does have?" She put her arm through the crook of his and hugged it lightly before turning them to head out the door.

"I'm sure we'll all have a different perspective from now on. There's nothing like a 'near miss' to make you appreciate the little things in life."

"I think you're right. I hope we've all learned something."

They joined the rest of the group, now chattering loudly with Libby and Matt who were standing arm-in-arm in the middle of them.

Matt patted his belly and asked Emily, "What's for lunch? I'm starving."

Chuck laughed and told him the menu. "If y'all will give me a few minutes, I'll get the biscuits on and we can sit down and eat. There's plenty for everyone." He looked down at Morgan, who was still at his side. "Will you stay for lunch? We'd love to have you, especially after what our family has put you through. We sort of owe it to you."

She agreed and they all visited a few minutes while Chuck put biscuits in the oven and brewed a fresh pot of tea. Emily joined him and started putting ice in glasses and setting plates out near the roaster to form an informal buffet line. The rest of the group followed as soon as the top was removed from the roaster. The smell of roast and vegetables permeated the office.

The room was filled with happy people and joyous sounds of a family meal. Matt and Libby kept touching each other under the table. Neither could believe how foolish they had been. Mary Beth and Lauren kept leaning together, giggling and sharing some secret that kept the rest of the family in suspense. Chuck entertained Morgan, while Charlie, Clay, and Ham carried on a lively discussion at the other end of the table.

For an hour, they enjoyed the company of friends and family. For Morgan, who had barely spent an hour with her family in the past 20 years, it was the most remarkable experience of her life. She vowed to herself to take them up on their offer to return whenever she'd like.

She had come to understand and respect these people. When she moved to Ainsley, she had thought it was just another small town where everyone knew everyone else's business and life remained constant from decade to decade. Today she had learned that being close to your friends and family could be the most rewarding part of one's life. This family had managed to save a marriage that in any other place and time would have been bound for the trash heap. Two boys would have grown up with visitation schedules and custody fights. If more people 'interfered' when they could, maybe more families would find the bliss this one had.

Life in the country was going to be a lot better than she had planned.

Chapter 17

Libby pulled the turkey from the oven and placed the roaster on the bar. She put a huge pan of cornbread dressing in the oven and closed the door. The kitchen was humid and the steam from her cooking had fogged the windows. The house smelled like Christmas. The boys were bouncing off the walls waiting for the family to arrive. She had talked them all into coming to their house tonight. They had so much to celebrate and she was determined to share this holiday in their home.

Matt walked into the kitchen and watched her in silence. He thanked God everyday that they had managed to keep their marriage together. They were better than they had ever been. They had each spent eleven years assuming that the other didn't want the marriage. It was a rocky foundation. Today, he looked at her with a heart full of love and respect. He would tell her every five minutes how much he loved her if that's what she needed to believe him. He would never again take her for granted.

She looked up from where she was whipping sweet potatoes for a soufflé and caught him watching her. She smiled at him through glassy eyes. He walked over and, taking her face in his hands, placed sweet kisses over her cheeks and lips. She tasted salty from the sweat she had worked up in the humid kitchen. He took the mixer from her hand and turned her into his embrace. She slid her arms around him and rested her head against his chest. Nothing had ever felt this good.

That's where Chuck found them. "That's enough. You two need to get over it. You're going to warp your children."

"I'll have you know that our children are thrilled to see their parents kissing and hugging." Libby laughed and pulled away from Matt to finish her potatoes.

Chuck walked over and put his head on her shoulder. He pulled a Christmas floral arrangement from behind his back and held it in front of her. "Would you let me stay if I gave you this?"

"Oh, it's beautiful! It'll look great on the table." She hugged him and instructed him where it was to be placed in the dining room.

He wandered from the kitchen into the dining room and admired the table setting. She had used all of the 'good stuff' that she and Matt had received as wedding presents. He knew he had seen all of it when they were getting married, but he wasn't sure he had seen it since. It was a shame they had never let her do this before. His mother had always held Christmas Eve dinner at her house. Change was good. He was looking forward to the rest of the evening.

The boys heard him in the house and ran around until they found him. Collin was jumping up and down, talking as fast as his words would come out. "You have to come see the tree. Mom said we can't touch anything, but you can. You need to shake the green package for me. I think I know what it is, but I won't know until you shake it."

"Your mom would take my head off if I touched a thing under that tree."

"You're right. She would." Matt had felt the thundering footsteps and knew the boys were up to no good. He put a hand atop each head and led them from the room. "You best stay out of the way. If you mess up her day, she'll shoot you both and block off the chimney so Santa can't get in."

They both looked at him in horror and simultaneously shouted, "NO!"

"Then find something to do that doesn't put you in her path."

"Yes, sir!" They skipped toward the stairs and went up to their rooms.

"Everything okay, here?" Chuck put his arm around his brother's neck in a mock wrestling hold.

"Better than okay. I hate that we put the whole family through hell for all that time we were separated, but in the long run, I think we're better off for it. If I had to do it over, I'd find an easier way to fix our marriage, but I'm glad we were able to do it, despite the pain we caused." He wrenched his way free of his brother's grasp and looked back at him.

"I didn't realize who all was being hurt. It sucks that you can't even keep your misery to yourself." They walked toward the game room where he pulled two beers from the fridge and handed Chuck one. He climbed onto a barstool and picked up the remote to the big screen television. He found a football game and watched it absently.

"Are you sure you're okay? You don't look like it."

"Yeah, I'm great. We've just got a bunch of things going on. We'll tell everyone about it later. It's kind of our present to everyone."

"That's not even fair. Now I'll never make it through the day. I'll be some kind of nut."

"Whine all you want, but you'll know when everyone else does." He chuckled. "It's great. You'll be glad I made you wait."

"Fine!"

Clay walked in and headed straight for the bar. "I need a drink. I've just spent the last two days shopping with Lauren and Velda, and the last two hours riding in the car with them. There isn't enough whiskey in Tennessee to make that bearable."

Charlie entered the room and slapped Clay on the back. "Welcome to the Men's lounge. I'm not leaving here until there's food on the table or a present with my name on it. It's not safe out there. If I go back, she'll find something else for me to do or carry or she'll need more money. All I want is food and presents."

"Dad, you're worse than the boys. They were trying to get Chuck to shake the packages for them." He laughed as he poured his father a drink.

"I'll tell you, son, I wouldn't have guessed two months ago that we would be having a holiday celebration at your house with your family still intact." He exchanged nods with Chuck and Clay.

"Me either. I'm just glad we're all here. It meant a lot to Libby that Mom let her have the family dinner. She feels more a part of the family than she ever did before."

"I'm glad. When I get ready to go to bed, we can just leave."

Brad joined them a few minutes later. "I'm not carrying in another package. She can do it herself or leave them in the car." He took the beer he was offered and reported on the progress from the kitchen. "It looks like we're getting close to dinner. Gosh, it smells good. If they don't call us soon, I'm going to go foraging for scraps."

"They'll take your hand off if you stick it anywhere in there." Matt laughed and led his brother-in-law over to the pool table.

Lauren, Clay, and Velda arrived at the door with packages piled under each of their chins. The boys were pressed into service carrying bags and packages from the car while Velda and Lauren brought in pies and other goodies. Libby was too busy finishing in the kitchen to notice anything but that they were there.

When she finally saw her mother, she was initially too shocked to say anything. She and Mary Beth were standing at the Christmas tree arranging the packages that had spilled out into the middle of the room. They were wearing identical sweaters with Santas and elves on them. She had commented on how cute the sweater was when Mary Beth had come in earlier. But her mother? Something was going on.

"Mother!" She walked over and hugged her, then held her at arms length. "What a lovely sweater. Don't you two just look precious?"

They both laughed. Mary Beth Spoke first, "Don't we, though? I talked her into buying it on our last shopping trip." She put her hand over her mouth and looked at Lauren with wide eyes. "Oops."

"I guess it's time we let the cat out of the bag. If any of them had a bit of sense they would have figured it out already."

"Figured out what?" Emily walked into the room and stared at them. "What's with the matching sweaters? You look like sisters." She barely suppressed a cackling laugh.

"We feel like sisters. We've been friends since the kids have been married. We talk a couple of times a week and go shopping whenever we can. Last week we spent the night at the Opryland Hotel and went to see the Nutcracker at TPAC." Mary Beth hugged her friend around the waist.

"Why have you kept it such a secret? I think it's fantastic. Lord knows, I can relate to the need for a close friend." Libby put her arm through Emily's and looked at her with tearful eyes.

"At first, we didn't want you kids to feel pressured because we were friends. After a while, it just became fun to keep our secret. I guess it's out, now." She gave Mary Beth a sidelong glance and grinned. "I've never had a friend as close, whose friendship I value as much. I'm truly blessed that she is my daughter's other mother."

"Y'all have to stop or I won't be able to finish dinner." Libby grabbed a tissue from a box on the coffee table and wiped her leaking eyes.

Lauren and Mary Beth exchanged looks; then led the group back into the kitchen. Mary Beth grabbed a dish and started toward the dining room. "Let's get this on the table and call the men in! Collin, Ben, go get everyone from the game room."

Collin and Ben ran into the game room and announced dinner. The men put down their drinks and walked en masse to the dining room.

So much food covered the table that not a single inch of tablecloth was visible. It was the ultimate goal of a fine Southern hostess. Velda looked at Libby's spread and nodded at her with pride. She had learned well.

All of them sat down and reverently looked to Charlie to ask the blessing. He looked at Matt. "This is your home, son, you do the honors."

They bowed their heads and he began, "Heavenly Father, thanks so much for all You have done for our family throughout this year. We are so blessed to have each other. Thank You for guiding us through the hard times and giving us an appreciation for the good times. Thank You for sending Your son to show us the true meaning of love and sacrifice. Please be with us throughout the coming year. Help us to grow as a family, but most of all, be with Libby and the baby. Keep them both healthy. Bless this food to the nourishment of our bodies. Amen."

He raised his head and looked around the table, not sure how much anyone had picked up. The kids were all reaching for dishes. Every adult eye at the table was on Libby or Matt, or looking back and forth between them.

Lauren spoke first. "Could you repeat that last part, please?"

"Bless this food…"

"Not that part, just before that."

"Oh, …be with Libby and the baby. Keep them both healthy. Is that the part you meant?"

Mary Beth jumped up and ran around the table to hug Libby. "I can't believe it! When? WHEN?"

Libby smiled sheepishly. "July 12th."

Her mother looked at her with a raised eyebrow. "Really?"

"Yeah, um, it seems our getting back together was uh, rather timely. We almost messed up even more than we all thought." Matt shrugged his shoulders and reached over to take Libby's hand. "I'm thrilled. I hope this time we get a sweet little girl."

"Libby, honey, what are you going to do about your new job? Will you be able to get childcare?" Her mother was concerned that she would resent giving up her career again.

Matt answered the question, "Actually, we won't need daycare."

Lauren snapped at him sternly, "She's not quitting her job!"

"No, she's not. I'm going to care for the baby. She'll stay home for the six weeks of recovery, and then I'll take over until 3:30 each day. I'll work from the house in the morning, take the boys to school, then the baby and I will head for the office. We'll stay there until time to pick up the boys. I'll run the afternoon bus and meet her at the house with all of them. After that, I'll go back to the office until 6:00. If necessary, I'll take work home at night."

"Are you sure that's going to work?" Charlie looked at him in disbelief.

"Do you think I'm going to shirk my responsibilities?"

"No, I just don't want you to get in over your head."

"I've never been more prepared for something in my life. The past few months of working with Libby to take care of the boys have been great. I've learned to work from ball practice. Most of our customers and subs know how to call me on my cell. Nobody seems to mind where I am, as long as I can get the job done. This is what we want to do."

"I think they'll do just fine. I'll be at the office to help with the baby."

Emily chimed in, "So will I. I'll be glad to help. I'm just so happy for you." She wiped her eyes with her napkin.

Libby started to cry. "Please don't start that. My hormones are so crazy I'm like a fountain. It's embarrassing." She wiped her eyes. Matt's tender look started a new spring of tears.

"Oh, honey, it's okay."

"I know. I'm not sad, I just can't stop," she replied in a watery laugh.

Collin spoke up, "Hey, I know we're all happy because we're going to have a baby, but could we PLEASE eat? I'm starving."

They laughed and started passing dishes. Several hours later, after the meal was finished and the dishes put away, they sat around the Christmas tree. The fireplace cast an amber glow around the room. The lamps had been lowered so that the fireplace and a few candles were all the light besides the blinking white twinkles of the huge tree. Collin and Ben sat squished together in their father's lap. With a flashlight to help them see, Libby's three men read the Christmas story from the Bible. When they finished, the room was still and quiet as they all reflected on the meaning of the season.

Collin, Ben, Meghan, and Allysan jumped up in a frenzy and turned on a lamp to give them all some light. Collin looked at his Grandpa Clayton, "Can we start?" He hopped from one foot to the other in frantic anticipation.

"Ask your dad; it's his house."

"Please, Daddy, we're dying here!" He flailed his arms in a dramatic plea.

"Pass 'em out. I want some presents!" He shouted as the kids ran to the tree and started delivering packages to the family.

Matt sat down on the floor and pulled Libby into his lap. They sat together, enjoying the closeness while they watched the kids. When the last child had ripped open the last present, the adults leisurely opened their gifts.

Brad and Emily loaded up their gifts and took the girls home so Santa could come. Everyone but Libby's parents and Velda followed suit. All of the grownups tucked the boys in. Grandpa Clay made a production of seeing Santa's sleigh coming through the night sky.

Libby and Matt returned downstairs while everyone else retired. They snuggled for a while in front of the fire, silently enjoying the peaceful glow of the flames. After giving the boys plenty of time to fall asleep, they rose and began to put out the Santa gifts. This had always been their favorite part of the holiday. They knew that Collin would soon become too old to do anything but pretend belief for the sake of his siblings, so they went to great lengths to ensure that this Christmas would be magical.

When they finished putting out the toys, video games, DVD's, and boxes of clothes, Matt hung an envelope bearing Collin's name on the tree. He would be absolutely convinced that Momma and Daddy had not purchased this particular gift.

He took Libby's hand and led her to bed. They spent an hour in slow loving before they drifted off to sleep.

At 5:30, Ben jumped into bed with them. "Can we go in? Please!"

Collin joined them, and they played in bed for a few minutes before Matt and Libby crawled out and threw on some sweats. Matt went into the living room with the boys while Libby poured them coffee and started a breakfast casserole and some sweet rolls.

The boys stared at the tree, anxious to tear into the boxes waiting for them. Grandma, Grandpa, and Velda came downstairs when they heard the commotion. They joined the vigil around the tree.

Libby brought in a tray of coffee and the grownups watched while the boys dug in. They ripped and tore and squealed their way through dozens of presents. Lauren and Clay had added a huge crop of new boxes, and Velda shamelessly brought in two more bags. The boys were wild with Christmas glee.

When all the boxes were opened and the paper crammed into garbage bags, Collin sat dejected and stared at their booty. Matt knew exactly what he was thinking.

"What's wrong, buddy?"

"Nothing. I just thought Santa would bring me one more thing." He shook his head. "I guess the kids at school were right about him."

"What's that up there on the tree?" He pointed at the envelope.

"I guess it's for me." He shrugged and reached up to pluck it off the tree. "What is it?"

"I don't know, open it." Libby was antsy. She wanted to see his face when he saw his present.

"It's a note."

"Well, read it!" She couldn't stand it anymore.

"It says to go out to the patio and look behind the garage. That's weird." He dropped the note and walked to the French doors leading to the back. Everyone followed.

Matt wished he could have taken a picture of Collin's face when he saw the bright yellow four-wheeler with the big red bow. He stopped dead in his tracks and stared at it with his mouth gaping and his eyes as big as saucers. "Cool," was all he said.

Matt pushed him forward until he was standing next to it. Still stunned and wide-eyed, he climbed on and looked it over, pretending to ride it.

"Who told Santa this was okay?" Libby asked in her most stern Mommy voice.

"Oh, please, Mom, can't I keep it? I asked Santa for it a hundred times. I sent e-mails and letters. It's all I wanted."

"Well, Matt, what do you think?" She crossed her arms and looked at her husband, trying not to give them away with her grin.

"I guess since Santa brought it, we'll have to let him keep it. I think he's old enough. It's just a little one."

"Okay, he can keep it as long as he takes the safety class."

"I promise I will. I'll be responsible and everything." He was hopping on the seat, making motor noises.

"Let's get back inside and eat some breakfast. You and Daddy can take it out later."

"Ben, you can ride with me." Matt wanted to assure Ben he wouldn't be left behind.

"It's okay, Daddy, I already got what I asked Santa for."

"You did? What was that?"

"Oh, it was nothin'."

"Really, big guy? Are you sure it was nothing?"

"Well, not nothin', but I already got it."

"What? What did you get?" They all looked at him, waiting for his answer.

"I got my family back."

www.ingramcontent.com/pod-product-compliance
Lightning Source LLC
Chambersburg PA
CBHW070554130626
46556CB00001B/155